"Why are you afraid?
He should be afraid of you!
It's your wife he killed..."

Harry and Pamela are man and wife. Ralph and Ruth are, too. Ralph and Pamela are lovers. Harry and Ruth are locked in an even more passionate embrace, with a kitchen knife and a Luger... And so the dance begins.

Now it is ten years later, and Harry is free. Ruth is dead. Pamela is alone. And Ralph is afraid.

So let the dance begin again...

SQUARE DANCE

JOHN WAINRIGHT

Berkley Books by John Wainwright

DEATH OF A BIG MAN
THE HARD HIT
SQUARE DANCE

SQUARE DANCE

JOHN WAINWRIGHT

A BERKLEY BOOK

published by

BERKLEY PUBLISHING CORPORATION

Extract from *The Simple Art of Murder* by Raymond
Chandler. © 1950 Raymond Chandler, published by
Hamish Hamilton, London and by permission of
Helga Greene Literary Agency.

This Berkley book contains the complete
text of the original hardcover edition.
It has been completely reset in a type face
designed for easy reading, and was printed
from new film.

SQUARE DANCE

A Berkley Book / published by arrangement with
St. Martin's Press

PRINTING HISTORY
St. Martin's edition published 1975
Berkley edition / December 1979

ISBN: 0-425-04160-3

A BERKLEY BOOK ® TM 757,375
Berkley Books are published by Berkley Publishing Corporation,
200 Madison Avenue, New York, New York 10016.
PRINTED IN THE UNITED STATES OF AMERICA

Four be the things I'd be better without;
Love, curiosity, freckles and doubt.

Dorothy Parker,
Inventory

It is not a very fragrant world, but it is the world you live in...It is not funny that a man should be killed, but it is sometimes funny that he should be killed for so little, and that his death should be the coin of what we call civilization.

Raymond Chandler,
The Simple Art of Murder

THE PLAYERS—

> *The Man*
> > Harry Ogden
> > > partnered by
> > > > Tom Harding

> *The Woman*
> > Pamela Ogden
> > > partnered by
> > > > Thelma Simpson

> *The Husband*
> > Ralph Watford
> > > partnered by
> > > > Angela Watford

> *The Cop*
> > Chief Inspector Sawyer
> > > partnered by
> > > > Detective Superintendent
> > > > > > Lennox

THE PRIZE—

> *The truth, the whole truth and
> nothing but the truth...*

THE MAN

THEY all knew what he was, and from where he'd come. His clothes told them; the crumpled, slightly-out-of-date cut of the suit, the shirt, the cuff-links, the matching waistcoat. His appearance; the pallor of his skin, the short-back-and-sides hair style, the half-worried-half-frightened expression which, however hard he tried, he couldn't sponge from his face. Even the shoes . . . ten years out of date. And the brown paper carrier-bag. And the time of day, and the fact that the cafe was less than half a mile from the prison gates.

They all knew what he was, and from where he'd come . . . and they all pretended *not* to know.

It was as if he had a deformity—a terrible deformity, of which everybody who saw him was immediately aware . . . a deformity which, out of humane politeness, everybody studiously ignored. And, by ignoring it, they magnified it. They made *him* aware of it . . . more than

1

ever aware of it. They didn't look at him, and he wished they would; not stare, but just look at him. He wished they wouldn't deliberately *not* look at him... because, by not looking at him, they made him feel abnormal. Subnormal. Unclean.

As if he suffered a terrible deformity. And he didn't—he was like them—he was as much a complete man as...

'Yes, luv?'

He pushed aside the curtain of his thoughts as the waitress spoke.

She was a young woman—young and blowsy, and with a bosom which stretched and spilled out of a low-cut sweater—a tease, and one reason why the cafe was a popular stopping-place for many drivers. Beyond the sweater was her skin, with nothing between. The outline of the nipples showed, like tiny pyramids of promised eroticism and, as she moved, the breasts swayed and bounced under the thin wool.

Not counting Pamela, to whom he'd talked, across a table and under the watchful eyes of a guard, four times—not counting the prison medic, who was a bespectacled, sexless creature—not counting the visiting do-gooders who had sought to buy an easy conscience with cigarettes and small-talk—this woman was the first woman he'd seen for ten years. The first woman he'd been near. The first *woman*!

The waitress repeated her question.

'Yes, luv? What is it you want?'

And she knew. This tart—this tease... she *knew*. It was there in the subtle emphasis on the last word. In the not-quite-hidden mockery on the painted lips. In the fractional lift of the brow, above the made-up eyes. She knew what he was looking at; knew what thoughts were racing through his head; knew what emotions he was having to control.

She knew—gloried in her knowledge... and gloried in what she was making him go through.

He cleared his throat, and muttered, 'Tea. Tea... please.'

She smiled, lifted the second brow into line with the first and turned to the urn, on the shelf beyond the counter. She picked a cup from a stack of crockery, and began to fill it.

And still she teased.

She watched his face, in the tilted mirror, above the urn; watched his eyes as they fastened themselves on the short skirt stretched tight across the cheeks of her backside; watched them drop to the hemline and, from there, to the back of the unstockinged thighs; watched the tiny quiver which, although he tried, he could not erase from his nostrils and from the corners of his mouth.

She watched and, in the mirror, her eyes reflected mocking laughter.

She placed the filled cup onto a saucer, turned and placed the purchase on the counter top.

'Milk?' she asked.

'Please.'

She poured milk into the dark tea and, even as she did that, she glanced at his face, and her expression was filled with knowledge and mocking confidence.

She said, 'Sugar's on the table.'

'Thanks.'

'Owt else?' And, again, the innuendo. The double-meaning. The tease.

'Er...' He moistened his lips, read the list, printed on the card at one end of the counter, and said, 'A—er—a sandwich...cheese. Please.'

The pantomine continued as she served him—as she took the coin and returned the change—and, as he walked to an empty table, he knew she was still watching him. Still with that half-smile. Still with the look of the whore who is supremely confident of the power of what she flaunts.

He sat with his back to the counter—deliberately—and this, too, was a mistake. There was another mirror...the damn place was rotten with mirrors! The mirror advertised beer, and she seemed to know just where to stand...her tits were there, mocking him, immediately above the word 'COURAGE.'

Christ, and all His angels!
And this was *freedom*.

He'd almost finished the snack—and taught himself not
to stare into the mirror—when the driver joined him at the
table.

The driver was a huge man; he was what a
heavy-weight prize-fighter is supposed to look
like . . . despite the fact that few of them do. He topped six
foot, by at least three inches and, if he weighed less than
fifteen stone, the loss could have been measured in
ounces. He had dark, tight-curled hair, above a face
which conjured up visions of broken granite; a face which
was muscular, contoured and clean-shaven, but not
smooth; a face which formed the perfect frame for the
broken and part-flattened nose and the white-healed scar
which bridged the nose, diagonally, from below the left
eye to above the right corner of the mouth.

The man had seen other such faces—battered faces and
scarred—but never one quite like this. The other savage
quality, and they had been the faces of men of whom
society had said 'Enough!' . . . men who had been caged,
like animals, because they *were* animals.

But not the owner of this face; not the owner of these
wide-spaced, cornflower-blue eyes from which radiated
smile-lines which softened the face and gave ugliness
character.

The driver gulped tea, unwrapped the foil from a
chocolate biscuit and munched.

For a moment, the driver chewed in silence and, as he
chewed, he watched his table companion.

Then, the driver said, 'Which way?'

'Eh?' The man didn't understand the question.

The driver glanced at the carrier-bag, which the man
had placed at one end of the table top, and said, 'You'll be
going home. North, or south?'

The man hesitated, then said, 'North.'

'I'm for Newcastle,' said the driver. 'Any good?'

'I'd—I'd like to get to Leeds,' said the man.

The driver said, 'I'll drop you. Wetherby—on the A.1.
You'll be within a few miles.'

'Thanks. Thanks a lot.'

The driver grunted and nodded. The nod was a form of introduction; the sealing of a temporary pact of friendship.

They ate and drank their tea. The driver took out a packet of cigarettes, offered the opened packet to the man and, when the man took one, produced a homemade lighter and lighted the cigarettes. They smoked and sipped what was left of their tea and, occasionally, the man's eyes strayed to the mirror and the reflection of the waitress.

The driver growled, 'She's brass, mate. Don't let her get you down.'

'No. I—er—I . . .' The man was embarrassed that his interest in the reflection of the waitress was so obvious.

'She does it,' said the driver, disgustedly. 'Every time. Every time one of you blokes comes in. And she'll do it one time too many . . . one day, one of 'em'll put his boot right up her snatch.'

The man smoked his cigarette, sipped at the dregs of his tea, kept his eyes away from the mirror and said nothing.

The driver squashed what was left of his cigarette into the saucer, wiped his mouth with his hand, and said, 'Ready when you are, mate.'

'Ready.' The man picked up his carrier-bag.

They stood up from the table and walked from the cafe.

THE COP

SAWYER was in early. Not too early—not before the sparrows stretched and yawned...but, for a man like Sawyer, thirty minutes was a small lifetime. Sawyer was a man whose whole existence was nailed firmly to two things. The clock, and 'the book'. He was punctual, to the minute and, unless it was there, in black and white—within the covers of *Stone's Justices' Manual*, or with the covers of *Archbold's Criminal Pleading Evidence and Practice*—it was ignored...and, if it *was* there, it was sacred writ.

By all acknowledged rules of the game, Sawyer should have been a chief superintendent. At least a chief superintendent—with luck, an A.C.C....or even a chief constable. He wasn't and he'd never been able to understand why; he was incapable of seeing that these things (the very things which had shot him up to the rank

6

of chief inspector) were also the things which blocked any hope of further advancement. He was (to use an Americanism) an ideal 'middle-ground-exec'. He took orders, and obeyed those orders to the letter. He passed instructions down the chain of command, and ensured that those instructions were carried out without a hint of deviation or initiative. In other words he was no decision-maker. His decisions (what he called 'decisions') came from textbooks; they were the end product of other men's weighing of pro's and con's, and they could always be justified by precedent . . . and, if they weren't available, Sawyer sought immediate advice from his superiors. Thus, Sawyer was never wrong, and for the simple reason that he never allowed himself the opportunity to *be* wrong.

Which (and although he didn't know it) was one reason why he was only a chief inspector . . . and lucky to be that!

He walked across the waxed, parquet floor of the main office, from the public-counter recess to his own sanctum, and a younger man, wearing the twin pips of inspector on the epaulets of his tunic, rounded a corner from the stairs leading to the upper floors.

The younger man said, 'Morning, Tom. You're in early.'

It was a cheerful enough greeting, but it brought a wince of annoyance to Sawyer's face. Sawyer's Christian name was 'Bardoph'. It was an unusual name, and a name whose very unusualness gave Sawyer a ridiculous and petty pride; there were not many 'Bardophs' around . . . which, if you cared to argue along those lines, made the few men who carried that name anything but run-of-the-mill. But, with the surname 'Sawyer', any Christian name other than 'Tom' was, it seemed, unthinkable. It had been 'Tom' all his service and, all his service, he'd hated this splash of the commonplace with which he'd been smeared.

He said, 'My office, inspector . . . if you please.'

The young man swerved in his path and followed Sawyer into Sawyer's office.

Sawyer closed the door, took off his peaked cap and his uniform mac and hung those garments on the rack which stood in one corner of the room.

He walked to the desk, sat down, fiddled old-womanishly with the blotter, the telephone, the 'In' and 'Out' trays, then looked up at the younger man.

'Anything during the night?' he asked.

'Not much.' The younger man moved his shoulders.

'Arrests?'

'A drunk. D and D ... he's on the court sheet, for this morning.'

'Bailed?'

'Uhu.' The younger man nodded.

'Straightforward?'

'He hasn't much option.' The younger man grinned. 'He was as pissed as a newt. He wanted to ...'

'He was *drunk*, Fenton,' said Sawyer, disapprovingly.

The younger man—Inspector Fenton—killed a sigh, and said, 'Yes, sir ... he was drunk.'

'Use the correct terminology ... please.'

Fenton let it ride; it wasn't worth arguing about.

Sawyer said, 'Is he defended?'

'No, sir.'

'Do we know what he'll plead?'

'"Guilty" ... if he has any sense.'

'Ah, but will he?'

Fenton used a flat, 'official' tone, and said, 'In my considered opinion he'll plead "Guilty", sir.'

'Good. Anything else?'

'A Missing from Home. A girl—sixteen years old—she went astray at just before midnight ... that's when we got the report. She got back home at a few minutes past six.'

'The circulation's been cancelled?'

'Yes, sir.'

'Has she been seen?'

Fenton said, 'It's been arranged. The policewoman's coming on duty at nine ... she's detailed to see the girl, and take a statement.'

'Good.' Sawyer nodded his approval. 'Remind her of

possible sexual offences which might be disclosed.'

Fenton said, 'She'll know, sir . . . but I'll remind her.'

'Good. Anything else?'

'A couple of stolen cars. One in Ronsdale Section, one in Bagdon Section. An Austin and a V.W. Nobody of any . . . importance.' Fenton hesitated a split-second, before the last word; he was, he knew, using Sawyer's own yardstick of 'importance'—a yardstick measured by the amount of official influence the owner of each stolen vehicle could bring to bear—and it was a yardstick which he, Fenton, disapproved of.

If Sawyer noticed the hesitation, he gave no sign.

He said, 'C.I.D.?'

'They're already dealing with it, sir.'

'Good. Anything else?'

'No, sir.'

'Sickness?'

'Nobody's off duty sick, sir,' said Fenton. 'A couple of men on Annual Leave. Three on Weekly Rest Day. One away on a Driving Course. Otherwise, all present and correct.'

'Good.' Sawyer fiddled with the desk blotter. He kept his eyes lowered—scowling slightly at the green surface of the blotting-paper—as he continued. 'Sergeant Goodman.'

'Sir?'

'He's in the main office. As I came through, I noticed . . .'

'He's doing the Overtime Cards, sir. It's a time-consuming . . .'

'He should be on the street.'

Fenton said, 'The Overtime Cards have to be kept up to date, sir. He's not wasting time.'

'He should be on the street, inspector.' Sawyer's voice was tight and petulant. 'If anybody from D.H.Q. happened to pay us an unexpected visit, they'd . . .'

'That's not likely, sir. Not at this time in the morning.'

'Inspector.' Sawyer's voice notched itself a semitone higher as the pique burned deeper. "Don't argue. Be advised . . . do not argue with a senior officer. Especially when that senior officer happens to be right.'

'No, sir,' murmured Fenton, wearily.

'And chase Goodman out of that office. His place is on the street. His job is to make sure the constables are performing their duty.'

'I'll tell him, sir.'

'No—don't tell him, Fenton . . . make it an order.'

'Yes, sir,' sighed Fenton.

The inspector turned, to leave the office.

Sawyer looked up from the desk blotter, and said, 'You'll be taking court, this morning.'

'Sir?' Fenton looked surprised.

'I have an appointment—at headquarters . . . at ten o'clock.'

'Oh! Er—yes, sir. In that case . . .'

'You'll take court, inspector.'

'Of course.'

'I—er . . .' Sawyer paused then, in a voice heavy with meaning, said, 'I want convictions, Fenton. There are no committals. Nothing out of the ordinary.'

'I've glanced through the list,' said Fenton.

'In that case . . . convictions.' Sawyer allowed himself a quick, tight-lipped smile. 'You understand, inspector? If anybody gets away with it—with *anything*—I shall be very displeased.'

Fenton nodded.

He left the office, and closed the door.

The thought struck him that, if that was being a copper—if *that* was what policing brought you down to—he'd picked a particularly lousy profession.

THE MAN

'COMFORTABLE?' asked the driver.

The man said, 'Yes. Very comfortable...thanks.'

The man felt the vibrating power of the engine on the underside of his resting forearm. The eight-wheeler shuddered as it took the first strain of its massive, tarpaulin-lashed load. The wheels crept forward. The cab swayed, gently, as they moved over the uneven surface of the car park.

'Shift some of the junk,' suggested the driver. 'Those spare overalls and that towing-chain...shove 'em behind the seat. It'll give you more leg-room.'

The man said, 'No...it's all right. I'm fine. I'm comfortable, thank you.'

The lorry eased its nose to the kerb edge. It waited...trembling and ready to move. As a gap approached, it rolled forward, turned left and entered the stream of traffic.

The driver moved up the gears as the lorry built speed, and the man left him to his concentration.

It was good in the cab. Warm, and safe; as warm and as safe as the cell had sometimes seemed, but without the claustrophobic walls, and without the louts who shared the cell. And without the forever clanging of unseen doors, and the everlasting ringing of hidden bells, and the eternal tread of slow-pacing shoes on steel-shod floors... and, above all else, without the stench.

That stench... that bloody *smell*!

He would never rid himself of it; it was there, until the day he died. It was part of him—deep inside—and, for the rest of his life, and no matter how hard he scrubbed or how many times he bathed, it would continue to ooze out through every pore of his body... like an invisible, but indelible, vapour.

The smell of jail.

It was the stink of mixed urine, in slop-buckets, combined with carbolic and bodily sweat... and hatred. Hatred was the basic smell of all; the stench upon which all the other smells rested and grew.

Hatred... it had its own odour, and each hatred had, in turn, its own subtle sourness. Bitterness. Rebellion. Self-hate. Contempt. Disgust. All forms of hatred, and every shade of each hatred, and each carrying its own odour. The prison reeked of it; it impregnated the walls and choked all sense of pride, and all sense of human dignity. The hatred of the prisoners for the screws. The reciprocal hatred. The hatreds of prisoners for fellow-prisoners. Individual hatreds. Universal hatreds. Crazy, illogical hatreds.

They were all there... and each hatred was necessary.

Because hatred gave the mind something to work at. It provided thought, albeit twisted thought. It prevented madness... even if it substituted a lesser and more bearable madness.

And it stank... always!

Like fear, it could be smelled, and all these stupid, petty hatreds added their measured quota to the one monumental and terrifying stench which the outside world could never understand.

But here, in the cab, there was a cleaner smell. The sweet smell of hot diesel and, from the open window alongside the driver, the rush of passing air ... and (God forgive him for even thinking such a thought!) the last ten years had almost been worth the suffering for this one exquisite moment.

'Home?'

'What?' The man snapped his thoughts from their abstract wanderings.

'Home?' repeated the driver. 'That where you're making for?'

'Er—yes ... home,' said the man.

The driver drove with the elbow of his right arm resting on the sill of the cab window. He caressed the rim of the steering wheel with the tips of his muscular fingers and, as he talked, his eyes never left the road ahead.

He said, 'My name's Tom ... Tom Harding.'

'Harry,' countered the man. 'Harry Ogden.'

'Pleased to meet you, Harry.' Harding grinned at the rear bumper of the sports car which was pulling away, ahead of the lorry.

'Thanks. Me, too.'

The eight-wheeler growled north for another half-mile. Harding changed down as they approached a traffic roundabout, then back to top gear when the dual-carriageway pointed, like a broad-surfaced rail, ahead of the windscreen. He made the gear-change with an easy—almost off-handed—movement; the hand finding the gear-stick as readily as a cup finding the lips, and mesh finding mesh as smoothly, and as naturally, as liquid from that cup finding the mouth.

Ogden said, 'You can handle this thing.'

'I should.' Harding kept his eyes on the road. 'Every day—six, sometimes seven, days a week ... I'd be a mug if I couldn't.'

'Still ...' The single, meaningless word was a compliment.

A white and blue sign pointed its squat arrow towards the M.1, and the dual-carriageway took a wide left sweep between high, grassed banks. The green showed the first freshness of a new spring, and clusters of bulbs had been planted to give border beauty to the stark, hard-surfaced artery of civilisation. Some of the buds had already burst, and the new-born daffodils bobbed their heads in the breeze from passing traffic.

And this simple movement was beauty, and far more than beauty...it was freedom.

'How long?' asked Harding, then, in an apologetic tone, 'I'm not being nosey. Just—y'know...summat to say. Tell me to mind my own bloody business.'

Ogden hesitated then, in a low voice, said 'Ten.'

'Months?'

'Years.'

'Christ!' For the first time since they'd left the cafe, Harding took his eyes from the road. He shot a quick glance at his passenger, then returned his eyes to the road, and repeated, 'Christ!'

'It's a long time,' said Ogden flatly.

'It's a *bloody* long time.'

Beyond the banks the land flattened out. Good land, with rich, chocolate soil, and freshly turned furrows where some farmer had left his ploughing until after the winter. And, chequer-boarded with the areas of brown, fields in which cattle stood, heads-lowered, and ate grass.

And this, too, was beauty...and this, was part of freedom.

Harding left the fingers of his right hand resting on the wheel while, with his left hand he explored the pockets of his jacket.

'My turn,' said Odgen, and fished cigarettes from the carrier-bag between his feet.

'Ta.'

As he opened the packet, Ogden said, 'I hope they're like wine. Like violins.'

'Eh?' Harding cocked his head slightly to one side, while still keeping his eyes trained ahead of the vehicle.

'That they improve with age,' explained Ogden. 'They were returned to me, this morning.'

'Oh!'

They lighted the cigarettes, using Harding's lighter. Ogden handled the lighter; he used it on his own cigarette first, then he leaned across the cab and brought the flame to the tip of the cigarette which Harding held between his lips.

Harding said, 'Ta,' took back the lighter, inhaled smoke, removed the cigarette from his mouth and exhaled into the whip of the slipstream of air beyond the cab's open window. He said, 'Not bad. Not bad, at all.'

And the warmth of friendship which Ogden already felt for the huge, ugly but gentle man increased.

The cigarettes were ten years old. They were as dry as rotten sticks. They burned the tongue and rasped at the throat...and they tasted lousy.

THE WOMAN

HER name was Pamela Gertrude Ogden—but the 'Gertrude' was never mentioned . . . indeed, it had come as something of a surprise to Harry, at the wedding ceremony.

'Wilt thou, Pamela Gertrude . . .'

And she'd felt him stiffen slightly, and almost expected him to break into a giggle. It was what he did, when he was unexpectedly amused. What he'd done . . . what he'd *used* to do. A suppressed explosion of laughter . . . which always ended up as a giggle.

But not any more.

She doubted whether he laughed much, these days; whether he'd laughed much for ten years. Whether he'd even smiled very often.

On the four visits—the four times she'd seen him—he hadn't smiled. He'd looked sombre. Haggard. He'd looked an old man . . . years past his years. Greying hair

16

and lined, long before grey hairs and lines should have been noticeable.

And now?

'Pick up the pieces'... that was the expression everybody used. That's what they'd told her; that, when he came back, he'd be able to 'pick up the pieces'. That's what they'd said ... the 'experts' who claimed expertise in something they knew nothing at all about; who touched your hand, reassuringly, and tut-tutted whenever the bottled-in truth burst out, and didn't know (didn't know *at all*!) what soul-destroying agony really added up to.

He'd be able to 'pick up the pieces'.

What bloody pieces? Because the pieces weren't there any more. There wasn't a single piece left... not one of them. Their marriage... *what* marriage? They shared the same name on an official document, but they hadn't shared the same bed for a decade... so *what* marriage? Their love for each other... *what* love for each other? She'd said all the expected things, at the trial—she'd 'stood by him'—but, after what he'd done, how could any self-respecting wife forgive him... so *what* love for each other?

What *anything*?

Four years ago—the last time she'd seen him—he'd looked what he was... what he must have been. Finished. Smashed. An empty shell of a man, without hope and without future.

And that was four years ago... when they'd met, with the solicitor, to sign the papers giving her legal possession of the house, and the right to sell the house and every stick of its contents. And he'd signed, without a murmur. Without a question. Without even reading what he was putting his name on.

God!

And that was four years ago.

And the fools—the stupid, empty-minded fools—still talked about 'picking up the pieces'.

She walked slowly across the living room of the cottage, and into the tiny, lean-to kitchen at the rear. She took a kettle from its place on the shelf and filled it with water from the brass tap, above the sink. She placed the kettle on one of the rings of the cooker, struck a match and plopped the coronet of blue flame into life under the kettle's base. She returned to the sink and ran water onto the tea-dregs in the bottom of a brown porcelain teapot, then opened the rear door of the cottage and threw the dreg-swimming water onto the soil surrounding the clematis outside the door. She re-entered the kitchen, closed the door, spooned fresh tea into the teapot from a cheap, tin caddy, then placed the teapot ready, alongside the kettle, on one of the dead rings of the cooker.

She did these things automatically and with the slow deliberation of a sleep-walker; unable to concentrate because of her thoughts... unwilling to push aside her thoughts, in order that she might concentrate.

She prepared tea... the great British panacea for all sicknesses of the mind.

When the tea was made, she sat at the plain-topped deal table which stood by the window of the kitchen, sipped the liquid, smoked a cigarette and tried to marshal her thoughts into something approaching a decision.

She sought out the questions, and tried to find the answers... but the questions multiplied and over-whelmed her, and none of the answers came out straight. None of them made sense... any sort of sense.

Except...

Except one answer. *That* one made sense—terrifying sense... a sense which tightened her throat and dried her mouth.

She breathed, 'Oh, my God!'

She stood up from the table and walked back into the living room. She hunted around until she found her handbag, took out her purse and checked the loose change. She held the half-smoked cigarette between her lips as she shrugged her arms through the sleeves of a coat.

She left the cottage, without closing the door, and hurried towards the post office, near the centre of the village.

She held the coin ready as she began to dial the number.

She fumbled, mis-dialled, dropped the receiver back onto its rest and, as she did so, the coin slipped from her fingers and rattled on the floor of the call box.

She groaned, 'Damn. Damn! *Damn*!'

She pushed a lock of her straying hair from her eyes, bent, retrieved the coin, pushed the hair clear of her face again then, once more, dialled.

A man's voice preceded the bleeps.

She thrust the coin into the slot, and said, 'Ralph. This is me... Pamela.'

THE COP

'NOT,' snarled Sugden, 'that I give a solitary monkey's toss what the hell you wear.'

'Nice of you,' murmured Lennox. 'Y'know... magnanimous.'

'For me, you could come on duty in a bloody bikini.'

'I'll bear that in mind, if we have a particularly hot summer.'

Sugden's eyes popped, and he roared, 'Don't you bloody-well *dare*!'

Lennox grinned, and said, 'I'll bear that in mind, too.'

It was, of course, unseemly. Detective chief superintendents—Heads of C.I.D.—should not sit behind their desks, surrounded by the polished paraphernalia of their fancy offices, and blow every gasket in their whole high-powered engines, before 10 A.M. on nice, Wednesday mornings in early March. It isn't 'done'... especially when the gasket-blowing exercise is directed at

their seconds-in-command. Detective chief superintendents are (reputedly) solid people. They are plodding,
pedestrian people, with an abundance of grey stuff
packed away under their skulls, who never lose their
'cool'. They are men with great influence, whose
subordinates tremble at their slightest frown.

At least...thus goes the fiction.

But even detective chief superintendents are human
beings, with basic human frailties, and Sugden had been
up and about all night, fannying around at a cafe fire
which the forensic science clowns had provisionally
earmarked as 'arson'...and the blasted headquarters
canteen had closed shop at 7 A.M. thus denying Sugden
even the dubious solace of a yearned-for cuppa...and
then he'd dropped his pipe, and some beetle-booted
copper had thumped his size-tens onto it and snapped the
stem into three separate pieces...and even Sugden hadn't
been able to think up a single offence under the Police
Disciplinary Code which might cover ham-footed
pavement-bashers who ruined detective chief superintendents' vital smoking equipment...and...

And—we-ell—taking it all round (taking everything
into consideration)...it had been a sod of a night.

And now, plus-fours.

Plus-fours, for Christ's sake!

All right...Lennox was an odd-ball. He was a
fat-gutted, bald-headed slob, with the dress sense of a
moulting hyena. He was an animated barrel, with
armour-plating for a hide, and damn-all respect for his
superiors. But (God damn and blast it!) he was now a
detective superintendent. He carried rank and responsibility in large lumps. He was also (by all the saints in
heaven, and all the damned in hell!) Sugden's immediate
lieutenant—second only to Sugden himself in the C.I.D.
hierarchy—and here he was, first day on duty after a spell
of Annual Leave...*and wearing plus-fours.*

'You are,' choked Sugden, 'expected to dress the
bloody part.'

'What part?' Lennox looked mildly interested.

'You aren't still buggering about with your bucket and
spade.'

'Eh?'

'Surrounded by equally barmy idiots, all wearing togs they wouldn't be seen dead in, at home.'

'It was out of season,' observed Lennox.

'Eh?'

'Quiet.'

'I always thought,' said Sugden, nastily, 'that you millionaire-types formed a clique.'

'Naughty,' murmured Lennox.

'I always thought you chased the sun.'

'It was cool... even for Kamena Vourla.'

'Cold?'

'Cool,' corrected Lennox.

'In Greece? All that lovely ultra-violet stuff?' Sugden's sarcasm was as subtle as a Marciano uppercut.

'Cool,' repeated Lennox, 'but relaxing. The Erechtheum was almost deserted... even the Erechtheum.'

'I'm not surprised.' Sugden lowered his eyes and looked hard at the offending plus-fours. 'If you were wearing those bloody things—if you were traipsing about, looking like *that*—I wouldn't be surprised if the whole population of...'

'Oh, no... no.' Lennox chuckled. His pot-belly danced a horizontal jig in time with his mirth. He said, 'I found these, before we went. Y'know... sorting out the suitcases. I came across 'em. Harris tweed. As good as new.' He leaned forward and peered at a point south of where his waist should have been. He looked remarkably like a man peeping over the edge of a cliff. He murmured, 'Natty... eh?'

Sugden breathed, 'Oh, my Christ!' and acknowledged defeat. He said, 'Sawyer's waiting downstairs. In the Billiard Room.'

'Sawyer?'

'From Ellerfield.'

'Oh... *that* Sawyer.'

'He phoned yesterday,' grumbled Sugden. 'Something he wanted to see me about. Something urgent.'

Lennox made as if to leave the office.

He said, 'In that case, I'll push off. See what...'

'You,' interrupted Sugden.

'Eh?'

'He's seeing you, instead. I'm not going to let a nebulous clown like Sawyer keep me from my bed...not after last night.'

'Oh!'

'The glories of high office.' Sugden grinned, wolfishly. 'Get used to 'em, Lennox. They come thick, fast and heavy.'

Lennox said, 'Any idea what he wants to discuss?'

'Knowing Sawyer,' said Sugden, sourly, 'he probably wants to pee...and doesn't know which stall to use.'

Chief Inspector Bardoph Sawyer was displeased. He was (he fully realised) at County Constabulary Headquarters and (he also fully realised) the displeasures of mere uniformed chief inspectors didn't count for much within these gilded walls. Unlike when he was at Ellerfield Sub-Divisional Headquarters, here he was one hell of a long way short of being the Grand Panjandrum. Here he was (if anything) a superfluous nuisance...and slightly less important than the cadet responsible for delivering the chief constable's mid-morning tea and biscuits.

Nevertheless—and, we-ell, accepting all these things...a Billiard Room!

Nor was it a very posh Billiard Room, or even very clean. It was, in fact, distinctly dog-eared and (as Sawyer well knew) rarely used, except as a handy receptacle for unwanted guests. It was a makeshift waiting room for non-V.I.P. personnel; a gathering place (for example) in which to dump the monthly intake of new recruits, pending Headquarters Stores being ready to issue them with uniforms; a handy spot in which to shepherd dazed-eyed pedestrians, dragged in from the street, until the required number with which to make up an Identification Parade was arrived at.

That sort of place.

There was a billiard table...obviously. But the cloth was stained, and with a neat triangular tear up by the top, right-hand pocket. There were cues—all twisted and all tipless—stacked in a broken rack, in one corner. There were even balls—a billiard set, and a snooker set—but the whites were yellowed and veined, like a sick man's face, and the reds had all faded to a colour which made them almost indistinguishable from the snooker set's pink.

What there certainly was was dust. Everywhere! It hung in the air and floated in the shafts of March sunlight which slanted through the windows. It surfaced the moulded plywood of the wall-benches. It gave the hint of a grey veneer to the green of the baize. It agitated the tiny hairs of the nostrils, and made you want to sneeze.

All in all, it was a very dilapidated Billiard Room—a very mucky Billiard Room—and not at all an appropriate place in which to dump a police chief inspector who has red-hot news to impart to his superiors.

The door of the Billiard Room opened and, pushing his bay-window gut ahead of him, Lennox entered.

Sawyer eyed the plus-fours. He eyed the dazzling pullover, then the candy-striped shirt, then the bow tie...then he returned his attention to the plus-fours.

'Nice day, chief inspector,' greeted Lennox.

'Yes, sir.' Sawyer seemed to be having difficulty in dragging his eyes away from Lennox's legs.

'Cool but nice,' amplified Lennox.

'Yes, sir.'

Lennox followed the line of Sawyer's vision, grinned happily and said, 'Like 'em?'

'S-sir?'

'The bags.' Lennox had his hands in his pockets. He moved them, and the plus-fours took on an even more pronounced effect of pantaloons. 'Very snazzy...eh?'

'Yes, sir.' Sawyer swallowed. 'Very—er...snazzy.'

'Nothing like being smart, old son. Smart—but comfortable...that's what I...'

'Er—sir,' interposed Sawyer.

'Yes.'

'I have an appointment—*had* an appointment—at ten o'clock. With Detective Chief Superintendent Sugden. I wonder if you know whether he's been...'

'He can't make it.' This time Lennox interrupted. 'He's otherwise engaged...very important. He's sent me, instead.'

'Oh!'

Sawyer looked crestfallen.

Lennox didn't seem to notice the disappointment on the other man's face. He hitched an overweight buttock onto a corner of the billiard table, fished into the inside pocket of his jacket and brought out a carton of cheroots. He opened the slide of the carton and held the carton offeringly, towards Sawyer.

Sawyer said, 'No—er—no, thanks.'

'No?' Lennox sounded mildly surprised.

'I don't smoke,' explained Sawyer.

'Is that a fact?' Lennox's surprise increased a notch.

'It's bad for the health,' pronounced Sawyer.

'That,' said Lennox, 'is what they tell me.' He stripped the cellophane from one of the cheroots as he continued, 'Myself . . . I have my doubts. I know—the whizz-kids say you live longer if you don't smoke—but I dunno . . . maybe it just *seems* longer.'

'Nevertheless, medical statistics . . .'

'I remember a couple of years ago,' mused Lennox. He lighted the cheroot as he reminisced and, gradually, the dust of the Billiard Room was joined by some of the most foul-smelling smoke Sawyer had ever breathed into his lungs. Lennox said, 'The missus decided we needed a spot of culture. Y'know . . . music—so-called 'serious' music—and a play or two, now and again. I remember the D'Oyly Carte people did a week in Leeds. Gilbert and Sullivan—y'know . . . Gilbert and Sullivan. All that tumty-tumty-tum stuff.'

'Yes, sir. But what I came to tell you is that . . .'

'Every bloody night.' Lennox bulldozed ahead with his memories. 'She carted me to that blasted theatre every blasted night. And I remember one night in particular—what was it? . . . *H.M.S. Ruddigore*, I think they called it.'

'Sir, there's no such . . .'

'I know there was this fancy, dressed-up prat, marching around with his chopper in his hand. An *axe*, you understand—don't get me wrong . . . not his . . .'

'Sir, I'd like to . . .'

'And the bloody theatre was plastered, from floor to

ceiling, with 'No smoking' notices. And there was I, bursting for a quick draw. And this bloke—this Lord High something-or-other...'

'Executioner,' supplied Sawyer, in a tired voice.

'Eh?'

'Lord High Executioner, sir. The opera was *The Mikado*.'

'Was it?' Lennox looked puzzled.

'Yes, sir. I'm sure it was *The*...'

'I do believe you're right, old son.' Lennox beamed at the suffering Sawyer.

'Yes, sir. Now, can we...'

'That's clever. Y'know that?...that's *bloody* clever. You know your kit, lad, when it comes to music. Whatever else, you..."

'Sir,' said Sawyer, tightly, 'I think I should inform you...'

'What I'm getting at, though,' insisted Lennox, 'is that that blasted hour—when I couldn't smoke—was just about the longest hour of my life. Never-ending. So—what I'm getting at, is this—if I was never allowed to smoke again—*ever*—I might not live any longer, but by God...'

'Sir,' said Sawyer in a loud and desperate voice, 'I feel it is my duty to report that a murderer is on the loose.'

It stopped Lennox...even Lennox.

The fat detective removed the cheroot from his mouth and blew a long, thin feather of smoke. He watched Sawyer's reddened face for a moment, then lowered his eyes and examined the well-worn lino of the Billiard Room, then he raised his eyes once more and did a second visual tour of the uniformed chief inspector's features.

After which, he spoke...slowly, quietly and distinctly.

'Y'know,' he said, 'that is quite an interesting proposition, Chief Inspector Sawyer. It beats Monopoly into a cocked hat.'

'Sir, what I mean is...'

'It would help—at the very least, it wouldn't do any harm—if you spelled out the details a little more carefully.'

THE HUSBAND

His name was Ralph Watford. He was a local authority employee—a fully paid up member of N.A.L.G.O.—and he had an office, complete with desk, filing-cabinets, official stationery, an ebony ruler, departmental ballpoints and a telephone. He was 'attached to' the local Youth Employment Office—which meant he was but, at the same time, wasn't . . . a very fluid state of affairs which suited him fine. Officially, he wasn't 'on the strength' of that department; which, being the case, meant he couldn't very well be sacked . . . at worst, he could only be 'transferred'. Which made him happy in the knowledge that, however much he slacked, and whoever found him with his feet up on the desk, he was dead safe. The situation had, built into it, a second chance which, as a long-stop against things going wrong, was as safe and as solid as a brick wall.

But, at this particular moment, Watford was not his

usual happy self. He was holding a telephone conversation, and he was glad he had his office to himself—and that the door was closed... and he only hoped that nosey little cow on the switchboard wasn't listening.

Watford said, 'Look... what the hell can I do?'

'Somebody!' The woman's voice was plaintive. Pathetically plaintive. 'I don't know which way to turn. I need help. I need *somebody*.'

'Well—for God's sake—why me?'

'Who else? Who else can I ask?'

'How do I know?'

'They don't know me. The people here—those in the village—they don't know me.'

'He'll—he'll...' Watford flickered his eyes around the walls of the office, as if seeking inspiration. 'Look... he might not even *come*.'

'He will.'

'Has he said?'

'He will... I *know* he will.'

He chewed at his lower lip, and his eyes went out of focus as he concentrated his mind upon some way in which to rid himself of this near-hysterical woman.

Over the line, her voice said, 'Ralph! Ralph... are you still there?'

'Yes, I'm still here,' he muttered.

'What are we going to do, Ralph? For God's sake... what are we going to *do*?'

'Nothing.' He put brittle certainty into his voice... a brittle certainty which was a lie. 'I'm going to do nothing. I don't see why the deuce I should get...'

'You gave evidence,' she cut in, and her voice was as ugly as his was hard. 'The main witness... remember?'

'I answered questions. I told the truth. That's all.'

'He might not call it that.'

'What the hell else can he...'

'He's a violent man, Ralph. You know him. He's a violent man.'

'Just what...' He swallowed, then said, 'What are you getting at?'

'He knows how to hate. That's all. And he can be *very* violent.'

'Why should...' Again, he swallowed to ease the sudden parchedness of his throat. He said, 'Let me think about it, Pamela. Let me ring you back.'

'Don't be silly.' There was contempt—bitterness—in the rejoinder.

'How do you mean? What's...'

'I'm in a call box. Telephones cost money.'

'Oh!'

'Get out here,' she said. 'You know where I live...you *should* know. Get out here, then...'

The conversation was cut short by the bleeps. He waited, hoping she'd feed another coin into the slot, at her end...but she didn't.

He replaced the receiver onto its rest, frowned, then pushed his fingers through his hair.

He breathed, 'Oh, Christ!' sighed, heavily, then repeated, 'Oh, my Christ! Now, what?'

THE MAN

THEY hit the M.1 at Junction Number 15 and, from then on, the engine which shared the cab with them rose in pitch to a steady, deep-throated throb and stayed there. In effect, distance was replaced by time; the needle on the speedo settled itself at the 45 mark and miles could be accurately measured by hours, and even minutes. Motorway driving—a connubial experience...the modern marriage of time and space.

At first, the traffic worried Ogden. So much of it—so many vehicles...so much concentrated speed. He'd known motorways before but, ten years back, they'd still been near-novelties; people—even motorists had stayed conservative...they'd plumped for the A-class routes when there'd been a choice. But no more. Today (or so it seemed) every vehicle in the world belted, foot hard down, along triple-lane dual-carriageways. It made him nervous...just a little.

The nervousness was offset by the cab; the warmth and the friendliness of the driver; the size of the vehicle in which he rode, and the easy control exercised by Harding; the feeling of indestructability... which, in turn, was part of the growing feeling of freedom.

'What do you do?' asked Harding.

'Eh?'

They'd driven in silence for the past thirty minutes, and the question caught Ogden unready. It wasn't an awkward question—not a nosey question—just a conversational question... but it *was* a question.

'Your job,' said Harding. 'What do you do for a living?'

'Butcher... master butcher,' said Ogden. Then, as an afterthought, added, 'Was.'

'A handy trade,' observed Harding.

'I thought so.'

'Shouldn't be too difficult to find work.'

'No?' The question had a core of sour doubt.

'Skilled work.' Harding put deliberate encouragement into his words. 'I know a bloke... a driver. He tells me. Meat-cutting. Slaughterhouse work. Not much skill—y'know... not a lot to it. But a butcher's different. He does all of it... and more. That's what he tells me.'

'He's right,' said Ogden, flatly.

'So-o...' Harding moved his muscle-heavy shoulders.

Ogden stared ahead at the ribbon of the motorway. He saw things—things he couldn't see with his eyes—and, gradually, his face softened a little. Some of the scowl-lines between his brows became less deep. Something which was almost a smile—but not quite a smile—gave his mouth contours which were less sullen.

And, when he spoke, he spoke to two people. He spoke to Harding, and he spoke to himself. It was a combined telling and a reminding... the forcing of a long-locked door, and a tentative peep at what was beyond.

His voice held little emotion; a touch of reflective sadness, perhaps... but little else.

He said, 'We had shops—three shops... my brother-in-law and me. My sister's husband. We have these three shops. Good shops—busy... we'd worked up a good reputation. Three towns—y'know...small towns. Market towns, really. Not the cities. We didn't want the cities. We had it all worked out. Small towns—on the edge of the country... between the industrial belt and the rural communities. Fresh meat. Straight from the cattle markets. Kill it, and sell it...no middle-man. Give value, give service...and nothing second-best.

'We started with one. Then two. Then three. We were onto a gold-mine...because we gave value. As simple as that. We gave what the others couldn't give—*wouldn't* give...because we weren't greedy. We never went back—not once...all the time, we improved. Never once...not once, in the red. After we'd paid off the first loan—to get us started...after that, we couldn't go wrong. Even with the new shops, we didn't have to borrow. We ploughed it all back and it made more. All it needed was work. Work, and giving value for money...that's all. The profits followed. More profits than we'd thought possible. Because we didn't covet...that's why.' Ogden moved his head, looked across the cab and spoke directly to Harding. He said, 'Y'know that, mate? "Thou shalt not covet"...bloody good advice. I know. Coveting—it caused more bloody aggravation...more aggravation than *that*.'

The junction with the M.6 was, to Ogden, like an explosion of traffic lanes; a Bedlam of vehicles, all racing north or nudging left before peeling off to the west...a Roman candle of internal combustion, with each coloured spark a car, or a van or a lorry.

He found himself holding his breath until the junction was behind them, and they were once more held firmly within the comparatively simple confines of the M.1.

He'd wanted freedom. For years, he'd dreamed of freedom...and now he had it. But the motorway junction was symptomatic. In its own mad way it represented too much freedom...far more freedom than he could yet handle.

Harding seemed to sense his unease.

He said, 'First time?'

'What?'

'Motorway driving?' said Harding. 'You'll have been on 'em before?'

'Yes...oh, yes. A few times.'

'But not the full dose...eh?' Harding grinned at the windscreen.

'Not...Not like that lot.' Ogden found himself smiling. A shy—almost sheepish—smile, in return for Harding's grin.

Harding said, 'You'll get used.'

'Eventually...I suppose.'

'When you're...' Harding frowned and closed his mouth.

'What?' asked Ogden.

'Nothing, mate...sorry.' The driver was suddenly embarrassed.

'Tell me,' insisted Ogden.

'Look—I talk too bloody much...it's summat I...'

'Please!' There was quiet, but concentrated, savagery in Ogden's voice.

Harding took a deep breath, sighed, moved one hand from the steering wheel long enough to make a quick gesture of reluctant capitulation, then said, 'All right, mate—when you get back into gear...that's all I meant.'

'Into gear?'

'Get back to your shops. You'll need to travel. You'll be...'

'No shops,' interrupted Ogden, harshly.

'Oh!'

'No shops. No home...no nothing.'

Harding muttered, 'I'm sorry, mate. I—y'know...I talk to much.'

There was a moment or two of silence then, in a gentle voice, Ogden said, 'Don't apologise. It isn't necessary...you're a good man.'

'Look—for God's sake—I shouldn't have...'

'I've met the other sort.'

'I—er—I reckon.'

'And not just behind bars.'

'No. I—er—I reckon not.' Harding looked awkward. Uncomfortable.

'Bastards,' said Ogden, softly. 'The *real* bastards... they never get caught.'

THE COP

LENNOX did circuits of the billiard table as he talked. He waved the partly smoked cheroot, whenever he wanted to emphasise a point. With his free hand he rubbed the bald dome of his skull, massaged the back of his neck, scratched his multi-chinned jaw, pulled the lobe of his ear and, generally, behaved much like a dog suffering from a surfeit of fleas.

Sawyer on the other hand, stood motionless. Not quite at attention, but certainly not at ease. He hated this overweight superintendent but, being Sawyer, wouldn't allow himself to show his hatred; he hated the matey-matey mannerisms—the outrageous mode of dress—the choking stink from the cheap cheroot . . . but most of all, and like so many other people, he hated the truth when he heard it and consequently, hated the deliverer of that truth.

'It's a good job,' said Lennox, 'old Sugden didn't come down.'

'Sir—with respect—I can't agree with...'

'All this guff about murderers being on the loose. The poor bugger's done his time. Leave it at that.'

'He's a convicted murderer.'

'All that... but that's all,' agreed Lennox. 'Convicted. Punished. Finished with. If prison means owt, he won't do it again.'

'Ah, but if he does?'

'If he does,' said Lennox, cheerfully, 'and if you catch him. If—like the last time you nail him... back he goes inside. And you can carve another notch on your gunbutt. It'll go with the first.'

'Sir—with respect—that's not a very nice thing to...'

'Sawyer!' Lennox stopped his pacing. He eyed the uniformed chief inspector warningly, and said, 'All this periodic bullshit about "with respect". If you want to be respectful, *be* respectful...don't crawl. I don't go for prayer-mats. I don't use 'em myself...I don't expect other people to use 'em when they're arguing with *me*. But—I'm telling you, son—if you'd spun this cackhanded yarn to Sugden, he'd have had you certified. Look at it—what's it boil down to?—just this: Harry Ogden's out... big bloody deal! So, who's Harry Ogden?... he's a miserable little squirt who once killed a woman he was having it off with. Again... big bloody deal! It happens all the time. He isn't unique... he isn't even out of the ordinary. But what makes him special?—I'll tell you, Sawyer... he represents the only fair-to-middling case you ever handled. As far as *you're* concerned the Mafia come a bloody poor second to Harry Ogden. And that's why you're here. And that's why you're wasting everybody's time. And that's why—if Sugden had come down to listen to all this crap—you wouldn't know whether your arse-hole was punched, bored or counter-sunk.'

Having delivered himself of an honest opinion, Lennox resumed his marathon walk around the billiard table.

Sawyer stood as still as ever; half-rigid and almost trembling with offended rage.

He fought back.

He said, 'The man's a murderer, sir.'

'Was.'

'Still is. He's killed. For the rest of his life, he's a murderer.'

'We're all potential murderers, son.'

'I wouldn't agree, sir.'

'No,' murmured Lennox, 'I didn't expect you would.'

'The man's a murderer,' insisted Sawyer. 'He should be watched.'

'Hounded?'

'Watched.'

'Victimised?'

'Watched, sir . . . I said *watched*.'

'Son,' sighed Lennox, 'the poor devil's been "watched"—as you call it—for ten long years. If "watching" him is going to hold him back from committing another murder, he's had enough of it . . . if it won't work after all that time, it won't work ever."

'I don't mean that,' protested Sawyer.

'I know what you mean, son . . . and you will not— repeat *not*—get my blessing.'

'Preventive policing,' argued Sawyer. 'It's what . . .'

'Preventive ballocks,' said Lennox, irreverently. 'Catching 'em and convicting 'em . . . *that's* preventive policing. And he's already been caught and convicted.'

'The textbooks all . . .'

'The textbooks,' interrupted Lennox airily, 'are all written by nutters, read by dummies and followed by raving lunatics. Show me a "book-bobby", and I'll show you a copper who shouldn't be paid out in tap-washers.'

Sawyer breathed heavily, then said, 'And that's your last word, sir . . . is it?'

'On this particular subject,' agreed Lennox.

'I can take it as a specific order? . . . *not* to keep an eye on Ogden?'

'Tighten your corsets, son.' Lennox stopped his walk. He leaned his broad-beamed backside against the surround of the billiard table, cocked an eye at the indignant uniformed chief inspector, and said, 'You came

asking for advice ... not orders. That's what I've given
you ... advice. An opinion. Take it ... or leave it. You put
him inside. He's now out again. He's likely to make for
your patch. If there's a problem, it's *your* problem. It's a
decision ... and decision-making goes with those three
pips you carry on your shoulders. He's your pigeon,
Sawyer. Cage him or let him fly free ... but *you* decide.'

'This—this conversation,' choked Sawyer. 'I find it
offensive.'

Lennox drew thoughtfully on the cheroot.

'I—I came here, with the intention of reporting to
Detective Chief Superintedent Sugden, certain facts ...'

'He wouldn't have thanked you.'

'Certain facts,' insisted Sawyer, in a strangled voice,
'which, in my opinion needed bringing to his notice.'

'That Ogden's out?'

'That a man, convicted of murder ...'

'Ten years ago.'

'... has been released from prison and, in all probability, will return to this police area.'

'I'll pass your message.'

Sawyer swallowed, stiffened and, in an officious tone,
said, 'For doing what I considered to be my duty, I have
been treated—spoken to—in an offensive manner. I have
been subjected to humiliation ... in my opinion, deliberate humiliation. I must inform you, sir, that a record of
this conversation will be made and a report of it
forwarded to the chief constable.'

'Good lad!' Lennox's face split. The grin was as
complete and as uncomplicated, as a melon with a thin
V-slice removed. He dropped what was left of the cheroot
onto the lino, squashed it dead with the sole of a brogue,
and said, 'It'll add to his collection. Every day, old
son ... a complaint about this bastard Lennox. The mail
wouldn't be complete, without one. One day he'll get one
that'll worry me ... and he'll frame it.'

Lennox shoved his hands into the pockets of his
ridiculous plus-fours, turned and rolled out of the Billiard
Room. And never did a man look more sure of
himself ... never did a man look so bloody *sure*!

Sawyer drove his Citroën Diane back, towards Ellerfield. A Citroën Diane because (to quote the ad, in the *Observer* colour supplement) 'The Citroën Diane looks like no other car on the road'...which made it a dead cinch for a man ridiculously jealous of his own unusual Christian name. It wasn't a bad car—just a poor reason for choosing a car...but, as far as Sawyer was concerned, a perfectly adequate reason.

He therefore drove his Citroën Diane, towards Ellerfield, and seethed at the manner in which his tiding regarding the recently released Harry Ogden had been received by at least one of Headquarters hot-shots.

But Lennox was a fool. He was an idiot. He was a bloated moron, puffed out with self-importance...beyond reasoning with. God only knew how he'd scrambled up the promotion slope, to the rank of detective superintendent...God *only* knew! Ten years ago, he'd been a detective sergeant; a roly-poly joke, tucked away in some backwoods sub-division; good for a guffaw, as his outrageous antics gradually became the talking-point of the rest of the force.

Lennox—*Sergeant* Lennox...and, today, *Superintendent* Lennox had had the impudence to call him 'son'. Had the gall to put on a hail-fellow, condescending act, when he must have known—he *must* have remembered—that he (Sawyer) was already a detective inspector, when he (Lennox) was only an adult Billy Bunter masquerading as a detective sergeant.

Because (and make no mistake about it) talent didn't mean a thing in this force. Not one damn thing. Talent—devotion to duty—a natural flair for police work...they all counted for nothing! It was always who-you-knew, and never what-you-did. It was always a matter of pissing in the same pot—having pals in the same Masonic Lodge—getting stinking drunk together—and, if all else failed, quietly sawing a length off with the right man's wife.

Christ!

But not for him. Not for Sawyer...not for a man like Sawyer. Sawyer did it the hard way. The honourable way.

The decent way. Sawyer reached the top, on sheer ability...that, or he didn't get there.

Sawyer was a uniformed police chief inspector, because Sawyer *deserved* to be a uniformed police chief inspector.

And Sawyer was—Sawyer was—Sawyer is...Sawyer is...

Detective Inspector Sawyer feels like throwing up.

There is (the book says so, therefore it must be a fact) approximately ten pints of blood in the body of the average adult person. But this adult person must have had far more than her fair quota. Blood is everywhere. Miniature seas of it lie, like irregularly-shaped scarlet rugs, about the lino-tiled floor of the kitchen. Great spillings of it discolour Formica-topped working surfaces and drip slow and sticky globules onto the paintwork of drawers and sliding-doors. The walls are streaked and smeared with it, and it has even flown high, slashed the ceiling and dried, scarlet-black, on one of the strip-lighting tubes.

This kitchen, with all its modern accoutrements and gadgets, is decorated in blood. The sweet, sickly smell assaults the nostrils. The thick, horrific sight shocks the eyes.

And Detective Inspector Sawyer feels like throwing up.

He does not throw up because, to throw up would be a sign of weakness. It would lower his jealously guarded prestige. The uniformed constables, and the detective constable, and the uniformed sergeant—all of whom, he knows, are watching him—would count him weak and gutless if he followed his natural inclination and went outside to vomit.

Therefore, instead of throwing up, he speaks to the uniformed sergeant.

He asks, 'Has anybody touched the body?'

'No, sir.' The uniformed sergeant qualifies his answer, by adding, 'Not while I've been here.'

'Good.' Detective Inspector Sawyer mentally flicks his

*way through the textbook pages and, as the do's and
don'ts appear, he gives his orders. 'Post men at front and
rear. Allow no person into the house, without my
authority. Notify a medical practitioner—we need formal
certification of death. Notify the coroner. Notify
Photography Section. Notify Fingerprint Section. Notify
the Forensic Science Laboratory. Notify the Dog Section.
Notify Headquarters C.I.D. Notify the Divisional
Superintendent—and request more men, as soon as
possible. Contact Divisional C.I.D.—get all C.I.D.
personnel on duty, immediately, and tell them to report
here, as soon as possible. Nothing to the Press ... refer
them to the Press Relations Officer. She's a married
woman?'*

'Yes, sir,' says the uniformed sergeant.

*'Contact him. Tell him what's happened. Note his
reply— his immediate reaction—make a recorded note of
his reply and reaction. Don't allow him to contact
anybody, until he's been interviewed. Got all that?'*

*'Yes, sir.' The uniformed sergeant. murmurs, tenta-
tively, 'The—er—Plan Drawing Section, sir?'*

*'I've already told you to notify them,' lies Sawyer,
petulantly.*

*'Yes, sir ... I'm sorry, sir.' The uniformed sergeant is in
no mood for argument.*

'Do it, then,' snaps Sawyer. 'Don't just stand there.'

*The uniformed sergeant leaves the kitchen. The
uniformed constables follow.*

Sawyer turns to the detective constable.

'Who found her?' he asks. 'Who reported it?'

'The next-door neighbour.'

'The name, man? The name?' says Sawyer, irritably.

'Ogden, sir ... Harry Ogden.'

... Sawyer—Detective Inspector Sawyer—was a man
who did his job well. Without fear or favour. Without
hesitation. He was a damn good detective and, as far as he
was concerned, murder was just one more crime—to be
detected—and *he* could detect it.

And the same with Uniformed Police Chief Inspector

Sawyer. He was the same man. As good as ever. As conscientious as ever. As ruthless as ever.

And, irregardless of the stupid arrogance of a certain fat-gutted detective superintendent, Uniformed Police Chief Inspector Sawyer was going to do his duty...he was going to treat a murderer *as* a murderer.

Because he was a copper...and a damn good copper!

THE HUSBAND

HAVING made his excuses—having lied to the Senior Youth Employment Officer, about the sudden onset of a severe migraine—Ralph Watford let himself into his home, made a bee-line for the drinks cabinet and poured himself a triple whisky... neat.

Whatever other faults he had, Watford was not given to undue worry concerning the opinions of other people. He was a firm believer in the sticks-and-stones adage. He had one life—just the one—and, if so-called 'principles' clogged up the smooth running of the machinery and, in so doing, switched the journey through that life from a Rolls to a pogo-stick, the hell with 'principles'. The world (according to Ralph Watford) owed Ralph Watford a living—a comfortable living, at that—and for the very good reason that the world (as far as Ralph Watford was concerned) ceased to exist, the moment the said Ralph Watford snuffed it.

It was a philosophy and, so far, it had worked.

It had steered him towards his first wife—because she'd been the only child, and pampered daughter, of a local up-and-coming industrialist—and, when his first wife 'died' (indeed, before her death) his sights had shifted to his present wife... which, in view of the fact that the local industrialist had, in the event, neither upped nor come but, instead had fouled everything by going into voluntary liquidation, showed certain long-term planning on the part of Mr Ralph Watford.

Admittedly, his present wife was a mite older than he was. Almost twenty years older, to be precise. But hard cash, and good living, could make amends for anything... at least, they could to a man like Ralph Watford.

That he 'worked' for a living was, of course, something of a private joke... a joke he kept strictly to himself. He left home for a specified number of hours each week; he lounged around in an office, at the Youth Employment Centre; he drew a salary, which he used as loose change. Fine—if that was 'working for a living'... he 'worked for a living'.

He found it a bore—but a bore he was, unfortunately, lumbered with—because Angela 'believed' in these things. That the man-of-the-house should be the 'breadwinner'... even though she happily provided the jam, the cake and even the caviare from her own purse. She was a great one for 'beliefs' was Angela. A sucker for 'causes'. A never-ending do-gooder and a very ardent Socialist. Indeed, the only real row they'd ever had had blown up from a remark he'd made, when he'd been tongue-loosened by booze... 'Y'know, Angela, you're the only Socialist I've ever met who has enough money to *be* a bloody Socialist.'

He'd thought the remark witty.

She hadn't... and, because she was old and set in her ways, it had taken him almost a week to smooch her back into her normal receptive mood.

And now, when he wanted her—when he was pushed for time—the silly bitch was out somewhere... up some bloody back street, feeding the poor, no doubt!

He slumped into the deep comfort of an armchair and swung his feet up onto a strategically-placed ottoman.

It was a great life, if he didn't weaken . . . and, by Christ, he wasn't going to weaken. Not after all this! Not after bedding a woman old enough to be his mother; not after dancing attendance upon a female ancient monument . . . a sexless cow who 'acquiesced to his rights as a husband' (her own monumentally prim expression) with about as much enthusiasm as a patient in a dentist's chair. Who was so bloody boring.

But who (unfortunately) was also so bloody well-heeled.

Not like Pamela . . . for example.

Pity about Pamela. With money, she'd have been perfect—we-ell . . . almost perfect.

Jealousy and nubility. He supposed they went together—except, of course, in whores . . . but, whatever else, Pamela wasn't a whore. Hadn't been. What she was now, was anybody's guess. But, in those days, she hadn't been a whore. She'd been eager . . . sometimes too bloody eager. Sometimes, Harry had hardly closed the front gate before she'd been in and at it. 'To see if Ruth was in.' That had always been her excuse—always . . . when she'd known damn well that Ruth was out. When he'd seen her, peeping at the window, watching for Ruth to leave. 'To see if Ruth was in' . . . the randy, lying bitch.

Then the pantomime. His suggestion that she stay and join him in mid-morning coffee. Her token humming and hawing—that she had housework to do—that she didn't think she could spare the time—that she'd 'only popped in for a minute, to ask Ruth something' . . . and, finally, the pseudo-reluctant acceptance of the offer.

And then . . .

Easy! She'd trembled—quivered in delightful anticipation—the second his fingers had touched the nape of her neck. She'd made muttered objections—empty, but conventional, objections—as he'd unbuttoned, or unzipped, her dress and eased it clear of her shoulders; as he'd unhooked her brassière and cupped her full and hard-nippled breasts in his palms.

And then . . .

She'd clenched her teeth onto a corner of her lower lip. And, sometimes, she'd bitten hard enough—deep enough—to draw blood. And she'd moaned to herself— soft, animal noises—as he'd gradually and lingeringly stripped her. And sometimes—often—her first orgasm had occurred before he'd even mounted her.

Easy... so bloody easy!

There'd been a rug—a wool rug—a soft, large, kitchen rug in front of the closed-in fire... and he'd called it 'their rug'. He'd called it their 'passion spot'. And he'd laughed, as he'd used these expressions, but she'd never joined his laughter.

Because she was Pamela—Pamela Ogden—and a suburban housewife... with a kink. With a weakness she couldn't control. Like drugs. Like alcoholism. It was bigger—stronger—than she was... and she was ashamed of it.

And, when it was over—when they were both spent and breathless—she'd stand there, on 'their rug', and the tears would roll down her cheeks, and she'd dress herself while he watched.

And he'd—and he'd—and he... and he...

She is attractive. Make no mistake about it, she is attractive. With decent grooming, she could be beautiful. She has a better figure—a trimmer figure—than Ruth. She is a young, red blooded, exciting animal—with all the explosive passions of such an animal—imprisoned within the 'respectable' exterior of a normal, middle-class housewife.

And she stands there, dressing herself, with the glow from the fire high-lighting the thin sheen of perspiration, and giving her whole body a colouring which personifies her secret self. Glowing and scarlet. Primitive and savage.

And she weeps. Because of what she is... because the civilisation, of which she is a part, would vilify her and call her emotions sinful.

Watford smokes a cigarette as he watches. And he always watches, because this, too, is part of his pleasure; part of the excitement part of the hold which he exercises over this young wife whose secret shame he uses.

He reaches a hand to where he knows there is a kitchen chair. He makes the movement without taking his eyes from her. He draws the chair closer, and sits down ... less than a yard from where she is sorting out the clothing she hurled aside less than quarter of an hour ago.

'Why the tears?' he asks. 'Why the waterworks? You enjoyed yourself. Why the hell cry about it?'

She bends, threads her feet into her panties, and pulls them up above her hips.

'You enjoyed yourself,' he insists. 'I know—you always do ... so who the hell are you kidding?'

She sniffs, wipes her eyes with the back of her hand, and whispers, 'Damn you, Ralph. You're—you're a ...'

He draws on the cigarette, smiles, then says, 'I'm a man. You're a woman. We have appetites ... similar appetites. We—er—"feed" ourselves. Is that wrong?'

'I don't want to talk about it.'

'Until next time,' he mocks, gently.

'There isn't going to be a "next time",' she chokes.

'Oh, come on!' He grins. 'There never is ... until next time arrives.'

'Damn you, Ralph. If you weren't Harry's-friend ... Damn you for what you are.'

'And what am I?' he asks ... and the mockery is still there.

'I don't have to tell you. I don't have to ...'

She gags on her own disgust.

She threads her arms through the tapes of her brassière. She hooks it into place, at the back. One at a time, she nestles her breasts into the unnecessarily moulding stricture of the cups.

And still she weeps. The tears roll down her cheeks. They gather at her chin. They drop, and the drop splashes moisture onto the fabric of the brassière.

'I am,' says Watford, airily, 'A voyeur. That, and nothing more. I take my pleasure—what pleasures I require—as they are offered. You, my sweetheart, are handy ... and offer them, regularly.'

'You're filthy. You're immoral. You're ...'

'*I am neither "filthy" nor "immoral".*' He smiles,
condescendingly. '*I am not—I freely admit—the Arch-
bishop of Canterbury . . . anything like that. But consider,
sweetheart, if I'm filthy—if I'm immoral—what does that
make you?*'

'*I'm a married woman.*'

'*Oh, dear!*'

'*With a good husband.*'

'*Whom you forget, very easily . . . as easily as I forget
my "good" wife.*'

She struggles into her underskirt.

She says, '*He loves me—Harry loves me—and I don't
deserve . . .*'

'*Loves you . . . but can't satisfy you, sweetheart.*'

'*Damn you. Don't call me "sweetheart". I'm not
your . . .*'

'*You—presumably—"love" him,*' teased Watford.

'*Yes. I do. You wouldn't understand such things,
but . . .*'

'*I wonder,*' muses Watford, slyly, '*whether this
"love"— this great "love" he has for you—precludes him
from . . . we-ell.*' He moves his shoulders, expressively. He
murmurs, '*Ruth says the same. That I "love" her. You
should ask her. She'd tell you. We all "love" each other.
It's what makes the world go round . . . that, and a little
variety, to relieve the boredom.*'

The shock hits her—the contemplation that what he is
saying might, conceivably, have a seed of truth—and the
shock freezes her expression into a mask of outraged
horror.

She stoops, scoops up her skirt, blouse and shoes into
one untidy bundle, and runs out of the kitchen.

Out of the house.

Home.

. . . he'd been happy in those days. Those far-away days,
before Ruth had 'died'—before Angela, and her loot, had
eased themselves into his life—when he'd had a wife, and
a mistress, and odd bits and pieces scattered about the
district. All unbeknown to Ruth . . . or so he'd thought.

And Ruth—good old, reliable old Ruth—always on tap, to feed him his oats when all else failed . . . or (again) so he'd thought.

Nevertheless . . . Happy Days!

He gulped some of the whisky, and wondered where that stupid cow Angela was, and why the hell she couldn't be home when he wanted her.

THE WOMAN

LITTLE MOYSELL—that was the name of the
village...often deliberately mispronounced 'Little
Mouse-hole'. A joke. Something meant to bring a smile,
or even a chuckle; nothing snide—nothing
disparaging...just a gentle leg-pull concerning a village
which typified genuine rural beauty.

'Genuine rural beauty'... up a bloody flagpole!

It was a slum, with grass. Two-thirds of the village
didn't have baths, or even water-closets. Half of it didn't
have hot water. Just under a quarter of the place didn't
have *any* water—not as far as indoor taps were
concerned...and every drop had to be carted in buckets,
filled at a communal stand-pipe, or from a nearby spring.
Good water—pure water—very healthy water...if only
because carrying the damn stuff kept you fit!

She hated the village. She hated the squalor which
crouched, hidden, behind the rose-covered frontage. She

hated the stinking stackyards, and the even more stinking piles of rotting mangles which seemed to fill every odd corner of every field. She hated the village green; the shapeless mush of damp and soggy grass, where the village dogs left their droppings and where passing motorists tossed their litter. The church, with its moss-scarred walls and tilting headstones; the school, with its piffling tarmac playground and narrow, porched door; the back lanes . . . mud-heavy after a shower, or with ankle-twisting ruts after a dry spell.

'Genuine rural beauty' . . . up a fifty-foot bloody flagpole!

That was Little Moysell—that was the village . . . and the village deserved the villagers every bit as much as the villagers deserved their village.

The men . . . oafs, to the last one; heavy-booted and slow-plodding; with expressions as stupid as their sheep, movement as dreary as their cattle's and manners on a par with their pigs. The woman . . . fit mates for their men; round or straight, but always shapeless; bare-armed and forever busy; slow to speak but, when they did speak, spiteful. The children . . . sullen as their sires and spiteful as their dams; conceived in procreative lassitude—with as much love as a boar feels for a sow—and raised to adulthood in monotonous tedium.

Thus the considered opinions of Pamela Ogden. Biased, beyond all reason but (as far as she was concerned) honest. She hated the village, she hated the villagers . . . she hated everything.

Life . . . particularly did she hate life. Especially her own life. Solitude did not become her; as far as she was concerned, solitude was synonymous with loneliness, and loneliness was something reserved for the grave. Solitude was the very antipathy of life.

And (God help her!) the cottage was the most solitary building in the whole village.

Somebody—some wild-headed fool, with an imagination way beyond the realms of reality—had named the cottage 'The Swan's Nest'. But it had never housed a swan, nor (come to that) had ever even *seen* a swan from its doors or windows . . . and it was certainly no *nest*!

It was built of stone, with a flagged roof and crumbling brick chimney stack which jutted out from one of its end walls. It had a single main room, downstairs, with a lean-to kitchen at the rear. It had one bedroom, dimensionally identical with the downstairs room and, like the downstairs room, the bedroom had an open fire . . . smaller than the one downstairs and, also unlike the one downstairs, non-functional. It had a tap; one large brass tap, fixed to the wall above the stone sink in the lean-to kitchen . . . and that was all. When hot water was needed, the water had to be heated on the Calor gas stove, alongside the sink. It had electricity . . . one fifteen-amp plug in the living room, and two ceiling roses (one in the living room, one in the bedroom) from which dangled lengths of worn flex and, at the ends of the flex, bulb-holders. The electricity did not reach the kitchen; after dark, you either left the door open and worked in the dim glow which filtered through from the living room, or you used a lamp or a candle. It had a toilet—a 'privy'—at the bottom of the rear garden; an abomination, reached via a treck through a neat mixture of mud, twitch-grass and brambles; a primitive and disgusting depository of human refuse, consisting of a brick-built shed which contained a low shelf, with a hole at its centre and, under the hole, a galvanised container which was emptied, twice a week, by a man some few rungs lower in status than the village idiot.

This, then, was the cottage and its amenities . . . this was 'The Swan's Nest'.

It stood in its own garden . . . so called *garden*! A hawthorn-hedged rectangle of weed-choked rankness. A place of midges and flies, in summer, and snails and frogs in autumn and spring. A place of drifts and icicles—freezing mist and rock-hard earth—in winter.

Her home . . . and this, too, she hated.

It was pokey. It smelled of damp. It was comfortless, and it stood, alone, more than fifty yards from any other building . . . as if the village (even this, run-down, dilapidated village) was holding it at arm's length as something it wished to disown.

It was home... and she was making her way back to it. Her feet slithered a couple of times in the thick and greasy March mud. She cursed as she stubbed a toe against a hidden stone—a stone almost as big as a football... and the damn things worked their way to the surface, every year, as if secret, underground creatures forever eased them higher whenever the softness of the ground permitted. It was one more thing to hate; the mysteries— the creepiness—of the countryside.

The door of the cottage was still open.

She entered, and was unbuttoning her coat before she saw the woman.

'What the hell...' She bit the exclamation off and, in a calmer voice, said, 'Thelma—I'm sorry... I didn't expect anybody to be here.'

The woman waid, 'Hello, Pamela,' and her voice was neither pleasant nor unpleasant; neither friendly nor unfriendly. It was neutral. It said, by its tone, that it was ready to be whatever Pamela Ogden wanted it to be.

She removed her coat and threw it over the back of a kitchen chair while the woman, Thelma, watched and waited for the next move.

Thelma Simpson. Corseted and coiffured—or was it wigged?... you never could tell, these days. Dressed in simple, but expensive, clothes. Supremely sure of herself. Of the same age—of the same style of upbringing—as Pamela Ogden. Separated, by a million miles, from Pamela Ogden.

Except...

Except for the name. 'Ogden.' Before her marriage, Thelma Simpson had been Thelma Ogden. Harry's sister.

She squatted in front of the ash-strewn fireplace; sitting on her heels and jabbing extra life into the inadequate flickering with a poker. The flames became fractionally more agitated, but the split log on top merely smoked and smouldered. It wouldn't burn; it was still too damp.

'Bloody coal!' she muttered. 'It's never coal, in a thousand years.'

Thelma said, 'I thought I'd better come.'

She rattled the poker through the bars of the grate. Red-hot ash cleared a way for more draught, and the flames grew momentarily, more healthy.

'I thought,' repeated Thelma, 'I'd better come.'

She leaned the poker against a corner of the hearth, straightened and dusted her hands.

She said, 'Tea? It won't take much effort . . . I could do with a cup myself.'

'No, thank you.'

She walked across the room, to the door of the cottage, closed the door then returned to the hearth-rug. The closing of the door merely increased the gloom, but without noticeably increasing the warmth.

She looked down at Thelma, and said, 'You found the place?'

'I beg your pardon?'

'This dump . . . you found it?'

'I asked in the village.'

'Oh!'

'I left my car . . . parked by the green.'

'When you get back, you'll probably find it covered in hen-shit,' then, having said it, she moved her hands in a quick, open-palmed gesture and added, hurriedly, 'I'm sorry—I'm sorry . . . I shouldn't have said that. Forget it. It was silly—uncalled for . . . it was meant to shock you.' She gave a quick, half-smile and ended, 'Your car'll be safe enough. We don't run to thieves at this place.'

For the third time, Thelma said, 'Yes—well . . . I thought I'd better come.'

'So . . .' The half-smile flickered on and off again. 'Now you know.'

'What?'

'Where I live. What it's like.'

'It . . .' Thelma glanced at the walls of the room. At the ceiling. She said, 'It could be made attractive.'

'Oh, my God!'

'It would need repairs. Alterations.'

'It would need *money*.'

'Ye-es.' Thelma nodded, slowly . . . as if conceding a point which might still be open for debate. 'It would need some money spending on it.'

'Not just "some"... a lot.'

'But it could be made attractive. Very attractive.'

'That coat.' Pamela nodded towards the coat she'd thrown over the back of the chair. 'Like it?' she asked.

'Yes, it's...' Thelma hesitated, then said, 'It's rather nice.'

'Not as good as yours, of course. Don't get me wrong... I'm not making comparisons.'

'It's a nice coat,' insisted Thelma. 'It suits you.'

'It isn't mine.'

'Oh!'

'Not really... it's from a bloody jumble-sale.' She tried, but the anger—the bitterness—seeped out through the cracks in the conversation. 'It was bought—originally—by some other woman. Somebody I don't even know. She wore it—got tired of it—she gave it away... and then *I* could afford it. It cost me five bob... twenty-five new pence. And, having bought it, I couldn't even afford to have the bloody thing cleaned, before I wore it." She took a deep breath, and added, 'Thelma, you've come to see me. Today... when I might need somebody. I know—I should be grateful... I am grateful. But—for God's sake—now you're here talk on my level. Don't—don't go on about this hovel—how it could be "made attractive"... not when I can only afford second-hand clothes.'

Thelma moved her head in a series of slow nods. Solemn—perhaps a little embarrassed—as if realising, for the first time, what she'd let herself in for. She said nothing.

Pamela walked towards the kitchen.

She said, 'I'm making tea. I need it—I need a smoke... have some.'

'Yes.' Thelma allowed her facial muscles to relax a little. 'Thank you. I'll—er—I'll change my mind. I think we both need a drink and a cigarette... then we can talk.'

Woolworth's beakers. Cheap, supermarket tea. Milk—yesterday's milk, therefore not quite fresh—poured from a chipped jug. Sugar, from a soup bowl—which made a change... it usually stayed in the bag. A shared spoon.

And cigarettes—Woodbines—tipped Woodbines...
tipped, not because she kidded herself that tipped
cigarettes were any safer than untipped, but because the
length of the tip just about equalled the stub you usually
threw away, therefore you smoked all the tobacco you
paid for. And tipped Woodbines were the cheapest
popular brand available.

She wondered how long it had been since Thelma had
tasted such tea. Had smoked such cigarettes. Had used
such 'crockery'.

One hell of a long time. Donkey's years... and yet, to
now, she hadn't batted an eyelid. She hadn't been
condescending. She'd said 'Please' and 'Thank you' in all
the right places... and she'd even made me believe she
was quietly enjoying herself.

She was either a cunning bitch, or she was...

Leave it! Let it come—let things happen at their own
speed—then we'll see ... we'll see exactly what she is, and
exactly what she is not.

They sipped tea from cheap beakers and inhaled smoke
from inexpensive cigarettes. They sat close together—
almost side by side—on chairs drawn up to the meagre
fire. They stared at the puny flames and the smouldering
log and there, in the gloom of that broken-down cottage,
there built up a strange atmosphere of tête-à-tête. Not yet
friendly... but no longer antagonistic. A tentative
reaching towards each other. A gentle probing—
timed ... but exploratory.

Thelma murmured, 'He'll be out, by this time.'

'Yes.' Pamela moved her head in a single nod, at the
flames.

'He'll—er—he'll be well on his way.'

'I should think so ... by this time.'

'They let them out ...' Thelma paused, awkwardly, in
her musings. 'In the mornings, isn't it? Eight o'clock—I
think ... isn't it?'

'Something like that.'

'Or is that ...' She cut the sentence short.

'That's when they used to hang them.' Pamela ended
the other woman's thought.

'Thank God!' And it was far more than a whispered

exclamation. It was a genuine prayer of thanksgiving.

The fire spat as the heat touched a layer of shale in the cheap coal. A tiny ember flew from the grate and landed on the hearthrug. Pamela picked it up, quickly, between finger and thumb and dropped it onto the tiles of the hearth. She wiped her fingers on the rug, then ground the sole of her shoe over the spot where the ember had landed.

She removed the cigarette from her mouth, exhaled smoke, then sipped at the tea.

She said, 'I hope he doesn't come here... that's all.'

'Why?' There was surprise—almost shock—in the question.

'This place?' Pamela raised her head and glanced at the cheap wallpaper above the fireplace. There was real bitterness in her tone, as she said, 'This place—and me... what a bloody combination?'

'It's his home... surely?'

'Not if he's any sense.'

'Look—if we can help... George and I. George knows I'm here. He was all for it. He wants to...'

'He won't want charity,' interrupted Pamela.

'No—of course not—but...'

'Nor do I.'

'Not charity,' insisted Thelma. 'Just—y'know—the family helping each other... till things get better. Till you're both on your...'

'Thelma, I'm scared!' She blurted it out. The truth... loud and naked. 'I'm scared stupid. I've—I've seriously considered... doing away with myself. Before he arrives. Before he meets me. That's how scared I am. Truly... that's how *frightened*.'

'Of *Harry*?' Incredulity was in the words, and in her expression.

'Of—of somebody I don't know. Of a man I spoke to—for a few minutes—four years ago. Of somebody I haven't been with—haven't known—for ten years. Of a stranger, who... who might hate me. Who might really *hate* me.'

'Harry,' insisted Thelma. 'Your husband—my brother... Harry.'

'No... somebody who *was* Harry.'

'He's the same man, Pam. Older—embittered, perhaps . . . and probably, like you, frightened. Pam, he's the same man.'

The Christian name did it—the shortened version of the Christian name . . . 'Pam'. It had been years—so many years—since anybody had used it. Meant it . . . meant it as form of mild endearment. At school . . . she'd been 'Pam' at school. Then, to Harry—in their courting days, and after they were married . . . "Pam". 'My wife, Pam.' He'd said it so many times. And always with that hinted ring of pride. As if she was—she was—she is . . . she is . . .

She is not a good wife. She is good looking; she is the sort of woman any man might be proud to display as his mate—as his bedfellow—as the creature from whom he is legally entitled to demand sexual co-operation. She is bright-eyed and vivacious. She laughs easily, and is lively. She is a passably competent hostess and a reasonably good conversationalist. Agreed—she is all these things . . . but, and despite all these things, she is not a good wife.

The things that matter—the things that make marriage a success—the things that give marriage depth, and the foundations upon which to build eternity—are beyond her ken.

Ask her, and she will tell you . . . that there can never be love without jealousy. That the two emotions are inseparable; that one is the natural and inevitable product of the other. Love a man and, of necessity, you expect all other women to love him or, at least, to desire him. To fault that proposition is to fault your own love—to make that love suspect, even to yourself . . . and, at the same time, to throw doubt upon your own taste. You have landed the paragon—the best of them all—and the law of the female jungle insists that the other cats will be envious, and will do all in their power to take him away from you.

Ask her, and she will tell you . . . that no man can be completely trusted. That that which women call love, men call affection, and that which men call love, women call lust. There is a difference, and the difference is the basic difference between the sexes. That men are weak and, with them, it is not a kink—it is not a disease they cannot control, and something of which they are ashamed—with them it is part of their natural makeup. It is part of manhood. It is proof of their own virility. Men are, fundamentally polygamous. Monogamy is against their natural instinct which is why whores flourish ... which is why strip-shows and blue flims have a ready market ... which is why the girlie-girlie magazines fill the bookstalls. Which is why any woman, with sense, is jealous of the man she loves.

Ask her, and she will admit ... housework bores her. There is nothing romantic about washing dishes at a sink. The marriage contract makes no mention of hoovering the house every day—of washing dirty socks, or cleaning the tide-mark from the side of the bath—of making the beds, or dusting the furniture—of sweeping the path, or making three meals a day, forever-more. When you stand alongside him, at the altar, the parson does not even hint at such things; the nuts and bolts of married life are ignored; wide-armed generalities, wrapped up neatly in the pink ribbon of religious dogma, are his sole concern ... probably because the parson, too, is a man!

Ask her, and she will admit ... simple, household economics are beyond her understanding. Money is something a husband is there to provide. Credit cards are there to be used. Pound notes are merely pieces of paper, pending their being exchanged for something more attractive. A cheque-book is something which is capable of bringing happiness, at the cost of a simple signature.

And yet ...

She would be offended if you called her a shrew. She would be hurt if you called her a slut. She would be outraged if you called her a spendthrift.

She is just 'not a good wife' ... and she truly doesn't know why. She tries—by God, how she tries! ... but does not realise that her own, self-imposed limitations ensure that she will never succeed. She wants to be—by God, how she wants to be! ... but she cannot see that her own rigid rules will not allow it.

She does her best, but...

'...it's too late. I know it. You know it. It's ten years too late, and...'

'I know nothing of the sort.' Thelma's voice was firm. Almost brusque, but not unfriendly. She said, 'What I *do* know, is that you're Harry's wife. And that, for far too long, you've felt sorry for yourself. You've thought too much about yourself—what *you* want—and not enough about him... what he *needs*.'

'Thelma, it's not as easy as that. There's something...'

'It's as easy as *that*,' contradicted Thelma. 'Great heaven's woman, do you think I don't know? I'm married—I've been married longer than you have... and I've made a success of it. Which means I've worked. Connived, if you like. George—Christ!... there have been times when I could have cheerfully killed him. So infernally stupid. So monumentally pompous. I could have...'

'He hasn't...'

'How the hell do I know?' snapped Thelma, before Pamela's statement could be even half-spoken. 'He may have had another woman—sometime... somewhere. I don't know—I don't think so... but I don't *know*. Which wife ever *knows*?'

Pamela widened her eyes, and said, 'And you don't mind? You—of all people—don't mind?'

'Of course I mind.'

'But what you're saying is that...'

'What I'm saying is that I'm George's wife... and if some randy little tart thinks she's going to stop me being *that*, she's in for the biggest surprise of her life. I'll beat her at her own game, if necessary. I'll drag George to bed so many times, he won't have the energy to even unzip his fly. If that's the attraction, I'll sicken him with it. I'll do things—to him, and for him... things no textbook on sex would dare to print. If that's what he wants, he can have it... from *me*. Then—after that—I'll be his wife... but I'll still *be* his wife.'

'Jesus!' Pamela exploded into a quick chuckle. Near-tears and near-hysteria were both part of the explosion of non-mirth. She nipped her lower lip between her teeth, and whispered, 'Poor George.'

'All right,' said Thelma, gently, 'then why not join me? Why not make it "Poor Harry".'

'It's—it's . . .'

'No . . . it's not too late.' Thelma placed the beaker onto the hearth surround. She stood up, and said, 'I'm going for the car. I have cleaning materials—brushes, dusters—in the boot. This place is going to shine. Then we'll make a meal . . . a *real* meal. Then we'll make you pretty . . . prettier than he's ever seen you before. Then—when he arrives—I'll shake hands with him, give him a sisterly kiss and then make myself scarce. After that, it's up to you. Feed him first—give him a good meal . . . then make sure he's glad he had a good meal.'

'Th-Thelma.' She, too, placed her beaker on the hearth, and stood up. Her eyes shone, as she looked with wonder at the other woman . . . and much of the sheen was held-back tears. She said, 'I—I once thought you were . . .'

'I know. A stuck-up, cold-blooded bitch.'

Pamela nodded. She couldn't trust herself to speak.

Thelma smiled—and the smile wasn't far removed from a grin—as she said, 'Never let an exterior fool you, girl. I have all the necessary equipment . . . and I've known teasers who wouldn't take their spectacles off without a marriage-band firmly on their finger.'

'I—I *love* you,' whispered Pamela.

'No.' Thelma shook her head. 'Don't waste it on me . . . save it all for Harry.'

THE MAN

IT was odd. Motorway driving... it was the oddest—the strangest—thing on earth. It just couldn't *be*...but it *was*!

Speed. Speed, multiplied by more speed, equalled slow-motion. The vehicles—the cars, the vans, the lorries—were all belting along, coming and going, at damn-fool speeds. At suicidal speeds, sometimes. Certainly at speeds not normally touched, even when overtaking, on ordinary roads. Every damn vehicle going flat out. Every damn driver with his foot down. And yet the final sensation was all wrong. It wasn't a sensation of *speed*. Monotony—that was one part of it... and, when you thought about it, God bless God for car radios which, at least, pushed some of the monotony to one side. Hypnotism—that,too, could be part of it...staring at the same road, the same width, the same colour and with the same road markings, rushing towards you at the same

speed for hours on end. Acoustic stupor—nor could that
be ignored...no traffic roundabouts, no bends, no
corners, few gradients, therefore no gear-changes and a
constant speed, which meant a constant engine tone; no
variation of note or pitch; like an organ playing a single
low note on, and on, and on until it buries itself deeper
than the eardrums and impinges itself on the brain and
makes you temporarily punch-drunk.

These things added up. Plus a gentle soporific
vibration. Plus a subtle, painless cramp. Plus...hell only
knew what else, plus.

But the sum total was an illusion; a sensation the other
drivers didn't seem to notice.

Maybe it was because he'd been so *stationary* for such a
long time. So fixed. So unmoving. Maybe that was why
he noticed it...why it sent spiders up and down his spine.

Slow-motion. Everybody—every vehicle—*seemed* to
be travelling at a safe speed. Almost sedately...until you
glanced across the cab and checked the speedo. Until you
realised the possible m.p.h. of some of the cars in the fast,
and overtaking, lanes.

Then—and only then—you realised.

Slow!

Slow...up a bloody flagpole!

He blinked, as the expression flipped across the silent
conversation of his mind. 'Up a bloody flagpole'...one of
her expressions. She used it—she *had* used it—as a
favourite vehicle for her disgust. For her contempt. Not
often—not every day...but, whenever she'd been particularly outraged.

'Up a bloody flagpole.'

Jesus—he couldn't get away from her...whatever he
thought about, he always ended up alongside *her*!

Harding said, 'A slash and a tea, at the next service
area.'

'What?' Ogden closed the door of his daydreams.
'You'll be getting a bit cramped.'

'No...not really.'

'In a hurry, then?' Harding cocked a cheerfully
sardonic eyebrow at the road ahead.

'No...not really,' repeated Ogden. Then, in a softer tone, added, 'No hurry at all.'

'Great. We'll stretch our legs. These things need taking, length at a time.'

'Motorways?'

'Otherwise, you're knackered...and don't know it.'

'Ye-es,' said Ogden, thoughtfully. 'I was—y'know ...thinking the same.'

'Mugs.' Harding moved his head, to indicate the steady stream of overtaking cars. 'Driving like it was a bloody race track. Hours on end. And, when you ask 'em why they do it, they don't know.' He dropped his eyes for a split second, glanced at the fuel gauge, and added, 'We'll top her up while we're at it.'

It was a different cafe; different from the one where he'd met Harding. It reminded him of a cinema foyer; futuristic-style lighting, polished floor, near-avant garde wall-covering. The tables were arranged in ranks of low-partitioned alcoves. The self-service counter was a long, scrupulously clean barricade of piled-high food—all hygienically-wrapped...all with that 'untouched-by-human-hand' superiority which, in some daft way, affected the taste and gave everything the same basic constituency of flavoured pap.

A line of picture-windows looked out onto the motorway and the fields beyond; a nice view—an almost 'posed' view...and (again) with that awful air of organised cleanliness which typified the twentieth-century.

It was comfortable in the cafe. The heat was perfect—to the last degree—but even the heat was of its own kind. Modern heat—'plastic' heat...or so it seemed. From cunningly camouflaged ducts which breathed warm air...air which (like the sandwiches) seemed to be cellophane-wrapped.

They drank tea, from plastic beakers; tea whose sugar and milk they had mixed in with plastic spoons. They ate their snacks from pre-pressed cardboard plates. Harding had bought a pork pie. Ogden had opted for a repeat of his previous snack . . . a cheese sandwich.

Harding bit into the pie, chewed a couple of times then, before swallowing, said, 'Getting used to it, then?'

Ogden frowned a mild question.

'Getting out,' explained Harding. 'Y'know . . . being one of us, again.'

'Yes . . . oh, yes.' Ogden smiled. 'Gradually.'

Harding chewed, swallowed, then gulped tea before he said, 'You're not a crook.'

He made it a statement—not a question . . . an observation, the truth of which he was not quite sure.

Ogden's lips twisted . . . but not quite into a smile.

'Not a *villain*,' insisted Harding. 'Y'know . . . not one of these light-fingered buggers on the loose, these days.'

'Not a thief,' agreed Ogden.

'No . . . else you wouldn't have ridden in my cab.'

'You—er . . .' Ogden hesitated then, very mildly, said, 'You're a judge of character. Eh?'

'I can tell them bastards.' Harding helped himself to another bite from the pie. 'I can smell 'em a mile off. Thieving sods! Some of 'em . . . they ought to have their fingers chopped off.'

Ogden started on his sandwich. It was cheese—the same brand as last time . . . pure 'mousetrap'. Shredded and dry. One thing, at least, hadn't altered in the last ten years . . . transport-cafe cheese sandwiches.

Harding mused, 'Ten years, though . . . that's a hell of a time.'

'It passes,' said Ogden, flatly.

'Yer—but—y'know . . . ten *years*!'

They sat in silence for a few moments.

There was a question, straining to be asked, and an answer reluctant to leave its hiding place. They both knew it, but neither wanted to risk the sudden fracture of their tenuous, but temporary, friendship.

One of the employees—a thick, stubby woman wearing a white smock and peculiar bumps on her thick-stockinged legs—moved wearily from table to table; collecting trays and used beakers; wiping the top of each table with a cloth which was filthier than any table it touched. She arrived at their table, emptied ash and dog-ends from the heavy glass ash-tray, rearranged the cruet and passed on.

People entered the cafe. Singly, in pairs, in groups. Drivers. Private motorists. Families. They took their places behind the chrome barrier, picked up a tray, moved along like well-conducted tourists at a museum, chose their dishes, paid at the cash-desk then dispersed around the alcoved tables.

As fast as people entered, people left. Singly, in pairs, in groups... the same types of people. For all it mattered, the *same* people. The cafe never emptied... nor did it become any more crowded.

These (or so it seemed) were the 'extras'—the hopefuls from some huge Central Casting Agency paid to walk on and walk off. They represented 'the crowd scene' which was part of the main production... faceless, and unnoticed.

'The wife'll be interested.' Harding broke the silence. He added, 'When I tell her. Y'know... when I tell her.'

'What?' asked Ogden... although he knew.

'About you.'

'Oh?'

'About giving you a lift.'

'Why? Doesn't she approve? Of you giving lifts, I mean?'

'As long as they aren't the floozies... she doesn't mind.'

'Would she know?' asked Ogden, with a smile.

'What?'

'If you took on a... floozie.'

'You don't know my wife, mate.' Harding grinned. 'She'd bloody-well know... before I'd got my coat off.'

'As close as that?' A keen ear might have caught wistfulness in the question.

'Eh?' Harding chewed pork pie, and didn't understand.

'You—your wife... as close as *that*?'

'Oh?' Harding creased his forehead, concentrated his thoughts upon a completely novel idea for a moment, then said, 'Aye—I suppose we are... come to think about it.'

'Lucky man,' murmured Ogden.

'Aye—I reckon... come to think about it.'

Harding's frown ironed itself out. His craggy face gradually beamed. The grin returned then, momentarily, became audible as a quick chuckle.

Three tables away a child opened its mouth and bawled. A toddler, with its two young parents, it was tired of travelling and the cafe food, pulped and being fed to it on a plastic spoon by its mother, was not to its taste. It let fly, in protest, and the howl was loud enough to laser its way through the general mutter of background conversation.

Every head in the cafe turned to stare at the child.

The mother looked embarrassed.

The father looked cross.

The child (apparently realising that it could command universal attention) opened his mouth again, increased the decibel rate and screamed at the top of its voice.

Harding screwed his face, and murmured, 'Christ Almighty! They make 'em with leather lungs, these days.'

The father said something to the child; the words were not loud enough to hear, but the tone, and the look on his face, insisted that what he was saying was a threat.

For a third time, the child opened its mouth for yet one more yell.

The howl changed key—from one of protest to one of sharp pain—as the mother administered two hard slaps across the back of the child's thighs. The tears came. The mouth corners drooped. The mother lifted the child into her arms, stood up and hurried out of the cafe. The father resumed his meal; he put on a deliberate act... as if the child (still heard howling, faintly, in the distance) and the child's mother were no concern of his, therefore in no way his responsibility.

The cafe and its customers returned to the previous dull normality.

Harding glanced across the table and saw the look on Ogden's face.

He said, 'Kids! I dunno... some of 'em are real noisy buggers.'

'Not to me... not yet,' said Ogden, gently.

'What?'

Ogden's mouth moved as he fought the emotions.

He said, 'I—I hadn't realised. Y'know...something you don't *realise*. I've not heard a child cry—laugh—anything...not for ten years.'

'What d'you reckon, then?' asked Harding. 'Does it do any good?'

The question was not flippant. It was asked solemnly; as if Harding had given much, and long, thought to the problem, without reaching a solution. As if—now the opportunity presented itself—he was curious as to the conclusions of an expert.

'Prison?'

'Aye... *does* it do any good?'

They conducted their conversation without looking at each other. They each stared ahead, through their own half of the windscreen; watched the never-ending sweep and swing of the motorway; saw (but without consciously noting) the overtaking traffic pulling away, ahead of them. The steady thrum of the diesel, housed between the box-shaped cover which divided them, gave their talk a continuous background roar; forced them to speak a little louder than they might have otherwise have spoken and, perhaps a little slower, and gave their talk an air of abnormal deliberation.

Ogden countered question with question.

He said, 'What else?'

'Y'mean it *does* do some good?'

'No. I mean, if not prison...what else?'

'I dunno.'

'The choice is limited.'

'Aye. But the experts—some of 'em—swear blind prison's no bloody good.'

'That's a sweeping statement.'

'That's what some of 'em say.'

'They're the experts.'

'Aye...but what do you think?'

Ogden said, 'I wouldn't try to tell you how to drive this lorry...in that field you're the expert.'

'No.' Harding shook his head. 'That's not the same thing, mate. Because they're not—y'know...not the *real* experts.'

A petrol tanker overtook them on the fast lane. Beyond the tanker, in the overtaking lane, an Austin was travelling slightly faster than the tanker and, behind the Austin, a Bentley was obviously impatient to push ahead, past the comparatively slow-moving vehicles in its path.

Ogden said, 'Meaning the experts haven't served time?'

'We-ell—they haven't...have they?'

'No.' Ogden's tone was rueful. 'They're the theorists—good theorists, no doubt...but not the practitioners.'

'That's neat.' Harding held his head on one side, in thoughtful appreciation. 'Practitioners...that's a neat way of putting it.'

'One way,' agreed Ogden.

The tanker was past, and ahead of them, but it stayed in the fast lane. The driver of the Austin seemed to become timid—to be suddenly conscious of the speed of his car, and the proximity of the tanker—and reduced his speed slightly. The tanker and the Austin raced, neck-and-neck, along the fast and overtaking lanes. Behind the Austin, the Bentley flashed its lights in an impatient demand for passage.

'Take you,' said Harding. 'You're not a crook.'

'You keep saying that.'

'No—we-ell...y'know what I mean.'

Ogden said, 'I could name one judge who'd disagree.'

'No—I don't mean that...I mean not a *crook*.' Harding worked to explain himself. 'Y'know...not a villain. Not bent. I tell you—y'know what?...I reckon I've got your number. Middle-class...right? Very respectable...right?'

'Once,' agreed Ogden, softly. 'But not today. Not again...until I've worked at it a long time.'

'Why not?' demanded Harding. 'You're out. You've done your spell. Why the hell not?'

'Because of that. Because I've "done my spell"...and until people forget it.'

'All right. All right,' conceded Harding. 'Let's say it'll

take a bit of time. But you'll be back again. What you were. Member of the local golf club . . . summat like that.'

'Actually,' Ogden smiled, 'it was a rifle and pistol club.'

'We-ell—see what I mean? . . . same thing. It's what you were. What you'll be again. But—what I'm getting at—you've been there, mate. You've been inside. And you've got the brains. So, you're the expert . . . the only *real* expert.'

The driver of the Bentley was a fool. He couldn't wait. He eased the speed of his car, moved left into the fast lane—immediately behind the tanker—then left, again, into the slow lane, before gunning his car to overtake the tanker on the wrong side.

Harding took the first gentle pressure on the brakes as he talked.

He said, 'Now—what I want to know is this . . . *is* prison the answer?'

'Sometimes.' Ogden watched the movement of the vehicles ahead, as he spoke. 'It stops a thief from thieving . . . at least, for a limited time. It does that much good. If that's what you want, then . . .' He gripped the dashboard ledge, and gasped, 'For Christ's sake! Watch that flaming . . .'

'Hang on, mate!'

Harding braked hard—but progressively—as the tanker made a belated swing into the slow lane and almost nudged the overtaking Bentley. The driver of the tanker spotted the Bentley a shaved second before there was a side-to-side shunt, pulled right, over-reacted and, instead of hitting the Bentley, hit the Austin.

And then the pile-up happened as all such pile-ups happen. With nerve-jarring noise. (Rubber screaming its protest as it was burned or torn to shreds. The screech of steel locked with steel in a running battle for supremacy. The crashing explosion of shattering glass. A multi-octaved range of terrifying noise which formed the huge discord of cacophonic destruction.) With near-impossible speed. (Incapable of being separated into tiny fragments of a continuous happening. Not 'A' followed by 'B' followed by 'C' followed by 'D' but, instead, the whole alphabet hurling itself past the eyes in a single visual blur... but each letter a car, or the tanker, or a snapped-off mudguard, or a glimpse of the central crash-barrier, or another, impossible-to-identify piece of wreckage.) With surprising distance. (From a speed of more than fifty miles per hour, to zero, and the distance that deceleration takes. Which means long, curved skid-streaks on the surface of the motorway; battered headlamps, broken bumper-bars, torn-off doors and a spray of glass fragmentations—like the debris from some idiot paper-chase—and some of the contents of two cars and the cab of a petrol tanker scattered for a hundred yards along the north-bound carriageway.)

But, most of all, the speed. That, one moment it was not—that, at that moment, is was merely 'potential'— and, the next moment it *was*! Complete. Ended...and a sudden nightmare.

And then the silence.

A few seconds of complete hush—as if the world was holding its breath at the madness of this, the latest example of man-made catastrophy...and then, the realisation.

Harding had halted the lorry on the hard-standing, less than twenty yards from where the three wrecked vehicles had spewed their torn parts across all three traffic lanes. Ogden had his door open, had jumped down and was racing towards the wreckage as Harding grabbed the fire extinguisher from its clips above the lorry's windscreen. Then Harding was haring after Ogden.

As Ogden wrenched at the door of the tanker's cab, the first flames reached hungrily, from the exposed engine of the Austin.

THE COP

'You may not remember him,' said Sawyer, 'but—take it from me—he's a killer.'

Fenton said, 'No, sir...I don't remember him.'

'Oh!' Sawyer sounded vaguely disappointed. 'Before you came to Ellerfield, of course.'

'Yes, sir.'

'Indeed, before *I* came to Ellerfield. Ten years ago, to be precise. I was a detective inspector, at the time. It was one of my cases.' The casual, throw-away manner of the last remark was meant to give the impression that *all* 'Detective Inspector Sawyer's' cases had been murder enquiries...and that the one under discussion, while important and particularly gruesome was, nevertheless, only one of many. Sawyer continued, 'He killed the wife of his next-door neighbour...a Ruth Watford. He started the job with a knife. Finished her off with a bullet.'

'Good Lord!' Inspector Fenton was suitably shocked.

'His wife—Ogden's wife, that is—now lives at Little Moysell. A cottage, on the outskirts of the village..."The Swan's Nest".'

'I didn't know,' murmured Fenton.

Sawyer said, 'No—you wouldn't, inspector...she keeps herself very much to herself. Shame, I suppose.'

'Why?' Fenton raised mildly surprised eyebrows. 'I mean...why should *she* be ashamed?'

'Oh, come now, Fenton...the wife of a notorious murderer?'

'But *she* isn't. *She* hasn't murdered anybody.'

'There are times,' remarked Sawyer, airily, 'when the sheer naivety of you young officers staggers me. The man is a murderer. She's his wife...she shares his name. Of course she feels shame. She must do. It's why she's shut herself away...in a hole-in-the-corner spot like Little Moysell. She's ashamed of her husband. Probably scared of him...in fact, I'll lay money on it. And today—despite what he did ten years ago—he's a free man. He'll seek her out...bound to. Then..." Sawyer moved his shoulders, expressively.

Fenton looked worried.

'I want a watch put on the place,' said Sawyer.

'Y'mean...' Fenton hesitated, then said, 'You mean he might come up here, and kill his wife?'

'He's a dangerous man,' said Sawyer.

'Yes, sir. But...' Fenton hesitated, again. Then he said, 'I'm sorry, sir—maybe I'm thick—but why should he kill his wife? Is it something to do with the last time? Some evidence she gave? Something like that?'

'He's a killer, Fenton,' said Sawyer, wearily.

'Yes, sir. Once. But...'

'I've already discussed the matter with Detective Superintendent Lennox—Chief Superintendent Sugden was indisposed—and we've agreed...better to be safe than sorry.'

'We're short of men, sir,' said Fenton, tentatively. 'As it is, we're pushed for even token cover.'

'Find the men,' ordered Sawyer. 'Twenty-four-hour surveillance...till further notice.'

'But, sir ...'

'That's an order, inspector.'

'Yes sir,' sighed Fenton.

'And, when he arrives—the minute he arrives—I want notifying. I want to see him ... and give him the hard word.'

The officer of whom Sawyer had spoken (the officer who, according to Sawyer, had agreed upon a period of better-to-be-safe-than-sorry tactics ... but who would have been surprised at this interpretation of what he had said) was discovering things.

Specifically, he was discovering a series of vaults—cellars, and various sized underground rooms—beneath the outwardly imposing structure of County Constabulary Headquarters.

It had started with a nagging curiosity; a few remembered details, plus a desire to get the facts right ... plus (probably) the realisation that, as newly appointed second-kick to the force's C.I.D. Big Daddy, he ought to know these things. This feeling had directed him to the Records Office. (A 'Records Office'—or so argued Lennox—was a place where it should be possible to find 'records'. Not, of course *gramophone* records, but certainly records of activities, cases, incidents—call them what you will—upon which, over the years, the fame—or even the infamy—of the force had been built. It seemed a reasonable enough assumption. But—to Lennox's surprise—it had been an erroneous assumption.)

The R.O. bloke had said, 'No, sir. Not here. Criminal records—records of all the villains—and records of all the serving officers ... that's all we deal with.'

'You live and learn,' Lennox had murmured.

'Sir?' The R.O. bloke had raised slightly supercilious eyebrows.

'The bent bastards, and the bobbies—all sharing the same bed ... as it were.'

'I wouldn't quite put it like ...'

'Tell me,' Lennox had asked, interestedly, 'am *I* among all this lot, somewhere?'

'Yes, sir. Of course.'

'Along with all the rapists—all the old lags . . . eh?'

'We have a careful filing system, sir.' The R.O. bloke had looked slightly offended.

'Aye—well keep checking . . . eh? *Mine*, I mean. I'd hate to end up interviewing myself as main suspect in a major crime.'

'Sir?' The R.O. bloke had been flummoxed.

'Skip it, son.' Lennox had sighed. 'Now—this Archives Section . . . where d'you say it is?'

'In the basement, sir.'

'Not one corner of the Boiler House, I hope.'

'No, sir. It's . . .'

'Under the Firing Range counter, perhaps?'

'*Behind* the Firing Range, sir.' The R.O. bloke had put on an air of long-suffering patience. 'Alongside the range—towards the back of the range—there's a door. It's marked "Archives Section". It's where we keep . . .'

'I'll find it, son.' Lennox had waved a cheerful hand. 'Back you go to your filing-cabinets . . . otherwise, they'll start feeling neglected.'

And Lennox had, indeed, 'found it.'

'It' being a door, well within earshot of the crack of exploding .22 ammunition being fired on the indoor range; a door which lurked shyly—almost secretively—in shadows and which had, stencilled across its panels, the words 'COUNTY CONSTABULARY ARCHIVES'.

The door was locked. There was a bell-push, and Lennox poked its button with a forefinger. The door opened.

The door did not open with a creak, nor was there a rattle of chains or withdrawn bolts, prior to its being opened . . . but the impression was that there *should* have been.

The man who opened the door was a copper—a common-or-garden constable . . . but a very *old* common-or-garden constable. He was thin; thin enough to look as if he'd kicked the time-wasting habit of eating. He had dark eyes—watery eyes—which peered suspiciously from the rear of deep sockets. His voice had a distinctly funereal ring about it.

He said, 'Yers?'

'The Archives Section?' enquired Lennox.

'Yers.' The constable glanced at the writing on the door, for verification, then repeated, 'Yers.'

'Good...there's something I'd like to have a decko at.'

'Sorry,' said the constable, sadly.

'Eh?'

'You.' The constable lowered his eyes, studied Lennox's plus-fours, returned his gaze to Lennox's face, and said, 'You'll need authorisation—from the chief constable... *written* authorisation.'

'Is that a fact?' growled Lennox, dangerously.

'Yers.'

'Tell me,' said Lennox. 'What's your name, son?'

'That ain't nothing to do with it.'

'Why? Is *that* a secret, too?'

'Wot you need is...'

'What I need is your name. *Now*!'

Lennox was long-suffering; indeed, for a senior police officer, he was unbelievably long-suffering. Admittedly, his shape did nothing towards top-blowing exercises. Nor, come to that, did his normally chosen mode of dress. Nevertheless, he *was* a detective superintendent... and all detective superintendents (given reason enough) can spit sparks and demolish girders. It goes with rank... it is one reason why that particular man has attained that rank.

'Don't mess me about, lad,' said Lennox, harshly. 'What's your name?'

'Peel,' said the constable, reluctantly.

'It follows,' growled Lennox. He felt in his pockets, as he continued, 'I assume you can read... right? English— official English... not just Norman French. All these ancient documents you stand guard over. If so, read that.' He found what he was looking for—a small, folded pasteboard—his warrant card, giving his own rank, name and authority. He held it before P.C. Peel's waterlogged eyes, and snapped, 'Now, stop buggering me about Peel. That's who *I* am. I want to come into this sanctum of yours. I want a conducted tour... just in case you've got

Tutankhamun's twin sister in there, somewhere. I want to know where everything is—*what* everything is . . . then I want a file, for personal perusal. Right?'

Peel peered at the warrant card.

He sniffed then, without a change of tone, said, 'Yers.' and stood clear of the door.

'The responsibility,' explained Sawyer, 'is mine. It has to be. With a man like Lennox it's impossible to discuss even broad-based guide lines. He's an oaf. God in His high heaven knows how he got to be a detective superintendent. He hasn't the faintest idea what policing's all about. Not the faintest idea.'

Mrs Sawyer murmured, 'No, dear. Eat it, while it's warm.'

She placed a bowl of *Piccata con Funghi* on the table-mat in front of his chair. She was the type of woman who (almost as a matter of course) served *Piccata con Funghi* for lunch . . . and, moreover, always *called* it *Piccata con Funghi*, rather than veal cutlets in wine and mushroom sauce. Her weekly Bible and prayer book were expensive glossy magazines; magazines which purported to explain (with photographs, to assist the less literate) exactly how the 'better class' people lived and ate. What clothes they favoured. What dishes they preferred . . . and how to cook those dishes. Which restaurants they used . . . the assumption being that all such 'better class' people lived within a few minutes' drive of the West End!

She was a small woman; small in stature, small, and squeaky, in voice. The word 'mouse' sprang to mind, whenever she entered a room and whenever she said anything. Her face was long and narrow; with a protruding nose and a receding chin; with a forehead which tended to slope backwards and teeth which tended to protrude . . . a mouse's face. Her hands were tiny and quick-fingered; when she walked it was with a nervous, scuttering gait . . . the movements of a mouse. Even her hair had grown to a mousy grey and, to complete the illusion, she favoured greys and browns in her clothes.

And yet this timid, frightened-looking woman—this

mouse of a woman—yearned to be the *grande dame* of the
local community... and, indeed considered herself just
that. There wasn't an evening institute lesson on flower
arrangement—on advanced cookery—on homemak-
ing—on appreciation of the arts which did not have her
name enrolled as an eager pupil. There wasn't a W.I.
meeting held which she did not attend. There was not a
fashion show which did not have her sitting on a chair in
the front row. There was not a visiting lecturer who
(whatever his, or her, subject) did not have her undivided
attention... and, after the lecture, she was *always* one of
the first with a question.

She was a fit mate, for a man like Sawyer. It would be
unkind to suggest that they deserved each other... but it
would be no less than the truth to suggest that they were
the only types of man and woman capable of tolerating
each other for the span of their natural lifetime.

The fact that Sawyer was punctual, to the minute—
almost to the second—endeared him to her, and the fact
that lunch (it was always 'lunch'—never 'dinner'... only
the common herd had 'dinner' at midday) was always
ready on the dot of twelve-thirty evoked a similar
admiration in him, for her.

They loved each other.

Like hell they loved each other!... but they *thought*
they did.

She arranged the vegetable dishes to her liking, and
joined him at the table.

He said, 'Ogden is a dangerous man. Any man
incapable of self-control is dangerous. And loss of
self-control isn't something that happens once in a
lifetime. It's a weakness... and it's always there.'

'Yes, dear. Is it flavoured to your liking?'

'Perfectly, thank you.' He dabbed his lips with a
napkin. 'That point, of course, escaped Lennox's notice.
Assuming he's capable of appreciating it... which I
doubt.'

'The cutlets,' she said. 'I had some trouble with the
butcher, I'm afraid. He insisted they were fresh... but I
wasn't quite convinced.'

'Yes... I think they are.'

'Good.'

'And, therefore, the responsibility becomes mine... and mine, alone. A released murderer on one's conscience. Living in one's sub-division. It becomes a priority... it must. If the man runs riot again. Loses control again. Commits another murder. What then? Would Lennox be prepared to admit that, on his say-so, a potential killer had been given freedom enough to repeat his crime? Knowing Lennox, I doubt it. I doubt it very much indeed.'

She said, 'I think a touch more paprika. Not much. A pinch, though... just a pinch.'

'I remember,' mused Sawyer, 'the first time I saw him. That first interview. He was—he was—he is... he is...'

He is on edge. This, of course, is understandable. He found the body, and notified the police; he has seen the mess—the blood, the carnage—therefore it is understandable that he is shocked, and on edge.

There is blood on his clothes. Blood on his hands. Smears of blood where, no doubt, he touched the corpse, or brushed his coat against some of the crimson splashes. Nevertheless...

They are in Ogden's house—Detective Inspector Sawyer and the dective constable—and, for the time being, they are not included in the interweave of official activity which is taking place next door; the photographing, the dusting for fingerprints, the inch-by-inch examination of the kitchen, the plan-drawing, the careful scrutiny of the corpse... all the important initial steps which are vitally necessary as a basis upon which to build the intricate dance of a murder enquiry.

For a moment, they are alone—the three of them—and, for a moment, something approximate to objectivity can be enjoyed.

The detective constable has his notebook open. He has his pencil at the ready. His job is to record—to take it down... 'that which may be given in evidence.'

Sawyer says, 'Sit down, please, Mr. Ogden.' He waves

a hand towards one of the matching armchairs. 'We won't keep you any longer than necessary. Just a few questions ... to get the chronology right.'

Ogden sits down.

Sawyer seats himself on the edge of the armchair which is the pair to the one used by Ogden.

The detective constable remains standing. It would be easier to write, seated in a chair ... but, so far, nobody has suggested that he do other than stand.

Sawyer starts slowly. With fundamentals.

'Ogden?' *he says, gently.* 'Henry Ogden?'

'Harry,' *Ogden corrects him, and the voice is a little off pitch, and with a noticeable tremor.* 'Harry Ogden.'

'I see. Thank you.'

The detective constable writes it all down.

'And you live at this address?' *verifies Sawyer.*

Ogden nods.

'Married?'

'Yes.'

'Children?'

'No ... no children.'

'And your age, please?'

'Thirty-one.'

'And your occupation?'

'I'm a butcher. In partnership with my brother-in-law ... George Simpson.'

'Thank you, Mr. Ogden.' *Sawyer pauses, then says,* 'Now—let me see—you found the body? Then you notified the police?'

Ogden nods.

'What time would that be?'

'When I ...' *Ogden swallows. He makes an obvious attempt to pull himself together. He says,* 'When I found the body?'

'Yes. Did you notice the time?'

'A—a few minutes—a minute, or two—before I rang you.'

'Did you notice the time?' *repeats Sawyer.*

'No—not really. Half past eight—about ... about half past eight. I think.'

'*In what circumstances?*' asks Sawyer, quietly.

'*What?*' Ogden looks dazed.

Sawyer says, '*You found the body, Mr. Ogden. In what circumstances did you find the body?*'

'*I—I just went in. And she was there . . . on the floor. It was awful. I—I was stunned. I couldn't believe she'd . . .*'

Ogden claps the back of his hand to his mouth, as if to stop himself from being sick. Above the hand, his eyes are wide—frightened . . . and they are staring, imploringly, at Sawyer.

Sawyer studies the eyes for a moment, then says, '*Would you like a drink, Mr. Ogden?*'

Ogden shakes his head. He lowers his hand, swallows the word, '*No,*' then says, '*No . . . I'm all right now, thank you.*'

Sawyer gives him a few more seconds, then says, '*You went into the house—Watford's house—you went into the kitchen . . . you saw Ruth Watford's murdered body. Correct?*'

'*Y-yes. Then I came back in here, and telephoned . . .*'

'*Why?*' interrupts Sawyer.

'*What?*'

'*Why did you go into Watford's house, in the first place?*'

'*He's a—he's a friend . . . just about my best friend.*'

'*Ruth Watford?*' Sawyer plays it dumb . . . as if he's misheard the pronoun.

'*No—Ralph . . . Ralph Watford. Ruth's husband. He's . . .*' Ogden stops then, in a worried voice, says, '*Ralph—does he know? How's he taking it? I mean . . .*'

'*He doesn't yet know,*' says Sawyer.

'*Oh!*'

'*Can you help us, perhaps?*'

'*What?*' Ogden suddenly looks startled.

'*Do you know where he is? Where he might be? We'd like to contact him . . . notify him, as soon as possible.*'

'*No, I'm sorry.*' Ogden hesitates, then adds, '*The cinema, perhaps. He—er—goes . . . sometimes. Not often. But . . . sometimes.*'

'*Alone?*' asks Sawyer. '*I mean . . . without his wife?*'

'He must have...mustn't he?'

'You think that's where he is?' asks Sawyer, innocently.

'Yes,' replies Ogden. 'I think that's—y'know...where he is.'

'Which cinema?'

'The Ritz. I think he'll be at The Ritz.'

'Why,' asks Sawyer, gently, 'did you go into Watford's house?'

'I've told you. To see Ralph. I wanted to...'

'Knowing he was at the cinema?'

'I didn't say that,' protests Ogden. 'I said he might be.'

'As you wish,' Sawyer moves his shoulders. 'Knowing he might be at the cinema?'

'I didn't know.'

'Nevertheless...'

'I wanted to see him about something...that's all.' A gleam, which might be defiance, creeps into the back of Ogden's eyes. His replies take on the quality of terseness. He says, 'Haven't you ever done that? Gone to a house, and found the person you wanted to see isn't at home?'

'Often,' agrees Sawyer.

'Well, then...that's what happened.'

'I have yet,' says Sawyer, smoothly, 'to find a murdered woman...at a house where the person I called to see wasn't at home.'

Ogden frowns, but makes no rejoinder to the observation.

'What about witness?' asks Sawyer.

'Witnesses?' Ogden looks puzzled.

'Who saw you go to the Watford house? Who saw you go? Saw you leave? Who can verify what you have told us?'

'Does it need verification?' asks Ogden.

'Everything.' Sawyer smiles. It is a tight, self-assured smile. Condescending, and without humour. He says, 'This is a murder enquiry, Mr Ogden. Everything—every statement must be verified...if at all possible.'

'Nobody saw me go in,' says Ogden flatly. 'Nobody saw me leave.'

'You're sure?'

'I'm sure.'

'Your wife, perhaps?' suggests Sawyer.

'No!' There is the hint of urgency in Ogden's reply. He says, 'My wife hasn't come home yet.'

'Oh, dear,' murmurs Sawyer.

'She's . . .' Ogden hesitates, moistens his lips, then says, 'She's at the cinema.'

'With Watford?'

'No!' And, again, the hint of urgency. In a quieter tone, Ogden adds, 'I don't think so.'

'Which cinema' asks Sawyer.

'The Ritz . . . I think.'

'Same cinema?'

Ogden says, 'That doesn't mean much . . . surely? There's only two in the town. The Ritz and The Lyceum. It has to be one, or the other. I think it's The Ritz.'

'And she's alone?' presses Sawyer.

'Yes . . . I think so.'

'She isn't with Watford?'

'No . . . she isn't with Watford. Why on earth should she be with Watford?'

'No reason—unless, of course, I reverse the question, and ask you . . . is there any reason why she shouldn't be with Watford?'

'No. No reason at all. But—but I don't think she is . . . that's all.' Ogden takes a deep, shuddering breath, then repeats, 'That's all.'

And suddenly—as suddenly as the quick closing and opening of an eye—Ogden looks tired. Defeated.

He looks like a man who, for hours, has been hacking a way through a mass of jungle vines and creepers—slashing a path for himself, towards some dreamed-of destination—and whose strength has left him in a rush. He is lost. He is licked. The vines and the creepers have been words and questions, and Ogden's machete of answers and explanations is no longer effective. Its blade has been blunted, then broken.

And Sawyer knows . . . he is as certain as the tides, as sure as tomorrow's sunrise. The rest of the enquiry is going to be easy; a mere gathering of evidence. And a *confession. He is sure of that, too . . . that, with a few more questions—a little more probing—Ogden will admit to the murder of Ruth Watford.*

'. . . and I knew it, you see.' Sawyer dabbed his lips with his napkin, once more. He was, in fact, a congenital 'lip dabber'; he had been taught, and he firmly believed, that a true 'gentleman'(and, of course, a true 'gentlewoman') brought the napkin to the lips after each chewed and swallowed mouthful. He said, 'A born killer, I need hardly say. A rogue of the species . . . as it were. He'll never change. They can't . . . even if they try. Fortunately, he was a poor liar . . . probably still is. Transparent, to anybody blessed with a judge of character. We-ell . . .' He sighed, 'He's out. He'll do it again. Unless, of course, he's warned . . . *really* warned. Told, in no uncertain manner that, if he puts a foot wrong—makes one tiny move in the wrong direction—he's back inside. That's what policing's about, my dear. Prevention—not merely detection . . . an aspect of policing Lennox doesn't seem capable of grasping.'

Mrs Sawyer said, 'Yes, dear. Now—for sweet—I've made your favourite . . . *gateau aux fruits chantilly.*'

That officer (the officer of whom Sawyer had, once more, spoken—the officer incapable of grasping one 'aspect of policing') had, by this time, learned a lot.

He had learned (for example) that, from the point of view of sheer paper, a police force—or, at least, this particular police force—closely resembled an iceberg. That, however much was on top (and a hell of a lot *was* on top!) seven times as much was out of sight, and underneath. Those vaults—those cellars—that, so-called, 'Archives Section' . . . Judas Christ! If anybody ever removed all that paper, County Constabulary Headquarters would disappear into a hole; the bloody building wasn't anchored to decent, concrete foundations—like any normal, self-respecting building . . . it was standing on solid paper.

Every sort of paper. Every size, every thickness, every type—the lot . . . it was all there.

Maps. Every deviation to a boundary—every new boundary—since the creation of the county constabulary itself had demanded a map. Every change in the size, of shape, of every beat, of every section, of every subdivision, of every division and (more recently) of each 'district' and each 'task force area' had required a map... and this, for more than a century! And a copy of every such map had been solemnly lodged in the Archives Section.

Plans. Again, every police station, and every police house. Every Sub-D.H.Q. and every D.H.Q. Every Section Station. Every alteration, improvement or extension... and a copy of every plan was there, in the vaults. And the crazy thing was that half the plans—more than half the plans—concerned houses or police stations which had either been sold, or pulled down and replaced by newer and more modern buildings... but a copy of the plan was still there. More than a hundred years of architectural ancestry, much of which wasn't even useful as makeshift toilet-paper.

Lennox had stared, dumbfounded, at the hundreds—probably thousands—of carefully preserved maps and plans.

He'd gasped, 'Does anybody actually *look* at this bloody stuff?'

Peel had said, 'Yers.'

'Who, for Christ's sake?'

'Me.'

And Peel had meant it. Seriously. As far as Constable Peel was concerned, it had been a perfectly valid question which, in turn, had received a perfectly valid answer.

Lennox had blown out his cheeks and trotted along, behind this gaunt keeper of constabulary state-papers, and had been even further flabbergasted.

Incident Reports—before they'd been called 'Incident Reports' and, instead, had been called 'Occurrence Reports'—and (going back) before they'd even been called 'Occurrence Reports' and had been headed by the single word 'Happenings'... pale blue paper, stiff and with the force coat-of-arms embossed at the top; written in longhand, and always starting with the words

'Superintendent, Sir, I have the honour to report...' and ending 'Superintendent, Sir, I have the honour to be your obedient servant...'. Lickspittle stuff (that's what they'd call it, these days), but stuff upon which a kind of discipline had been built. Blind discipline... and, sometimes, a very necessary discipline. A discipline which had helped to create a unique Police Service; something to be found nowhere else on earth.

Lennox had read one of the pale blue foolscaps.

He'd said, 'Holy Cow! I dunno whether to kiss it, or spew all over it.'

He'd handed the foolscap back to Peel, and Peel had handled it with open reverence. He'd silently returned it to its place, along with all the other, tens of thousands of 'Happenings', merging into 'Occurrence Reports', merging into 'Incident Reports'.

'Everything?' Lennox had asked, in amazement.

'Except Lost and Found Reports... we keep them for fifty years. Same with Missings From Home... fifty years. Lost Dogs... ten years. Pocket Books... twenty years after the bloke's either resigned or retired.'

'And the rest?'

'We keep 'em,' Peel had said, simply.

'*Everything*?'

'Yers... the original, or a copy.'

And these were some of the things this officer—this officer incapable of grasping one 'aspect of policing'—had learned.

And now he'd had enough of it; the windowless, airless rooms; the smell of mustiness and warm paper; the silent weight of this great mass of long-gone bobbying was getting him down.

He turned to Peel, and said, 'Cases—crime files... a ten-year-old one. Can you help me?'

'Yers.' Peel nodded, sombrely.

'Regina versus Ogden. A murder job... it would be assize case, in those days. I'd like a decko. Everything you have on it.'

Ten minutes later Peel handed Lennox an East-Light box file. It had been taped shut, and it was surprisingly heavy. Figures and oblique-strokes had been stencilled on

the spine of the box file and, under the figures, the words
'R. V. OGDEN'.

'Wot about the Pocket Books?' asked Peel.

'The Pocket Books?'

Peel nodded at the box file, and said, 'They ain't in
there.'

'Do I need them?' asked Lennox.

'I dunno.'

Lennox said, 'All right ... if I need them, I'll let you
know.'

'Yers.'

They walked back to the entrance, and Peel unlocked
the door.

As he left the vaults, Lennox turned to speak to this
thin and elderly custodian of ancient constabulary
records.

He said, 'By the way, Peel. Things have altered since
you pounded the paving-stones. Occasionally—not too
often, but just occasionally—a constable says 'sir' to a
superintendent. Not that they mean it, you understand,
but it makes for ...'

The door had been closed—not slammed, but closed
very firmly—and Lennox had addressed the last few
words to a notice which read 'COUNTY CONSTABULARY
ARCHIVES'.

Lennox sighed, then grinned, then murmured, 'It's
your castle, son. Come to think of it, maybe it's *me* who
should have said "sir".'

Lennox carried the box file, containing the papers
relating to the case of Regina versus Ogden, from the
bowels of County Constabulary Headquarters and up
flights of stairs leading to his own office of Assistant Head
of C.I.D.

The office was on the third floor and, on the fourth
landing, he was panting a little.

A cadet met him on the landing.

Lennox said, 'Hold it, son.'

'Sir!' The cadet skidded to a halt and held himself at
attention.

'What's on in the canteen?' asked Lennox.

The cadet said, 'Bangers and mash, sir.'

'Followed by?'

'Spotted dick.'

'Any good?' asked Lennox.

The cadet was a very honest youth. He said, 'No sir . . . lousy.'

'Thanks.' Lennox fished in the pockets of his plus-fours, found a fifty-pence piece, handed it to the cadet, and said, 'Find a fish and chip shop . . . there should be one still open. Cod and chips. Not much salt, but plenty of vinegar. Get 'em well wrapped . . . to keep 'em warm. Then call at the H.Q. bar . . . if it's closed, tell 'em—from me—to open it long enough to sell you a couple of bottles of Guinness. Get that lot up to my office, as soon as possible. Right?'

'Right, sir.'

The cadet hared down the steps, towards street level.

Lennox paused long enough to regain his breath, then lumbered up the remaining stairs to his posh new office.

THE HUSBAND

WATFORD was in a foul mood.

He, too, was eating. It was a stand-up meal, in the large and almost clinically clean kitchen of the house (Angela's house); a snatch-snack of apple-pie, White Stilton and milk. He drank the milk straight from the bottle. It was a tasty meal, and a lesser man (or a bigger man, depending upon how you view these things—but certainly a more contented man) would have counted it a good and sufficient midday stoke-up.

Watford didn't.

As far as Watford was concerned it was merely 'something to eat'; something with which to occupy his hands, his mouth and, to a lesser degree, his mind. Something with which to pass the time, pending the return of that stupid bitch, Angela.

It had been one hell of a long time. Nine years... more than nine years, in fact. It felt like ninety... sometimes (for God's sake!) it felt more like nine-hundred and ninety. Nine years of playing a part; of acting a character, and being paid for it. There wasn't a West End actor under the sun who'd have touched the part with a barge-pole. Not because the pay wasn't good—he'd made bloody sure he was going to act in comfort, whatever else—but because the lines and the 'business', twenty-four hours a day, *every* day, for the rest of Angela's life, was a little like feeding your nerve-ends through a shredding machine. It got you down. It sent you hell-for-leather towards the nearest twist. It made you reach for the nearest booze-bottle.

He bit into the half-eaten slice of apple pie, crumbled a portion from the wedge of White Stilton on the cheese-dish and popped it in with the pie. He chewed the mixture for a moment, then drank from the milk bottle. Some of the milk escaped, before it reached his mouth. It ran down his chin and dropped onto the lapel of his jacket.

He muttered, 'Blast!' and rubbed at the white stain with the heel of the hand holding the pie. The stain became fainter... but larger.

He muttered, 'Sod it!' and decided to change his jacket, before he left for Little Moysell.

He sought consolation—some sort of relief, from his present mood—via the thoughts which always sustained him.

One day...

One day, the stupid bitch would die. She couldn't live forever.... even *she* couldn't live forever! And then, he'd bury her—or burn her... cremation being one of the things she 'believed in'. And then, he'd spend it. All of it. Every brass-bloody-farthing! He'd live like a prince and, because he had the loot, people who now tended to stick their stupid noses in the air when he was around—people who made no real pretence and treated him like some sort of high-class gigolo... just watch them *then*! My Christ they'd change their bloody tune once he had his hands on everything. Money, mate... it talked. It sang songs, it played symphonies, it made more noise than a Wagnerian opera. And he'd have it—more than he had ever hoped for ... and he'd crack it. By God, he'd crack it! And all those whey-faced hypocrites wouldn't be so bloody hoity-toity then. They'd be round the jam pot ... bet money on it. They'd be pushing their toffee-nosed daughters at him. They'd all be listening, eagerly for the spring-interior music, and rubbing their greedy hands in expectation. *And* he'd take 'em ... every one of 'em. He'd screw the starch out of 'em. He'd give 'em horse-riding. He'd make 'em think they'd just done the Grand National, bareback!

He finished the slice of apple pie, ended with another piece of cheese and slopped more milk into his mouth.

Meanwhile ...

We-ell—meanwhile Angela ... where the hell *she* was.

Funny that ... the most cockeyed thing on God's earth. Angela. He'd once thought something about her. Y'know—not *love* ... sod 'love' for a living! Love was something romantic novelists had invented ... like the S.F. writers had invented bug-eyed monsters. It wasn't real—it wasn't human—it was something dogs felt for their owners. Over and above that, 'love' belonged with the fairies, at the bottom of the garden. It was something kids thought they had—on a par with pimples and puppy-fat—but a few years of adulthood soon put the skids under that sort of stupidity.

Nevertheless—we-ell ... he'd had some sort of a feeling for her, in the early days. Something. Maybe because, in those days, she'd made him feel important. He was the first man she'd ever had—she'd told him so, and Angela never lied—and, because he was the first, she'd doted on him. She'd made him a god; treated him like a god and made him feel like a god. The best—nothing but the best ... and even the best hadn't really been good enough for him. They'd been golden days. She—stupid bitch that she was—had been in a permanent state of semi-coma. Nothing ... there had been *nothing* she wouldn't do for him. Physically. Financially. Socially. Emotionally. You name it ... *nothing*!

And (well, hell why not?) he'd been grateful. He was human, wasn't he? He wasn't some sort of a bloody ogre.

And when somebody—when a woman, even an old woman—treats you like she'd treated him, something happens. Gratitude... that, at least. Gratitude for the appreciation. A willingness to play along; an encouragement in the dumb belief that this is 'The Great Love Story'... if that's all it takes to make the old dame happy.

It wasn't much. Hell, in those days, she'd have believed anything. She'd even believed all the guff about Ruth. About Ruth not 'understanding' him... even that old gag! But she'd swallowed it, and it had made things that much easier. The secrecy—the dark-corner assignations—in case Ruth got to hear about things, and made life more difficult.... more(what was the way she'd put it?—what was the po-faced expression she'd used?) 'utterly unbearable'.

That was it. In case Ruth made his life 'more utterly unbearable than it is already'.

Jesus wept!

The innocence of some of these biddies who suddenly discover there are more exciting pastimes in this world than stroking a doctored tom.

Like that night—the night Ruth 'died'—when they went to the cinema. When they were—they were—they are... they are...

They are in the front row of the circle. Naturally. The seats which make up the first three rows of the circle are the most expensive seats in the cinema; there is a clear and uninterrupted view of the screen and, in these particular seats, the screen is at a perfect distance and at eye-level. They are very comfortable seats, and they are also the only seats in the cinema which can be made the subject of reserve booking.

Angela is paying. Angela has booked the seats. Angela is sitting on Watford's right. Watford is relaxing, and enjoying himself.

The film (Watford's choice) is Shane; *the film adaptation of Jack Schaefer's classic western. It is a return showing (by popular request) and although Angela does not like 'cowboys' (as she calls them), this one is the exception which breaks the general rule. She has seen it once, at its first showing at this same cinema, and she was surprised (even startled) to discover how much she enjoyed it. She liked the magnificence of the scenery. She liked the honesty of the dialogue and the acting. She liked the small boy, through whose eyes the story was told. And (most of all) she liked the central character... Shane, the quiet-spoken, teetotal, knight-errant in western garb, whose honour and loyalty prevents a small man from being frightened away from his own tiny plot of land.*

She is looking forward to seeing the film again.

Watford, too, has seen the film before. As with Angela, he saw it at its first showing at this same cinema... and, on that occasion, he was with his wife, Ruth.

Watford also liked the film. Mainly for the store-room brawl, and the final explosive gun-fight.

Each in their own way—each for their own reasons—are anxious for the lights to dim and the show to get under way.

Behind them the circle is slowly filling with cinema-goers. Beneath them—beyond the low, padded bow of the circle's frontage, and in the double-aisled stalls—a small crush of other customers are choosing their seats.

Watford watches the activity in the well of the cinema. He sweeps his eyes casually over the heads of those already seated.

Suddenly, he leans forward, and says, 'Pamela... that's Pamela, down there.'

'Who?'

Angela asks the question in a sharp-edged tone. She, too, leans forward in her seat and looks down, over the circle's frontage.

'Pamela,' says Watford. 'Pamela Ogden... Harry's wife.'

'Your next-door neighbour?' The question is asked in a softer voice, but with concern touching the edges.

'Yes... there.' Watford nods towards the bulk of the seats which make up the centre of the stalls; to where an auburn-haired young woman, wearing a light-coloured mac, with epaulets, is unbuckling the belt and unfastening

*the buttons of the mac, prior to settling back in her seat
for the show.*

*In a low voice, Angela says, 'Sit back, Ralph. Don't let
her see you.*

'It's okay.'

*'If she looks back—if she looks up here, and sees
you...with me,' whispers Angela, urgently. 'She'll tell
your wife. She'll tell Ruth.'*

*'No, she won't.' There is absolute confidence in
Watford's assurance.*

'Please!' pleads Angela.

Watford shrugs, and leans back in his seat.

'She—she can't see us...not now?' asks Angela.

'No. Not if we sit back.'

*'Good... I'm glad.' Angela breathes a sigh of relief. 'I'd
hate to be responsible. You know...for making your life
more utterly unbearable than it is already.'*

*'You're wonderful.' Watford turns on his special smile;
it is a smile which radiates adoration tinged with sadness.
He murmurs, 'You're a wonderful woman, sweetheart.
God knows what I'd do, without you.'*

*The lights dim. The beam from the projector cuts a
narrow V through the smoke and the dust motes. The
stage-curtains open and the first of the adverts flashes
onto the exposed screen.*

Angela entered the kitchen. Watford turned, startled as
her sudden arrival cut into his daydreaming.

They spoke together.

Angela said, 'What on earth are you doing home at this
time of day?'

Watford said, 'Where the hell have *you* been?'

Angela peeled off her gloves as she said, 'There was a
committee meeting of the Townswomen's Guild. I had to
attend—obviously...as their vice-president.'

'Obviously,' murmured Watford...and made little
effort to erase the slight sneer from the word.

As she took off her hat, Angela said, 'Now, please
answer my question. What are you doing home at this
time?'

Watford watched her face, as he said, 'Ogden's out, today.'

'Ogden?' She allowed herself a quick frown, then said, 'Oh!... Ogden. The man who murdered your first wife.'

'He was released from prison, this morning.'

'Really?'

Angela removed her coat, she draped it over her arm and, in the hand of that same arm, held her gloves and hat. She made as if to walk across the kitchen, towards the main body of the house.

'He's likely to come up here,' said Watford.

'Here? To this house?'

'No ... of course not. Not *here*.'

'As you say ... of course not.'

'To Little Moysell.'

'Isn't that where his wife lives, now?' she asked.

'Yes.' Watford paused, then added, 'She rang.'

'His wife?' Angela showed polite, but controlled, surprise.

'Uhu.' Watford nodded. 'She rang me—at the office ... she's scared.'

'Of her own husband?' This time *she* made no effort to hide the hint of contempt.

'He's a murderer,' Watford said, flatly.

'Of course.'

'He's also my friend ... *was*.'

'And still is?' she asked, with some interest.

'Ye-es.' Watford spoke slowly. Contemplatively. 'Ye-es ... I still consider him a friend.'

She looked at him for a moment then, in a quiet, cool tone, said, 'Your friend—the man who murdered your wife ... *why*? *Because* he murdered your wife?'

'Don't be a damned fool!'

'Forgive me. I'm not sophisticated in these matters. It seems odd ... that's all.'

Watford forced calmness into his voice, and said, 'Pamela telephoned. She's frightened. She asked me to be there—with her—when he arrives. I agreed ... I think I should be.'

She watched him for a moment, in silence. There was

knowledge in her gaze; knowledge, coupled with stoical acceptance.

She moved her arm, over which the coat was draped, and said, 'I—er—I need a quick wash. I feel grubby. I'll put these away—in the wardrobe... if you can spare the time to wait. Then I'll be back. You'll need money... for expenses, and a possible hotel bill.'

She walked out of the kitchen, along the passage, into the hall and up the stairs.

Angela Watford took her time. She didn't hurry because, these days, there was no point in her hurrying. Once ('once upon a time'... as with the case of all fairy tales!) she might have thrown the coat, hat and gloves onto the bed in order to rush back, downstairs, to make sure her beloved Ralph was still there, and lacked for nothing.

Now she *knew*.

He'd be there... as far as she was concerned, he'd be there forever!

He'd be there, because he'd chosen to be there and, whilever the cheques were honoured, he'd *be* there. His emotion, (assuming he was capable of any emotion, other than greed and selfishness) had fiscal foundations and, if she wished to keep him as a husband—and she knew she could never stand the humiliation of him leaving her, and the subsequent I-told-you-so commiserations—all she had to do was feed him cash. Like an old-fashioned 'What The Butler Saw' machine; keep pressing the pennies in the slot—keep turning the handle—and the scene was enacted over, and over again. All it needed was pennies... plus a minimum of effort.

She was prepared to give her life that, rather than be a laughing-stock.

Pennies... plus a minimum of effort.

She was an old woman. Not 'old' in the modern sense; not 'old' by the yardstick of today... today women (and men) were considered 'young' even when they were in their eighties. 'Young in heart' was the expression glibly mouthed, by those who were lucky enough to understand its meaning. But she was *old*. Because she was 'old-fashioned'. She'd been brought up to believe that age—old age—arrived somewhere in the mid-fifties, that, at sixty a woman was *really* old. Wrong? By today's standards, yes...but not by *her* standards. Not by the standards taught her when she was a child—when she was a teenage girl...therefore, by her standards she was most certainly 'old'.

And, nine years ago, she'd tried to abandon those standards. For a time—for a few months—she'd gone crazy.

Having put the coat, hat and gloves carefully away in the wardrobe, she took off her wrist watch and necklace and walked to the bathroom.

As she soaped her hands at the bowl she had, of necessity, to watch the wedding-ring...and, as always, it increased the hurt and magnified the contempt.

Her—Angela 'Watford'...despite every effort, at the beginning, she'd never been able to break the habit of putting her married name in mental quotation marks.

It wouldn't have been so bad—it wouldn't have been as monumentally crazy—had she chosen a man of her own age-group. A husband, for a companion...not a husband for a 'lover'. Oh, my God! The shame...the humiliation...the sickening foulness.

That first night!

He'd—he'd *invaded* her body. Nothing else—nothing less savage...he'd physically invaded what no man had previously even touched. He'd used words like 'love'—words like 'passion'...but, in fact, it had been bestial and disgusting. A ravishing, of which she could never complain. There had been no gentleness. No consideration. No attempt at slow awakening.

There had been '*it*'. Sudden, savage, nauseating and (not least of all) sickeningly painful. As painful as a surgeon's knife. As bloody. As offensive.

She scrubbed at her hands with the nail-brush, as if attempting to clean away some stain which would go with her to the grave.

And, after that—after that mockery of a 'honeymoon'...after that, she hadn't cared.

She'd insisted upon certain ground rules. She'd imposed a certain discipline, via the purse-strings...she had, at least, learned *that*.

That he take up token employment; that, at least on the face of it, she did not 'keep' him. That they had separate bedrooms; and that her own room be fitted with a lock, of which he did not have a key. That, whatever else he did—however many other women he enjoyed—however many prostitutes he visited—he must keep up a facade of respectability; that, publicly, their marriage must retain all the outward appearance of a happy and successful union.

The only things she had left in life were pride and money, and she was prepared to use one to keep the other intact...and Ralph was ready to oblige, if the payment was sufficient and regular.

She supposed she was a born 'old maid'. She supposed all men weren't like Ralph. She supposed she'd been unlucky...and she supposed she'd deserved all the ill-luck she'd got.

She looked into the mirror, above the bowl, and was surprised to see tears trickling down her cheeks.

Damn him! Damn any man who could do to another human being what he'd done to her! Damn him, for what he'd done—for what he was still doing—for what she knew he would continue to do!

Damn him!

She bent and sluiced her face with warm water.

She dried her hands and face, returned to the bedroom, took the coat, the hat and the gloves from the wardrobe and returned to the kitchen.

In the kitchen, she threaded her arms through the sleeves of the coat and, in a quietly controlled voice, said, 'When you're ready.'

'What?' He looked puzzled.

'I'm going with you,' she pronounced.

'What the hell...'

'I'm curious—vulgarly curious, if you like... I've never met a murderer.'

'Angela. Don't be such a fool. There's no need for you to go. It—it could be very distressing.'

'I know.' She fastened the coat, picked up the hat and positioned it carefully on her iron-grey hair. She said, 'I imagine it *will* be distressing... but interesting.'

'I forbid it. I...'

'Don't be such a damn fool!' she snapped.

He blinked then, in a harsh voice, said, 'You'll be sorry. You'll regret it. It isn't one of your polite little meetings of...'

'Ralph.' She concentrated upon working the fingers into her gloves as she spoke. 'I've regretted so many things, in my life, one more won't matter. However—the more I think about it, the more convinced I am... I *should* go with you. You may need moral support. You'll certainly need financial support.' She stroked the last wrinkles from the backs of the gloves, looked up and, in a tone which carried absolute finality, said, 'Right... when you're ready.'

THE WOMAN

THE place looked noticeably cleaner, and smelled noticeably sweeter. Thelma hadn't exaggerated when she'd said she'd brought cleaning materials in the boot of the car. Mops, brushes and dusters—polishes, detergents and soap-powders—plus pails, bowls and two rolls of cheese-muslin. The Calor-fed gas stove fed them a continual supply of hot water and, as the two women became progressively more soiled, 'The Swan's Nest' progressively took upon itself a sparkle and a shine.

Thelma had changed into sweater and trousers. Pamela wore a T-shirt and jeans. And they worked, and were happy . . . and (although neither of them might have either admitted, or even realised, the cause) their happiness, and their willingness to work, stemmed from a single and mutual cause.

Harry Ogden.

But the cause (although single and mutual) was not simple. It was a very complicated cause; it embraced nuances and shades of which neither woman was openly aware . . . some nuances, and some shades, which each would have vehemently denied.

Thelma Simpson—sister of Harry Ogden...and all that that meant.

It meant (among other things) that, for more than two decades, she had lived under the same roof as Ogden; that, for twice as long as Pamela, she and Ogden had shared the same house and shared the same family. She knew him intimately, as a person—knew how his mind worked, knew how his emotions swayed him him—whereas Pamela (in the opinion of Thelma) knew him intimately, only as a man...as a husband. Given time, Pamela might have grown to know him as well as she (Thelma) knew him, but their marriage had been interrupted...if 'interrupted' was the right word. 'Cut short'—probably 'ended'...because Pamela had an impatience which might prevent her from making necessary readjustments.

Which was one way of saying that Pamela didn't love Harry as much as she (Thelma) loved Harry. Differently...but not as much. How could she? She wasn't his sister; they hadn't been children together; in her school-days, he hadn't been her automatic, and accepted, champion against the hatefulness of other children ...and, later, other teenagers. She hadn't wept, for the loss, when he'd married; hurt beyond measure—beyond understanding—that this gallant of hers (this brother, this Harry) had given himself to another woman.

And, at the trial, Pamela had given evidence... *given evidence, against Harry*! Never mind that it had been the truth. Never mind that what she'd said had been a plea for mercy. Never mind that that stupid Watford man had seen her alone, in the cinema, at the time of the murder; that what Watford said would have been substantiated by that silly biddy who was now his wife. Never mind, even, that Harry had pleaded 'Guilty'; and the trial ('trial', for God's sake!) had lasted less than thirty minutes, and hadn't even needed a jury.

Never mind all these things... *Pamela had given evidence*.

She (Thelma) had gone quietly mad. She had offered to give evidence in the witness-box (to swear an oath, if necessary, on all the Bibles ever printed) that Harry had been with *her*, at the time of the murder. George would have gone along... George would have been *made* to go along! And, if Pamela had joined them—and Harry, himself—and if they could only have argued him into changing his plea ... it would have been four, against two.

They would have committed perjury ... but, what of it? They would have beaten the court. They would have forced a jury (any jury on earth) to the conclusion that Watford and his lady-friend had made a mistake; that there was an 'element of doubt' ... enough doubt to give Harry his freedom.

It could have been done. Easily. All it had needed was guts. All it had needed was love for Harry.

But, no! ... *Pamela had given evidence.*

Which meant?

We-ell, now—it could be argued (and despite all that had been said—and said in good faith—since her arrival) that Thelma's presence at 'The Swan's Nest' was not quite the good-neighbourly—the forgive-and-make-up—action of an ever-loving sister-in-law which, on the surface, it seemed to be.

There are dark and secret corners in every mind.

For example (just for example, of course) it is possible that she was there in order that she might be one of the first—if not *the* first— to greet Harry upon his arrival home. It is possible that she was there to illustrate that (at the very least) nobody loved him *more* than she did; to show that, whereas he had had to come to Pamela, she (Thelma) was prepared to do her share of the travelling in order to meet him, and complete the perfect homecoming.

For example (again, just for example, of course) it is possible that she was there in order that 'The Swan's Nest' might look particularly (and unusually) clean and particularly (and unusually) bright. It is possible that she knew—and also knew that Harry shared her knowledge—that Pamela was incapable of such superb housework; that she knew—and, again, knew that Harry shared that knowledge—that Pamela could not prepare a first-class meal. It is possible that Thelma knew these things—and knew that Harry knew them—and that, therefore, the comparison between herself and Pamela would leave Pamela deficient... and that this comparison, followed by a realisation of this deficiency, might easily be seen to reflect a corresponding deficiency in love.

Make no mistake. Thelma would have denied such motives. She would have considered them base, and offensive. But, denial or not, they were possibilities.

There are dark and secret corners in every mind, and people do things for strange reasons; reasons they will never admit, because they are ashamed of those reasons.

Thelma squeezed the last drops of grey-coloured water, from the cloth she'd been using, into a plastic bucket. She straightened from the hearth and, as she stood up, held her right, middle-ribs (towards the small of her back) and winced for a second as the first twinges of oncoming rheumatism reminded her of her age. She surveyed the newly-cleaned hearth and fire-surround with approval.

She said, 'Right, Pam... feeding-time.'

'Should we?' Pamela looked round from where she was polishing the panes of the window. 'Have we time?'

'I'm shagged,' said Thelma, in an unladylike tone. 'I usually have the proverbial 'little woman' come in and do all this stuff. A quick hoover-down... that's my normal limit.'

'Sorry.' Pamela looked embarrassed, then added, 'I'll—er—I'll nip down to the shop... the post office. They'll have something. What d'you fancy?'

'What I fancy is on the back seat of the car.' Thelma dropped the damp cloth into the bucket of soiled water. 'A Thermos jar of good, home-made soup. And some packets of sandwiches... teacakes, with home-boiled ham. Thick slices. All you need provide, girl, is cups—and good English mustard... got any?'

'Oddly enough... yes.'

'Good.' Thelma wiped her damp hands down the thighs of her trousers. 'That's it, then. We eat.'

While Thelma sprawled in the only decent armchair, in the living room of 'The Swan's Nest', Pamela stood at the door of the lean-to kitchen, stared out at the anarchy of vegetation which was the rear garden and waited for the kettle to boil.

The quick meal had been perfect...but, of course! Thick pea soup; piping hot and seasoned to a T. The ham had been meltingly delicious; sandwiched between cool, fresh butter and newly-baked bread-cakes, with the mustard adding the tongue-smarting bit which balanced the smoothness of all the other tastes.

Perfect—but of course...Thelma had organised it.

And now it was her (Pamela's) turn. A cup of tea and a cigarette, to round off the meal; cheap, supermarket tea in Woolworth's beakers; yesterday's milk and sugar spooned from a chipped soup bowl.

Christ!...the difference.

And yet, she was still Harry's wife...and *that* was the difference. That was the only difference that mattered; a difference which all the mouth-watering snacks, and all the efficient housekeeping, couldn't remove.

It was *her* (Pamela) he'd come home to...supposing he came home to anybody. Supposing he ever came home, again. Supposing he hadn't had a gutful.

And who could blame him, if he had?

Who could blame him?

Indeed, who could have blamed him that night, ten years ago, when he'd—when he'd—when he...when he...

He stands there. Looking a little ridiculous. At any other time—in any other circumstances—she would have been unable to hold back the laughter. What man can look dignified—what man can look truly outraged—wearing only socks and candy-striped underpants? —

And yet...

Even in the soft glow from the table-lamp which stands on the vanity-bureau his quivering, almost uncontrollable, fury can be seen. It can be felt. It electrifies the whole bedroom. It beats its way through all ridicule of dress, as easily as it beats its way through the silent sway which is the end-product of hard and prolonged drinking. It is a murderous fury—frightening...and she feels the fear far too much to laugh.

She holds the sheet up to her chin, raises her head an

*inch or two from the pillow and, very tentatively, says,
'Harry?'*

'Bitch!'

*The rejoinder is little more than a whisper, but harsh
with anger. The control almost breaks with that one
whispered exclamation, and she sees him tremble and
clench his jaw as he fights to overcome the passion which
threatens to drown him.*

She sits up in bed, still holding the sheet to her chin.

*She stares at him. She knows ... but hopes, even prays,
that the knowledge is false, and based upon her own guilty
conscience.*

She says, 'Where—where have you been, Harry?'

*'Out.' He moves his lips, but keeps his teeth
tight-closed.*

'Drinking?' she asks, meekly.

'Drinking,' he rasps.

'Who—who with?'

'Ralph.'

'Oh!'

*Such a short exchange ... but it explains everything. It
verifies her fear. It substantiates her knowledge. It tells
her that he, too, knows ... and magnifies the fear into
terror.*

*She glances down, from his face, and sees the stick he is
holding in his tightly-folded right fist. For a moment, she
does not recognise it—then she does ... it is the shaft of a
golf-club; one of a set which once belonged to her father
and which, when he died, her mother had given to Harry.
'As a momento—and in case you ever feel like taking up
golf.' And Harry has treasured them, because he admired
her father—he's treasured the clubs, although he's never
shown any interest in the game ... and now he's snapped
the head from one of the clubs and is holding the slim
shaft as a weapon with which to beat an appreciation of
wifely duty into the daughter of the man he admired.*

*Because that's what it is! She knows that—she knows
Harry ... and she knows the destructive rage of which he
is capable. She knows he is going to beat her—whip her
into submission, like an untrained animal—with the*

broken club he once treasured...she knows it, even though he's never raised a hand against her before.

Nor does she blame him...except, perhaps, for breaking the club. He could have used something else. A walking stick, perhaps. Even his fists. But, by smashing the club he has, somehow, increased the coming hurt; as if her dead father is aiding the whipping...and as if Harry, himself, is sharing the deserved pain.

But the pain is due—the pain is deserved—the pain is just...and, terrified though she is, she waits for it without complaint.

And then, she is aware that Harry is talking. Muttering, to himself. As if trying to justify what he is there to do...that, or talk himself out of it.

And she hopes the former. She requires pain—she yearns for suffering...if only, in part, to match his own.

He is mumbling, '...going to leave you. That was the big idea. Bitch! Sleep downstairs. On the sofa. Be away, before morning—before you got up...have done with you. Away. Sod you. Bitch! That's what I was going to do. I'd like to have done. Off...and blast you. But I couldn't sleep. Couldn't sleep. Hatred. Disgust. Summat...I couldn't sleep. You bloody bitch!'

He looks across at her; seems to see her for the first time. His eyes narrow and, for the first time, seem to focus in on her, sitting there in bed, with the sheet still held at her chin. Waiting. Watching. Listening. Making no excuse—making no denial...and, by her silence, tacitly admitting everything.

And, gradually, his voice strengthens. As the anger surges up again, and overwhelms the self-pity, the words become more accusing and the tone becomes more harsh and, progressively, more hate-filled. Fury feeds upon fury, and the talk tumbles out in broken sentences, from lips which show the gleam of spittle at the mouth-corners.

'Tonight,' he snarls. 'D'you know what happened, tonight? D'you know? Earlier?...this evening? I had it planned. I had everything planned. Nice—y'know...nice. To have an evening out, together. Y'know...just the two of us. You and me...just the two of us. A dinner, somewhere. Somewhere nice—maybe a *night-spot, somewhere . . . maybe Harrogate, maybe York, maybe Leeds. I was going to let you say. Let you decide, where. A treat—a nice change—a night out . . . just the two of us. That's what I planned. Y'know . . . that's what I bloody-well planned!*

'*Then Ralph phoned me. He was in a state. Worried . . . worried stupid. He wanted to see me. Urgently . . . that's what he said. That it was urgent. It couldn't wait. That's what he said . . . that it couldn't wait. Even till morning. Even till I got home, this evening . . . that's how urgent it was. He wanted to see me. And—y'know what, bitch? . . . I'll bet you know damn well what he wanted to see me about.*

'*All right . . . so I don't have to tell you. You know. You know what he wanted to tell me. You bloody-well know! But I didn't know. Even when he tried to tell me, I didn't know. I was stupid. I was dumb . . . I was like a big, dumb cow standing there, with my mouth open and not knowing what the hell he was trying to say. There—in the boozer—him, spluttering and stammering . . . and me not knowing what the hell it was all about. Not knowing. Not even guessing. And he was telling me—trying to tell me something . . . something the whole sodding district seems to know. Everybody, but me. I didn't know—how the hell was I supposed to know?—I'm too dumb to know these things. And it damn-near choked him . . . telling me. It took him twenty minutes—all of twenty minutes . . . to put it into words I could understand. Twenty minutes! Long enough . . . long enough for me to have guessed, before he got it properly out.*

'*Christ . . . you bitch. You bloody bitch!*'

The last word is a choked-off scream and, as he utters it, he moves. He takes two quick strides to the centre of the bedroom. He scythes the club-shaft and sends perfume bottles, cosmetic jars, tissue containers, brushes, combs and hair-lacquer cans flying from the surface of the vanity-bureau.

'*These!*' he chokes. '*This . . . this . . . this.*' And, with each word, he smashes the shaft onto a piece of furniture; the kidney-shaped dressing-table, the basket-weave bedroom armchair, the tiny, near-antique writing desk which *she uses as a stand for her collection of glass figurines. Under the fury of the onslaught, wood splits and scars, silk cushion-covers slice open and spill their contents, the glass of the figurines shatters and flies.*

His voice is midway between a sob and a scream, as he raves, 'I can't buy your love. I can't buy your decency. I can . . . I can give you these bloody things as presents. In exchange . . . but I can't buy the bloody stuff. You either do, or you don't. You're my wife . . . you're not a sodding prozzy. I can't—I can't—I can't . . .'

He suddenly hurls the shaft at the mirror of the dressing-table, and howls, 'Blast you! Blast you to hell, Pam. You're a bitch . . . you're a hurtful, lousy, unfaithful bitch.'

And the explosion passes. It dies, as if it has never been; as if the broken furniture, and the torn cushions, and the smashed mirror have been there since the beginning of time.

But the fury is still there, and the hurt is no less, and she watches from behind her puny shield of held-up sheet . . . and, as she watches, her terror notches even higher.

He walks like a robot—like a dream-walker—and he walks to his own wardrobe. He opens the door of the wardrobe, puts his hand to the rear of the top shelf and lifts out the leather-faced case. He opens the case and, from its red velvet nest, he takes out his Luger. His beloved Luger . . . with its special sight and its modified trigger-pull. The weapon with which he has won the cups, the medals, the tiny sliver plaques which fill the display cabinet in the lounge. The gun with which he is an acknowledged expert . . . a marksman, and one of the top dozen shots in the country.

He slams a magazine into the base of the handgrip, cocks the Luger and walks to the bed. With his left hand he grabs her hair and jerks her head back. He curls his right forefinger around the trigger and brings the snout of the gun up, until it touches her upper lip. A gentle, deadly kiss of cold steel under her nostrils and with the barrel slanted towards the back of her skull.

She can smell the sweet stench of gun-oil. She can feel

the tiny pressure on her teeth, as the Luger's muzzle is pushed harder against her lip.

She is terrified ... but she forces herself to hide the terror.

If this is what he wants, so be it ... and she deserves nothing better! The decision is his, and she will not influence him.

She releases the sheet and allows it to drop, in folds, on her lap. She leans back a little, on her straightened arms, in order to ease the tension he is exerting on her neck muscles.

She looks up at his face, and waits. She waits for whatever has had to be.

And then he speaks. Whispered words. Hoarse, and heartbroken. Trembling a little with emotion. Still overflowing with disgust and disappointment ... but without the previous explosive hatred.

'How easy,' he says, softly. 'How bloody easy. Messy—bloody ... but easy. One little squeeze. That's all. Then I'd be sure ... wouldn't I? No more Ralph. No more flaunting your favours to some other bloke. No more getting on your back for some other man. I'd know ... and maybe that's the only way I would know. The only way I'd be sure.'

He pauses, and she breathes, 'Please!' ... *and the word might just as easily be taken as a plea for him to kill her, as a plea for mercy.*

He says, 'Ruth knows. That's what he wanted to tell me. It's why he had to tell me. She's going to sue for divorce ... naming you as co-respondent. That makes you a whore ... and me a fool.'

'I—I didn't know,' *she whispers.*

'But more than me,' *he retorts, bitterly.* 'A damn sight more than me. You knew more than I knew ... a damn sight more than I even suspected.'

'I—I didnt' know about Ruth. I—I thought ...'

'That she was as dumb as me?'

'No ... not that.'

'What?' *There is a heaviness in his voice. The heaviness of defeat and weariness.* 'That neither of us would find out? Is that what you thought?'

'I—I didn't think anything,' she breathes. 'That's the awful thing—the frightening thing—that I didn't feel anything...about anything.'

He moves his mouth, then says, 'Just that he was better than me.'

'No!'

'For Christ's sake! You must have thought...'

'I don't know what I thought. I didn't love him—I don't love him...nothing like that. It's just that...'

Despite the Luger, she moves her head in a tiny shake. She doesn't know the answer; she cannot explain, therefore she doesn't try. She merely looks up at him, and waits for whatever he will do next.

His nostrils flare slightly, and he mutters, 'Because he can do it better than me. Because he can...'

'No!'

'Look! There has to be a bloody reason. Some bloody reason. A woman doesn't...'

'Nobody can do it better than you, Harry,' she says, softly.

He stares into her face, shudders, then removes the gun from her face. He uncurls his finger from the trigger, and drops the gun onto the bed, alongside her.

He says, 'She can't do it. I won't let her do it...not name you as co-respondent. She has to be seen. Convinced. Threatened, if necessary. Even frightened. But she's not going to name you—call you a whore...call me a fool. She has to be...'

He stops talking, clenches his teeth then closes the fist of his right hand over the neckline of her nightdress. He still holds her hair in his left hand and, with his right, he rips the nightdress from her.

They make love, as never before; as if this is the first and last time, and forever-more; as if he would purge her mind of all memory of Ralph Watford. He snarls obscenities—words she has never heard him use before—as he uses her body as a vehicle for ridding himself of his previous fury.

And, as they love, she feels the hard shape of the Luger in her back, as it lies where he dropped it. But it does not matter. She is not frightened that it is loaded and cocked,

ready to fire; that their convulsions might trigger it off. It
does not matter. It is not important.

Then she no longer feels it ... no longer cares whether,
or not, it sends a bullet through her her spine!

And the next day, Ruth Watford is murdered ... and
Harry makes his confession to the police.

'It's boiling.'

'What?' Pamela returned to 'The Swan's Nest' with a
rush.

'The kettle,' said Thelma. 'It's boiling ... I think it has
been for some time.'

'Oh ... I'm sorry.'

Thelma eyed her quizzically, from the door leading to
the main room.

'Daydreaming?' she asked.

'Yes.' Pamela walked to the stove and turned off the
gas tap.

'About Harry?'

'What else?' said Pamela, truthfully.

Thelma said, 'Let's have that tea, girl. He won't be
long, now ... and we've still things to do.'

Thelma returned to the living room.

Pamela busied herself with the tea, and worked to
exorcise her mind of ghosts. It wasn't the same place. The
same beakers—the same cheap tea—the same cigarettes
smoked in front of the same hearth ... but not the same
place. It was cleaner—brighter—and it smelled
sweeter ... it smelled of pine disinfectant, and lemon
furniture polish, and lavender air freshener. It smelled
more like a bloody florists' shop than a home.

But it wasn't just the smell.

It wasn't just the look of the place ... that it was cleaner
and brighter.

It was Thelma—who else? ... what else? She'd stamped
her personality onto the cottage, already. She'd made it
hers; the place where *she* was going to meet Harry. And
that it was her (Pamela's) home, where she (Pamela) had
waited seemed unimportant; as if she (Pamela) had
merely kept it—stood guard over it—pending the arrival

of Thelma, and Thelma's final decision concerning how it should look, and where everything should be.

Thelma mused, 'Y'know . . . I still don't think he did it.'

'What?' Pamela looked startled.

'What he said,' amplified Thelma. 'About having an affair with Ruth Watford. I think that part was a lie . . . an excuse.'

'Why should he lie?'

'It isn't Harry,' said Thelma, thoughtfully. 'He wouldn't do that.'

'Sisterly intuition,' murmured Pamela . . . and there was a sneering quality about the remark.

'Perhaps.' Thelma nodded. The sarcasm had missed her, by a mile. She said, 'I know him. I know him as well as—better than—most people . . . even you, Pam. He wasn't that way.'

'You mean—er—undersexed?' She looked, with mock-interest, at Thelma, and said, 'How would you know anything about *that*?'

'I know my own brother.'

'Better than I know my own husband?'

'That, too, is possible.'

'One of us knows him,' said Pamela, gently. 'The other only *thinks* she knows him . . . but doesn't know him at all.'

'Ruth Watford,' said Thelma, bluntly, 'was no sex-pot.' She had—to use your own expression—the "necessary equipment".'

'For a quick romp . . . not for an affair.'

'There's a difference?'

'As between a sip of wine, and getting roaring drunk.'

'A matter of degree . . . surely?'

'Not at all.'

Pamela murmured, 'You've obviously given much thought to these things.'

'Obviously.'

'They interest you?'

'I *make* them interest me . . . I'm a married woman.'

'Oh!'

Thelma drew on her cigarette, exhaled, then said, 'Pamela, a novelty is just that . . . a novelty. But an affair— which was what Harry claimed it was—is more than a mere novelty. It has depth. It has reason. With a married man, it needs two women—his wife and his mistress . . . they both contribute. One gives too little. The other makes up for what's missing.'

'Like buying apples,' said Pamela, cynically.

Thelma smiled, knowingly, at the other woman. She said, 'You had the apples, girl. You still have 'em . . . any red-blooded woman, with working antennae, can tell that a mile off. Harry didn't need anybody else. He certainly didn't need an 'affair' with a prissy-faced wet fish like Ruth Watford.'

'He killed her,' said Pamela, bluntly.

'I'm not denying that . . . but for what reason?'

'If she thought she was pregnant . . .'

'She wasn't. The P.M. established that.'

'Yes . . . but, if she told Harry she was.'

'What of it?'

'By *him*.'

'For God's sake!' Thelma threw her finished cigarette into the flames of the newly-built-up fire. The gesture was one of disgust and disbelief. She said, 'Harry—even Harry—knows the slice-off-a-cut-cake argument. Even if she was pregnant—she wasn't, but even if she *was*—how the deuce could she tell? Harry, or her own husband? Come to that, how was her own husband going to tell? He was no celibate . . . whatever else he was, Ralph Watford wasn't *that*!'

'He wasn't that,' agreed Pamela, softly.

'So-o . . . I don't believe him.'

'Harry?'

'I don't believe he had this stupid "affair" he told the police about. I think he used it as an excuse. To hide the real motive.'

'What motive?' asked Pamela, her tone was tinged with breathlessness.

'I don't know. But, when he gets here, I'm going to ask him.' Thelma stood up, dusted the crumbs from her trousers, then said, 'Right, girl—back to work . . . you start on the bedroom, I'll see what sort of a meal we can get organised.'

THE MAN

A HERO—an idiot...the dividing line is hair's-breadth fine. And the line disappears, and heroism becomes true idiocy when what is practised is heroics. The commando raid on St. Mazaire, to deny the *Tirpitz* the use of the only dry-dock in the world capable of taking her...that was heroism. The suicide sabre-charge of the Polish cavalry against advancing Panzer tanks on the outskirts of Warsaw...that was heroics. Romance has already threaded its weave into both incidents and, in time, each will become its own legend. But there is a difference. One had a purpose. One was a gesture. One might have shortened war...might even, in the long run, have won that war. The other shortened nothing, except the lives of the cavalrymen and their chargers...it was a minor annoyance, and swatted as easily (and as off-handedly) as a man swats a gnat.

One was the action of heroes, who had no desire to die. The other was the action of romantic fools, who had lost

114

the will to live. One gained an objective and five V.C.s. The other gained nothing... except perhaps, problematic immortality!

The argument continues, and will continue whilever realists and dreamers meet... and each will be sure the other is wrong.

But, by both yardsticks, Harry Ogden was a hero. He was not a *conscious* hero—he didn't say to himself, 'Here goes! This is my big moment. If I do this, or do that, people will call me a hero.'... He did what had to be done, and what many men caught in the same set of circumstances would also have done and, by doing just that, he became a hero.

Nor was he a hero on a wide canvas; the scope of his heroism was confined to a few feet of the M.1 motorway, witnessed by comparatively few people and would be forgotten within a few weeks. What he did was magnificent, but not glorious enough—not patriotic enough—to ever find its way into history.

Nevertheless, magnificent... and bloody painful!

The driver of the tanker was unconscious. He had broken bones; at the very least, his right leg was snapped and the jagged edge of bone had driven its way out beyond the skin and beyond the material of his trousers. He had a gash across his forehead, from which blood washed over his face. He was in a bad way, and he was knotted up inside the twisted wreckage of his cab.

There was God only knew how many gallons of petrol, within inches of the wrecked cab, the flames from the burning Austin were spreading and Harding's fire extinguisher was doing its best, but its best was not good enough and (unless something bigger, and better, arrived in a very short time) the tanker had to blow... and take with it both its driver and Ogden.

Ogden fought the torn metal, inside the cab. He prised, and ripped, and bent. He thrust his hand deep into what had once been the front of the cab, and felt the knife-edge of savaged steel slice, bone-deep, into his forearm; it was a sickening sensation, but without pain and he hadn't time to be sick!

The pain was in his legs. His trousers had caught some

of the petrol from the Austin, and the lower legs of his
trousers were on fire. Harding had used the extinguisher
on them, for a moment—but only for a moment, as the
main danger threatened was the possibility of the flames
touching off the contents of the tanker—and the
petrol-doused material burned merrily, and painfully,
and it was a little like having his legs encased in the
circular wicks of twin oil-lamps. And yet the pain was
bearable, because he made it bearable; he was able to
force that part of his mind which would otherwise have
screamed with pain to be silent—to ignore the pain—
much as, for the last ten years, he had forced part of his
mind to ignore memories which, if allowed to burn, would
have driven him mad.

He could do what he was doing—and continue to do
it—because of what he was, and he was what he was
because of the last ten years of his life . . . and if, because of
this, the life of the tanker driver could be saved, those last
ten years had not, after all, been for nothing.

It felt like a lifetime . . . in point of fact, it was less than
five minutes.

The fire service and the police arrived together. The
ambulance service arrived within the next thirty seconds.

Ogden had the driver half way from behind the broken
steering-wheel and the bent steering-column when the
first fireman climbed onto the side of the tilted cab and
elbowed him clear. Then he was soaked, from the waist
down, in extinguishing foam and his burning clothes
stopped burning.

Then there was a realisation that helping hands were
guiding him away from the immediate danger of the
overturned tanker. That he was being lowered, gently,
onto a stretcher. That a padded bandage was being
strapped to his arm, and that blankets covered his
suddenly pain-wracked body and that he was being lifted,
then slid through the rear entrance of an ambulance.

Then there was a gap—seconds, minutes,
hours . . . there was no means of measuring the passing of
time. There was only gathering pain which, in turn,
distorted time.

A voice spoke. It was a voice he knew—a voice he

should have remembered—a voice, not from his past, but from his present.

The voice said, 'Here, mate ... try this.'

The roof of the ambulance swam into half-focus ... and the blued windows ... and, beyond the windows, traffic and buildings being passed ... and the sway of well-sprung movement ...

Gentle fingers—rough-surfaced, but gentle—held a cigarette to his lips. He concentrated his thoughts long enough to close his lips around the slim cylinder of packed tobacco and inhale.

The smoke caught in his lungs.

He tried to mutter his thanks but, instead, burst into a spluttering cough.

And then there was another gap ... seconds, minutes, hours ... again, there was no means of measuring the passing of time.

Full consciousness came with the realisation that he was in bed. A strange bed, with clean, cool sheets. Wearing pyjamas which were not his. And the bed was in a room; and a strange room—which, like the bed and the pyjamas, was not *his* room—and a room with a large picture window, and gloss-washed walls, and a white ceiling, and small, but neat furniture. A pleasant room ... very clean, and very quiet.

A voice—the voice which had offered the cigarette—said, 'Feeling better, mate?'

Ogden turned his head.

Harding was sitting on a chair, alongside the bed. Harding's jacket was draped across his shoulders, the sleeves hanging empty like elongated epaulets. His right hand was a bandaged ball.

Ogden moved his head in a tiny nod, at the bandaged hand, and said, 'What happened?'

'I tried to pull the bloody Austin clear.' Harding grinned—an oddly shamefaced grin, as if making an admission of a foolhardy act—and added, 'Some hopes!'

'Where—where are we?' asked Ogden.

'You're in hospital, sir.'

The voice came from the other side of the bed. It was a

polite enough voice—not officious, not without sympathy and in no way harsh—but (to Ogden) it was
immediately recognisable.

It was a cop's voice.

Ogden rolled his head, and looked to the other side of
the bed.

The uniformed sergeant was sitting (like Harding) on a
chair alongside the bed. He was bareheaded, and looked
strangely incomplete without his helmet. He sat, straight-
backed and very obviously 'on duty'.

He smiled and although (again) the smile was genuine
enough, it was a cop's smile; not to be completely trusted.
He was a middle-aged man; weary-looking from untold
hours of night duty in lousy weather; sad-eyed from
listening to so much excuse for law-breaking; thin-lipped
and with that air of quiet, but supreme, confidence which
is the cop's trademark.

He said, 'When you're strong enough, Mr. Smith. I'd
like a short statement from you.'

Ogden looked puzzled.

From behind Ogden's head, Harding said, 'I've already
told them your name, Tom. Thomas Smith.'

'If you don't mind . . .' began the sergeant.

'I have also,' continued Harding, 'given them *my*
statement. Why the hell they need one from you, I don't
know.'

'Look—if you don't mind, sir.' The sergeant looked
across Ogden, at Harding, and said, 'We need as many
statements as possible. It was a bad accident . . . very bad.'

'Fatal?' asked Ogden.

'Not fatal.' Harding answered the question.

Ogden forced himself to think; to refuse to be hurried,
or conned into doing anything he might regret.

The sergeant spoke to Ogden, and said, 'We need a
short statement about what happened.'

'And, if I don't?' asked Ogden.

'Why shouldn't you?' countered the sergeant.

'Look mate—can't you see? . . . he's knackered.' This
time Harding talked across Ogden, to the police sergeant.
His voice was touched with anger, as he continued, 'Give

him a chance. He's just come out of it.'

The sergeant said, 'I'm in no hurry, sir. All I want is ...'

'I know—you want another bloody statement.'

'We need as many ...'

'And, he doesn't have to *give* you a bloody statement ... not if he doesn't want to. But you haven't told him that, yet. Have you?'

'He must know ...'

'He hasn't come round, yet,' snapped Harding. 'Not properly. Give him at least that much time.'

'I will,' said the sergeant, patiently, 'give him all the time in the world. I'll sit here, till he decides.'

Ogden stared at the ceiling throughout the exchange. Part of his mind wanted to back Harding's objections to being rushed. Part of his mind shied at the thought of having even a minor skirmish with the police, so soon after release from prison. But, most of all, he wanted peace; peace in which to think—in which to reach a decision—in which to work out some way of getting out of this damn bed, getting out of this damn hospital and continuing his journey north.

He heard, rather than saw, Harding stand up from his chair.

Then, Harding said, 'Don't say anything, mate—no statement, no nothing ... not till I get back.'

The sergeant said, 'Where are you going, Harding?'

'Who knows?' Harding spoke from the door. 'Maybe for a pee. Maybe to telephone a solicitor ... maybe that's what we need.'

Ogden heard the door of the room open and close.

The police sergeant was phlegmatic, like the rest of his kind. He sat silent, and waited ... he had (to use his own expression) 'all the time in the world'. Sitting on a chair, in a side ward of a hospital, was no hardship; he could be doing worse things.

Ogden could almost forget the presence of the police sergeant; he could almost ignore this representative of one part of an organisation which, for a decade, had robbed him of freedom, had caged him like a dangerous animal, had worked to strip him of every last vestige of human dignity.

He suddenly realised something.

It came as a surprise—something bordering upon traumatic shock—to discover that he hated the police. That he truly hated them, and that this hatred was not a passive emotion; that this loathing was an active thing, on a par with hating evil... on a par with the disgust which any decent man feels for wanton cruelty. It was an unrestrained hatred—and unreasonable... but it was there. And the realisation shocked him.

Nevertheless, he could almost forget the presence of the police sergeant.

Almost...

He had other things to worry about. Bodily discomforts, and a steadily increasing pain.

The feeling was that he was suspended on elastic—or, perhaps riding a yo-yo—first up, then down, then up again. He oscillated from clear-mindedness to near-unconsciousness and, with each grasp at perception, the pain washed a little higher... as if it, too, was rising and falling in wavelets which gradually covered and soaked his whole body.

He became aware of his arm—his right arm—heavy with bandage, from wrist to elbow, and resting in a broad-bandage sling; when he moved the hand, or the fingers, needles of pain rippled up the forearm...deadened pain which (he knew) had had its sharpness blunted by drugs but which, once the drugs wore off, would bite deeper and make the whole hand and arm useless.

His legs, too...they also sent warnings of dope-quietened agony along his nervous system. His legs were burned. He knew this—he remembered his burning trousers, and tried to recall the agony which (at the time) he had forced himself to ignore... but it was impossible. As always, total recall of pain was beyond the measure of the human mind. And yet he tried. Not for any masochistic reason, but as a means of assessment. How badly burned were his legs? How badly injured? Scars

didn't worry him . . . but had he complete control of his leg
muscles? Could he walk? Again, the pain was something
he would tolerate—even welcome—as long as he could
walk. And, if he *couldn't* walk—couldn't walk,
immediately—how long would it be, before he could?
Unaided, or with a stick, perhaps? Or even
crutches? . . . God grant that it wasn't as bad as that!

He wriggled his toes, experimentally, and jagged edges
of pure torment pierced the dope barrier and made him
wince.

Painful . . . but hopeful. The muscles—the muscles
between the upper leg and the foot—still functioned.
What was there, would mend—given time . . . whatever
else, there wasn't complete destruction.

The arm didn't matter. Sod the arm! . . . a cut (even the
deepest cut) would heal.

The legs posed the only problem. They were usable;
they'd carry him . . . he hoped! Start with the proposition
that they *would*. If so, the only question was how
far? . . . and with what degree of pain? He might be able to
walk a short distance. He was damn sure he was capable
of sitting up; of riding in a cab, or in a motor car.

Which, in turn, meant he could get a few miles farther
north; a few miles nearer home.

Which (again, in turn) raised the sixty-four-thousand-
dollar question. Where the hell *was* 'home'? Little
Moysell? Thelma's place? With his wife or his sister? Or,
come to that, with neither of them? Just 'home'—up
'north' back to his own stamping ground.

There came a second shock—a second realisation—
that, just as the motorway, and the traffic, had come as a
surprise, so 'home' (be it Little Moysell, Thelma's place or
merely up 'north') might come as a surprise. Ten years ago
was not yesterday. Changes—big changes—could have
taken place. Certainly a lot of people he'd known would
no longer be there; some would have died, some would
have moved and some (maybe most of those remaining)
wouldn't want to know him. Buildings would have been
pulled down, and other buildings would have been put up
in their place. High-rise flats, perhaps. Pedestrian
precincts, perhaps. Supermarkets . . . multi-level-car-

parks... market halls, instead of open markets... one-way-street systems... under-passes and over-passes...

Judas Christ!

He'd read of these things. Seen photographs of them. Seen them on a television screen.

But now, suddenly—in a single day—they were all reality... they were all part of *his* world.

Behind the thinning curtain of dope, his mind tried to grapple with certain possibilities he had not previously given much thought to; the impact of those possibilities upon the superficially simple act of 'going home'... and 'going home' wasn't simple any more. It was very complicated. It was frightening. It was like... It was like... Hell!—it was like stepping out, onto a lighted stage, in full view of a critical audience, and not knowing the bloody lines... not even knowing which character, in which play, you were supposed to be.

It was as frightening as *that*.

He closed his eyes, and tried to shut his mind to these thoughts; to these certainties, upon which were built possibilities, from which flowed a feeling of panic. From reality and certainties, to possibilities and panic... and this was 'going home', for Christ's sake!

He heard the door open and the soft squeak of rubber-tyred wheels on the lino.

He heard the sergeant say, 'What's up, now?'

A man's voice answered the question, brusquely and with the minimum of explanation.

'More X-rays. He'll be back when they've finished with him.'

He felt himself being lifted gently from the bed to the trolley; felt the blankets being folded and straightened over his legs and body; felt the smooth movement of the trolley out of the side ward and along the corridors.

Ogden kept his eyes closed.

It was not the X-ray Department.

It was a ward-sister's office and, when the porters who had delivered Ogden left, they were alone. Ogden, Harding and a young-looking medic who tried to hide his youthful looks behind a beard which, itself, was not yet robust enough to do other than give an impression of pseudo-age.

The medic eyed Ogden waggishly, and murmured, 'Mr—er—"Smith"? "Thomas Smith"?'

Ogden glanced at Harding.

Harding grinned, and said, 'Sorry, mate. It was a daft idea . . . me giving 'em your wrong name. I thought—y'know . . . you wouldn't want publicity. That's all.'

Ogden looked up at the medic, and said, 'Ogden. Harry Ogden. Don't blame him.' Ogden glanced at Harding. 'I'd have done the same.'

'The name isn't important, squire.' The medic sawed his forefinger, up and down, along the side of his nose. It was obviously a habit; it was also a habit which off-set any added impression of 'age' which the beard was meant to give . . . it was such a blatantly cheerful, and youthful, habit. He said, 'Your friend has told me . . . *why* he gave a wrong name.'

'Prison?'

The medic nodded.

'I see.'

'In strict confidence, of course,' said the medic.

This time Ogden nodded.

'You're on your way home, I understand?'

'I . . .' For a moment, Ogden almost tried to explain his present doubts about the meaning, and non-meaning, of the word 'home'. Then, he said, 'Yes.'

'Mmm.' The medic sawed away at his nose for a few seconds, then said, 'The situation, squire. I'll summarise it . . . then let you decide. The accident—bad enough, but not fatal . . . nobody's going to die. The tanker driver . . . he'll tell the police his story, when he's in a fit state. Same with the driver of the Austin . . . he'll tell *his* side. The two passengers from the Austin—as far as I know, they've already made statements . . . have, are doing, or are going to. The driver of the Bentley, and his passenger. Your friend, here. As I understand it, the police have collared two—it might even be three—independent witnesses, who were travelling south, and who saw the accident. No-ow . . .' The medic paused, eyed Ogden, then said, 'It's up to you, squire. If you think you can add anything to what these people can say. If you want to express an opinion. It's your choice.'

'And if I don't?' asked Ogden. 'If I don't want to make a statement . . . what then?'

'You just don't.' The medic shrugged. 'Thanks to your pal, they'll never trace you.'

'Ah . . . but *you* know.'

'The records, squire,' said the medic, solemnly. '"Thomas Smith" . . . address unknown. That's what the Emergency Intake Records say. I'll fix things. Have you transferred to another ward—forget to mention the transfer to the police . . . I'm not paid to do *their* job for them.'

'See?' Harding grinned his delight.

'If that's what you want,' insisted the medic.

The medic stopped sawing at his nose and, for the sake of variety, began to scratch his beard alongside the jaw.

'Thanks,' said Ogden. He looked hard at the medic, then added, 'I want more than that, though. I want out of here. I want to be on my way.'

'You're in bad shape, squire,' said the medic, solemnly. 'A couple of days—less than a week . . . then, if you can fix a car to collect you.'

'Today,' insisted Ogden. 'Now.'

'I can't justify an ambulance. Believe me, I would if I could, but . . .'

'I'm not asking for an ambulance.'

'One thing for sure,' said the medic, with finality. 'You can't walk—not yet . . . not on them legs.'

'I can try.'

'Squire—don't be a damn fool . . . please!' For the first time, impatience put an edge on the medic's voice. 'Those burns on your legs aren't just blisters. Some of them are second degree burns . . . a couple are third degree. Now, I don't know whether you know what that means, but . . .'

'I know,' said Ogden.

'Therefore, don't talk like an idiot. Destroyed tissue—flesh that's been burned away—isn't something to shrug off. You'll walk . . . be grateful for small mercies. But, if you walk too soon, you won't walk for long . . . after which, you won't walk at all.'

'As bad as that?' said Ogden, heavily.

'As bad as that,' agreed the medic.

Harding cleared his throat. He moved his unbandaged hand in a tiny gesture with which to attract their attention.

Ogden turned his head. The medic raised enquiring eyebrows.

Harding said, 'The—er—the lorry...*my* lorry. With this...' He moved his bandaged hand. 'I can't drive it, see? So, I've already telephoned head office. They're going to get onto the Leeds depot, to send a van down here, with a spare driver. Then, the van comes here, to pick me up and take me home...see? Now—er...' Harding glanced from the medic, to Ogden, then back to the medic. 'I could fix it. Y'know...we could take Harry home, first. In the back of the van. It'll be a mini—but a van...there'd be room enough for him to stretch out. If that's okay.'

'I would not,' said the medic, doubtfully, 'describe it as "okay".'

'I would,' said Ogden.

'It would be...' the medic paused, then selected the word, 'inadvisable.'

'Dangerous?' Harding pressed for a commitment.

'It could be dangerous,' said the medic.

'Could be?...or *would* be?' Ogden joined Harding in pinning the medic down.

The medic fought back. He said, 'Could very *well* be.'

'What you're saying,' said Ogden, 'is that, as a doctor, you're opposed to the idea of me travelling in the back of a van.'

'Precisely.' The medic nodded.

'And, as a man?' asked Ogden.

'What?'

'Not as a doctor—as a man...what would you say, as a *man*?'

'I'm a doctor, squire.' The medic began to saw the side of his nose, again. It was a habit—a sort of nervous tic—and both Ogden and Harding recognised it as an outward sign of indecision. He said, 'In this place, I'm a doctor...don't press me.'

'It's an answer,' said Ogden, with a smile.

'The nearest you're going to get to what you want me to say.'

'Fair enough.' Ogden nodded his satisfaction.

Harding said, 'A couple of hours— thereabouts...that's when the van should arrive.'

The medic dropped his hand from his face, shoved it and his other hand deep into the pockets of his white coat, and scowled.

'It's appreciated,' said Ogden, gently.

'What?' asked the medic.

'That you've gone out on a limb...as far as you dare.'

The medic grunted.

'It is appreciated,' repeated Ogden. 'There'll be no come-back. I promise. It's my decision, from now on.'

'You're going?' grunted the medic.

'What do you think?'

'I suppose.' The medic sighed. 'You'll need clothes— trousers at least...and slippers. Your feet aren't too bad. Your shoes saved them. But not socks...just slippers. And use those pyjamas as underclothes.'

'Look—there's no need to risk...'

'Don't be more of a bloody fool than you can help,' said the medic, irritably. 'In your place—all right...I might do the same. But don't make things harder than they are. We have spare clobber. I'll fix it.'

'Thanks.'

'I'll get the dressings changed. You might as well *start* clean.'

'Again—thanks. I'll...'

'And we have some old pillows somewhere. Stained...but clean. You'll ride more comfortably. Oh...and one more thing.'

'Yes?'

'You'll be discharging yourself...technically, that is.'

'Of course.'

'Leave it till the last minute. Until then, I'm justified...more, or less. After that, I'm helpless. Stay here...it's an empty ward, pending alterations, so you won't be disturbed. I'll fix the nurse to change the dressings, and porters to help you to the van. *Then,* discharge yourself...I'll be around.'

Ogden looked embarrassed.

He said, 'Look. What else can I say? I know what you're doing for me. I'm grateful... very grateful indeed. I'm—I'm...'

'Skip it.' The medic stared at Ogden's face for a moment, then said, 'Just remember it... that's all I ask. You people can be bitter. You can carry chips as big as railway sleepers—I know, squire... I've met a few. Don't! If you feel like it, remember this hospital. Not just me—not just here... but that, given a fair shake, most people want to help. Right?'

He turned on his heels, walked from the office and closed the door behind him.

Harding said, 'Nice bloke.'

'Uhu.' Ogden nodded, slowly. 'You too, Tom... you fixed it.'

'It'll amuse the wife,' muttered Harding. 'Y'know ... summat she can tell the neighbours.'

THE COP

HAD any fellow-copper been asked to give a serious character assessment of Chief Inspector Bardoph Sawyer certain words and expressions would, without doubt, have been used. Words like 'pompous'. Expressions like 'self-opinionated' and 'lacking a sense of humour'. Even the word 'fool' might have found its way into the assessment... but not the expression 'damn fool'.

The sad thing was that Sawyer, himself, might also have used those same words—those same expressions— had he been asked to strip his soul and provide some divine being with an honest self-assessment.

Sawyer knew his own weaknesses. He tended to ignore them—tended to either pretend they weren't there or that, instead of weaknesses, they were strengths—because he knew he couldn't rid himself of them. They were far more than 'part of him'... they *were* him. As much as a perpetual roaring temper was that which made Sugden (Head of C.I.D.) Sugden—as much as plus-fours made Lennox Lennox—so these not-very-nice foibles of

character made Sawyer. He loathed them, but had grown
to live with them. He had even grown to ignore
them ... except (just occasionally) at moments like this.

He looked up from his desk, shook his head sadly, and
tried to get through to the younger man.

He said, 'Fenton—believe me—I know what I'm
doing.'

'Yes, sir. But ...'

'Sit down, Fenton.' Sawyer waved to a spare chair, in a
corner of the office. 'Bring that chair up here. Sit down,
and let me tell you.'

Inspector Fenton carried the chair nearer to the desk,
sat down and waited.

'The Watford killing,' began Sawyer. 'When Ogden
killed Ruth Watford. It was more than murder ... it was
carnage. He used a carving knife ... from Watford's own
kitchen. He used a gun ... his own Luger. He stabbed
her—slashed deep into her—seven times. He shot her
twice. It was *carnage*. And I never want to see a human
body subjected to such violence, ever again ... ever!'

Fenton cleared his throat. He looked uncomfortable—
as if Sawyer had suddenly drawn aside a curtain, to give
him a glimpse of what he (Fenton) had previously been
too much of an oaf to appreciate—he moistened his lips,
prior to making a reply.

Before Fenton could speak, Sawyer continued, 'I was a
detective inspector at the time ... I've told you that,
already. I'm repeating it, because I wish to underline the
horror of that kitchen. I'd seen things ... like *you've* seen
things. Like every police officer sees things. Violence. The
end result of a vicious assault. The bodies of people killed
in road accidents. Every policeman sees these things—
they sicken him ... but, gradually, he gets accustomed to
them. He accepts them, and they don't turn his stomach.
I'd seen these things—as a detective inspector, I'd seen
them many times ... but never anything remotely like that
kitchen.'

'Sir ...' Fenton hesitated, then said, 'As I remember, he
put forward a plea of Diminished Responsibility ... that
she taunted him.'

Sawyer nodded.

'It could...' Fenton frowned, then added, 'It could have excused the savagery of the attack. Obviously, the court thought so.'

'The court,' said Sawyer, 'didn't see that kitchen.'

'Nevertheless—y'know...people can be driven to excess. Even that sort of excess.'

'Not if they're sane.' Sawyer's words were quietly spoken. They carried a ring of utter belief. He said, 'That kitchen—that murder—was proof of madness...and never mind what a good defence lawyer made it out to me. I saw it. Which means I know Ogden. I know what he's capable of...*and in my sub-division, he'll never do it again.*'

Fenton murmured, 'No, sir. Let's hope not, sir,' and knew what was coming next, but didn't know how to counter it.

Sawyer said, 'I want surveillance, inspector.'

'Yes, sir. But...'

'Twenty-four hours a day. Seven days a week.'

'Sir—we haven't the men. We're...'

'Joseph.' For one of the few times in his career, Sawyer addressed a subordinate by his Christian name. It was a yardstick of his concern. He said, 'Find the men. Rank doesn't matter...constables or sergeants. C.I.D. or uniformed. Just find the men. Round-the-clock surveillance, at Little Moysell. I want to know, the minute he arrives.'

'If he's coming,' ventured Fenton.

'Until we're sure—until I'm sure—he's *not* coming.'

'Yes, sir,' sighed Fenton.

'I'm not being an old woman, Joseph,' said Sawyer, heavily. 'Not this time...despite what Lennox might think.'

Lennox, of course, would not have agreed. Lennox was Lennox, and as far removed from Sawyer as it is possible for any copper to be removed from another. Lennox had panache (to put it politely)—to put it less politely, he was eccentric...Sawyer had as much panache as unleavened dough. If Lennox was a blazing sun, Sawyer was a Toc H candle. That was how far apart they were.

And yet Lennox could not put down the papers which made up the Regina versus Ogden file. The photographs, the statements, the forensic science reports. Scores of them—few of which had been necessary, as s result of Ogden's plea—and, every time, there was something wrong...something *wrong*!

The remains of his fish and chips were cold on his desk. The Guinness in the half-filled glass was flat and fast becoming stale. The air of the office was thick with the stench of smoke from cheap cheroots.

And Lennox was worried.

The photographs...

They were standard, ten-by-eight police blow-ups; carefully presented in book-folders, each folder holding half-a-dozen views; ready and handy for the jury to handle and examine. Black and white, and glossy. Sharp-edged and well-lighted. They showed the horror of the kitchen, the boneless, rag-doll posture of the victim. They showed close-ups of the knife wounds and the bullet-holes. They left nothing—*nothing*—to the imagination. They were good photographs—excellent photographs...and they were part of what was wrong!

Lennox studied the photographs. He gazed at them, one at a time, at arm's length, and then within inches of his nose. He sought an overall picture, and then he searched for each minute detail. He tore them from their folders, spread them on the desk and viewed them collectively.

He knew there was something—some little thing—that was wrong.

He didn't know *how* he knew—he didn't know *why* he knew—but his knowledge was no less positive because of this lack of supplementary knowledge.

The basic knowledge was an instinctive thing. It was what made him a good copper; what excused all his surface extrovertism. It was what (and despite everything else about him) had brought him the rank of detective superintendent.

Therefore, he knew...but, from hell, he didn't know *what* he knew.

He muttered, 'Bugger it!' bundled the photographs together, and started a re-read of the statements and reports.

The statement made by Harry Ogden...

...AND I RETURNED TO MY HOME. I THEN WENT NEXT DOOR, TO THE HOME OF MY MISTRESS, RUTH WATFORD. WE HELD A SHORT CONVERSATION DURING THE COURSE OF WHICH SHE INFORMED ME THAT SHE SUSPECTED THAT SHE WAS PREGNANT. SHE INFORMED ME THAT I WAS THE FATHER. I DID NOT DENY THIS. I KNEW I MIGHT WELL BE THE FATHER. SHE FURTHER INFORMED ME THAT SHE WAS GOING TO NOTIFY HER HUSBAND OF HER CONDITION. SHE SAID SHE WAS GOING TO TELL HIM I WAS THE FATHER OF THE CHILD. I TRIED TO REASON WITH HER, BUT SHE BECAME HYSTERICAL. SHE RAISED HER VOICE. SHE BEGAN TO SCREAM. I TRIED TO QUIETEN HER, BUT COULD NOT. I BECAME FRIGHTENED. I THINK I LOST CONTROL OF MYSELF. THE NEXT THING I REMEMBER WAS WHEN I WAS STABBING HER. I WAS USING A CARVING KNIFE WHICH I THINK I MUST HAVE PICKED UP FROM THE TABLE. I DO NOT REMEMBER PICKING UP THIS KNIFE. THEN I HAD MY LUGER PISTOL IN MY HAND AND I WAS SHOOTING HER. I DO NOT REMEMBER RETURNING TO MY HOME FOR THE LUGER. I REALISED THAT SHE WAS DEAD, AND THAT I HAD KILLED HER...

'Shakespeare,' murmured Lennox, 'would have been bloody proud!'

Sawyer was not proud...Sawyer was frightened. This was one day in his life he was going to remember; he realised this, as he realised his fear sprang from some spectral cause he could not put his finger upon. The problematic arrival of Harry Ogden at Little Moysell? Even the *certainty* of that arrival? So-o...what was there about the arrival of Harry Ogden which might give cause for fear?

He didn't know.

But what he did know was that it *was* fear. It wasn't worry. It wasn't apprehension. It wasn't just Sawyer-style panic.

It was fear...and without logical reason.

He sat at his desk, within the privacy of his office, and wrestled with thoughts which were less than thoughts; thoughts which were fading shadows of long-gone episodes; thoughts which, by this time, were near-healed wounds to his vanity. The thoughts touched upon a detective superintendent who had outpaced him in the promotion race; upon men over whom he wielded sub-divisional authority, but who despised him and did little to hide their contempt; upon the years ahead—the few years left, before his pension—and the increasing effort which was needed to keep abreast of modern police work and a rising crime rate.

It was a mental stocktaking...and he was shocked at the unexpected paucity of some of the shelves.

And all this—all this soul-searching—for what?

For the homecoming of Harry Ogden?

In heaven's name, what had Ogden to do with all this? Why the devil should a criminal—one criminal—a sub-human who had butchered his mistress have this effect?

Ogden was nothing... *nothing*!

Ogden—the man who killed women—was, like all his kind, a coward when the chips were down. He cringed. He almost fainted with terror. His bravery was paper-thin and, beneath it, he was cowering scum.

Good God, he couldn't even stand up to normal questioning. He'd caved in. He'd buckled—and before any sort of pressure had been exerted—and he'd blurted out—he'd blurted out—he blurted out...he blurted out...

'I...I...I...' The words stick in his throat but, like the cork of a shaken champagne bottle, they will force their way free. Given time, they will come. Given time, they will blast a way through the constriction of his throat. Meanwhile he tries. He gasps, 'I...I...I...'

Sawyer waits, knowing that Ogden's own conscience is

fermenting and building up the pressure.

The detective constable's pencil is poised over the notebook. He is straining to catch every word. He knows that what comes next is all-important.

Ogden's face is white. Shiny with a film of sweat. Tormented as the desire for silence fights the desire to confess. He is panting; as if breathing itself is a deliberate, physical effort. His eyes are wide, wild and panic-ridden.

He grips the arms of the chair with clawed fingers. Flops back into the chair, arches his spine, tilts his head and stares at the ceiling.

Sawyer leans forward a few inches, and says, 'Ogden, she was stabbed.'

Ogden's head moves, once, in a single, tight-muscled nod.

'She was shot.'

Ogden nods, again . . . once.

'You're a butcher,' says Sawyer, softly. 'Knives are the tools of your trade.'

Another single, jerky nod.

'You're a local celebrity. A marksman . . . of reputation. Who else, around here, has a gun? A pistol?'

Ogden stiffens. It is as if his whole body gives a tiny jerk as a prelude to complete immobility.

'Who else knows her?' insists Sawyer. 'Who has a gun? Who has a pistol?'

Ogden stares at the ceiling, and remains motionless.

The detective constable records every word of the conversation, in question and answer form.

Sawyer says, 'Ogden, there is an inference . . . a very obvious inference. It cannot be ignored. Somebody stabbed her—somebody shot her . . . and you're a butcher who owns, and knows how to handle, a pistol. There is an inference. Explain it away. This is your chance. If you don't—if you can't—it means we must work from that inference. It means we must ask the forensic science laboratory to make a special examination of the knife wounds. Of the bullet wounds. Of the bullets, and of your firearm. We must ask the scientist to make comparisons. We must . . .'

'I killed her.'

The three words are breathed from behind closed teeth and tightened jaw muscles. They are spoken to the ceiling above Ogden's head, and they are so softly spoken that it is doubtful if they even carry those few feet.

But Sawyer hears them, and the detective constable hears them.

Sawyer glances at the D.C.

The D.C. asks a silent question, with his eyes, and Sawyer nods.

The D.C. records the three words.

Sawyer speaks to Ogden.

He says, 'I'm sorry, Ogden. I didn't quite catch that . . . would you mind repeating it?'

Ogden brings forward his head. Slowly, until his eyes are level with Sawyer's eyes. Tears brim from the eyes and run in streaks down Ogden's face.

He says, 'I killed Ruth Watford. I stabbed her. I shot her. Then I telephoned the police, and pretended to have found the body.'

There is a silence. Deadly. Complete. As if all three men in this room have stopped breathing—have, for a few moments, stopped living—as if their hearts have stopped beating and their pulses have stopped pumping. There is a silence . . . utter and absolute . . .

Sawyer clears his throat, before speaking to the D.C.

He says, 'You've recorded that remark, constable?'

'Yes, sir.' *The detective constable's voice is off-key enough to be near falsetto.*

'Ogden,' *says Sawyer,* 'I must warn you. It is my intention to charge you with the murder of Ruth Watford. You are not obliged to say anything in answer to that charge. Whatever you say—whatever you say, from this moment—will be taken down in writing, and may be given in evidence.' *Sawyer pauses for a few seconds, then asks,* 'You may if you wish, contact your solicitor.'

'No solicitor.' *Ogden's voice is weary with defeat.*

'A note will be made of that reply.'

'One thing.' *Ogden brushes the tears from his eyes with the back of his hand.* 'One favour . . . please.'

'What?'

'I want to be away from here, when my wife gets back.'

'She'll have to be seen of course.'

'Not with me—not while I'm present . . . please.'

'As you wish." Sawyer bobs his head in agreement. 'I can leave a man here. Then, when she comes home, he can . . .'

'Not in the house. Tell him to wait for her . . . outside.'

'Ogden, you're in no position to make demands. On your own admission, you're a . . .'

'I know!' Ogden removes his hands from the arms of the chair. It is a slow movement; as if the hands are heavy, and he has lost all strength. He twists his fingers together, below his lap; body bent forward and head drooped. He pleads, and his pleas are wetted with the moisture of tears which periodically drip from the end of his chin and onto his writhing fingers. He says, 'What I've done—all right . . . I've done it. I'll tell you. Whatever you want to know . . . I'll tell you. I'm what you say I am . . . but not her! Spare her as much as you can. Spare her as much shock as you can. Get me away from here, before she comes back. Then, lock the door—don't leave anybody here to wait for her . . . it'll startle her. She'll see . . . she'll see your men next door. Let that be enough—please! . . . at the beginning. Don't make her come into her own home, and find the police waiting for her. Break it to her—y'know . . . gently. Let her get home, first—get over the first shock . . . then tell her. Please?'

'She has to be seen. She has to be told,' insists Sawyer, but the words are less aggressive than before.

Ogden mutters, 'I know. But gently—please . . . as gently as you can. She hasn't done anything.'

Sawyer hesitates, then says, 'All right. We'll leave, and lock the house. I'll tell one of the men—and a policewoman—to watch. When she gets home, they'll interview her. That's as far as I'm prepared to go, Ogden.'

'Yes, sir,' whispers Ogden. 'Thank you, sir.'

Sawyer does not smile—not even the ghost of a smile—but he feels the glow of satisfaction which, in less tragic circumstances, would have brought a smile to his lips. He has solved a murder. What has been said—what has been done—cannot be faulted. It is copybook—has been copybook, all along the line—and a commendation,

*either from the bench, or from the chief constable (quite
possibly both) is as near a certainty as anything is in this
life.*

His name will be in the newspapers.

His wife will be pleased.

His colleagues will be envious.

He is satisfied.

*He says, 'When you're ready, Ogden. We'll continue
this interview at the police station.'*

It had been a copybook case ... truly, a copybook case
and a model to be held up as an example of how a murder
enquiry should be approached, conducted and brought to
a successful conclusion.

He'd lived off that case. For years, he'd quoted it—to
recruits, to visiting friends, to anybody who cared to
listen—knowing it was faultless in execution and
complete in its final presentation. He'd taken statements,
and every statement had dovetailed into all the other
statements. He'd supervised the taking of the photographs, attending the post mortem examination, interviewed the dead woman's husband and the murderer's
wife. Compiled the file—Regina versus Ogden—
personally and meticulously ... re-typing and re-typing
until every last spelling mistake had been corrected, and
the whole edifice was solid and indestructible.
'Guilty' ... with proof up to the hilt, and beyond.

And the chief constable's commendation had been
deserved.

So-o ...

What the dickens was getting under his skin? Why the
deuce was he working himself up like this? And why—for
God's sake, *why*!—after all these years, did Ogden worry
him?

It could be done again. He didn't want to see another
corpse, like the corpse of Ruth Watford—heaven's above,
he didn't want *that* ... but, if it had to be done again (if,
despite everything, it all *had* to be done again) he was up
to it. He was still as good as ever. Better. Ten years better.
If necessary, he could stick Ogden back, behind
bars ... and, this time, forever!

So, what the devil was he worrying about?

It was a conclusion. If he was kidding himself, he was unaware of it, therefore the conclusion quietened his mind. He took a couple of deep breaths, to clear his system of what few cobwebs of doubt remained, then glanced at his watch and concentrated upon more important matters.

He lifted the receiver of the desk telephone, and spoke to the constable on switchboard duty.

He said, 'I make it three o'clock.'

'Yes, sir,' agreed the constable.

'Are we having any tea, today?'

'It's being made, sir.'

'That's nice to know.'

'Yes, sir,' said the constable, heavily. He jerked the plug from the socket marked 'C/Insp. Off.', turned to a nearby policewoman, and said, 'Bardoph. He wants to know where his mid-afternoon cuppa's got to.'

'I know where I'd like to pour it,' remarked the policewoman, vulgarly.

'What a waste of good tea that would be.'

'What's it worth,' mused the policewoman, 'for me to substitute strychnine for sugar?'

'The Queen's Police Medal?' suggested the constable.

'You must be joking...you get *that* for stopping runaway horses.'

'Who the hell,' muttered Lennox, 'was Angela Finkle?'

She was described, at the top of the statement form, as 'An Unmarried Person'—this under the heading 'Occupation'. Her age was given as 'Over 21'—which was quite acceptable ... but which left bags of room for manoeuvre. Angela Finkle (as far as Lennox was concerned) was a very enigmatic character, but also a very important character because (as far as Lennox was concerned) Angela Finkle gave Ralph Watford a complete and foolproof alibi. And Ralph Wartford was the sort of beauty who took 'Angela Finkles' to the pictures, leaving his wife alone at home to be murdered ... which (as far as Lennox was concerned) made Ralph Watford a very dicey type.

Lennox wasn't all that keen on the Ralph Watfords of this world.

Come to that—if it was possible to reach any sort of a decent conclusion upon such meagre evidence—he wouldn't cross too many streets to shake hands with Angela Finkle.

The statement made by Angela Finkle...

... TO THE CINIEMA. IT WOULD BE ABOUT 6.30P.M. WHEN WE ENTERED THE CINEMA. THE SHOW HAD NOT YET COMMENCED. THE HOUSE LIGHTS WERE STILL LIT. WE SAT ON THE FRONT ROW OF THE CIRCLE. NEAR THE MIDDLE. RALPH WATFORD WAS SITTING ON MY RIGHT. I REMEMBER THAT HE POINTED OUT TO ME THAT PAMELA OGDEN WAS IN THE DOWNSTAIRS SEATS. SHE WAS IN THE STALLS. AS FAR AS I COULD MAKE OUT, SHE WAS ALONE. SHE WAS STILL THERE, AT THE END OF THE FILM, WHEN THE LIGHTS CAME UP AGAIN. SHE WAS STILL ALONE. RALPH WATFORD DID NOT LEAVE MY SIDE THROUGHOUT THE SHOW. THE SHOW ENDED AT ABOUT 9.30 P.M. I CAN SAY, WITH ABSOLUTE CERTAINTY, THAT RALPH WATFORD WAS IN MY COMPANY FOR EVERY SECOND THROUGHOUT THE SHOWING OF THE FILM. WE DID NOT GO HOME IMMEDIATELY AFTER THE FILM. WE WENT TO A RESTAURANT, AND ATE A LATE MEAL. THE NAME OF THE RESTAURANT WAS...

Lennox finished reading the statement.

It could be said that the office was thick with tobacco smoke. It could be said (and without undue exaggeration) that, had a passing motorist wished to make a diversion through that office, he would have needed fog-lights in order to make sure he didn't collide with the furniture. That was what the air (so-called) of the office was like.

Lennox didn't notice it.

He fished a cheroot packet from his pocket, opened it and found it to be empty.

He growled, 'Damn!'

He pushed himself up from the chair, waddled to the door, changed the key from inside to outside, left the office, closed and locked the door, slipped the key into his pocket and began to descend the stairs leading from the third floor to the street . . . and, from there, to the nearest tobacconist.

THE HUSBAND

WATFORD drove the Merc. It was a nice car; it was Angela's car (Watford, himself, ran an Austin 1100) and Angela made sure it was always well serviced ... but, of course! Nevertheless, it *was* a nice car. It handled like a dream and turned even the roughest of road surfaces into a ride along oiled silk.

Angela sat in the front passenger seat. She sat (as usual) in a prim and upright posture; lets together, skirt pulled demurely down to an inch or two below her knees. She kept her hands linked together, on her lap, and kept her eyes motionless on the road ahead.

'The Immaculate Virgin.' The phrase sprang to mind. It was what she was—correction ... what she probably *wished* she was! What she pretended to be, after her Indian Summer of almost ten years ago. She played the part well, too. Anybody seeing them—would take them for mother and son; a moderately well-preserved mother and a doting son who looked slightly older than his years.

Except, of course, that 'immaculate virgins' don't *have* sons ... not these days! So-o—maybe aunt and nephew. Which made the relationship even more cosy. Even more hilarious ... or, perhaps, even more spew-making.

It started to rain. Quite suddenly, and quite heavily.

Watford flicked the wiper switch and the rubber blades swept the water from the windscreen with boring, metronomic monotony. Like life ... unbelievably boring. Left-right-left-right, unendingly—until the rain stopped ... until the stupid bitch died.

She said, 'It still puzzles me.'

'What!' He jerked his tone to its mock-honey-sweetness ... honey, laced with quinine. He said, 'What puzzles you, darling?'

'Why she needs you ... why *you*?'

'She's ...' He sought an appropriate word. He settled for, 'She's worried.'

'Has she never been "worried" before? If not, she's a most fortunate young ...'

'Of course she's been worried before.'

'In that case, why you? Why this time?'

'It's just that ...' He lifted his hand from the wheel; raised his fingers a few inches in a vague gesture, then returned the hand to the wheel. 'Y'know ... Harry. He's out, today.'

'That,' she said, quietly, 'is why I'm puzzled.'

'We were friends,' he said, tightly. 'We were next-door neighbours ... remember?'

'You and Ogden? Or you and Ogden's wife?'

'All of us—all four of us ... we were neighbours. Friends.'

'Up to—and beyond—death,' she said, softly. She spoke, as if to herself; as if quietly repeating something from memory. 'Up to—and beyond—murder.'

'We liked each other.' Watford changed down to third. He tucked the Merc close behind the tailboard of a lorry, as the lorry made heavy weather of a slight, but twisting, hill. He said, 'Harry and me—we were friends ... we got on well.'

'Obviously.'

'Sweetheart, you're meaning something. You're meaning something you're not actually saying.'

'You forgave him for murdering your wife...you forgave him very easily. Very readily. I sometimes wonder. Whether it was necessary for you to forgive him...or, perhaps, whether you *approved*.'

'What the hell sort of a...'

The lorry dropped down a gear and almost stalled. The bonnet of the Merc almost kissed the lorry's tailboard.

Watford snarled, 'Damn the man!' braked, flipped the gear-lever and allowed the Merc to crawl up the snaking incline, behind the lorry.

'I often wonder,' she said, musingly.

'What?'

'Whether *you* could have killed her.'

'Just what the hell...' He bit the explosion short and, in an over-controlled voice, said, 'Just what is that supposed to mean, sweetheart?'

'Please don't call me "sweetheart". It makes me feel cheap.'

'Answer my question.'

Her shoulders gave the hint of a movement, and she said, 'I think you could...I really think you *could*.'

'God damn it, Angela. I was with you. At the time of the murder, I was with *you*.'

'Yes,' she agreed.

'So, how the blazes could *I* kill her?'

'I used to read detective stories,' she said, dreamily. 'Not the hard-bitten kind. Not Chandler—Hammett—Peter Cheyney...not that kind. The—er—the "puzzle" kind. John Dickson Carr. Erle Stanley Gardner. Margery Allingham. I remember, they were my favourite authors. I was quite the little expert. Sometimes—not often, but sometimes—I could even solve the mystery, before the dénouement.'

'For the life of me, I can't see what...'

'It wasn't easy,' she insisted. 'You had to have a certain type of mind. Simple, but at the same time devious. The whodunits—that's what they're called, these days...they aren't what they used to be. They aren't as numerous.

They aren't as ingenious...not the few I have time to read.'

Watford rasped, 'Angela, will you please tell me what the devil you're getting at. Will you please answer my question. How the hell could I have murdered Ruth?'

Her face softened into a quick smile, and she said 'I could make a wager. John Dickson Carr—Erle Stanley Gardner—Ellery Queen—Margery Allingham...any of them could have worked out a way. A score of ways.'

'To murder Ruth? While I was with you?'

'A score of ways,' she repeated musingly. 'They could make their murderers walk through walls...apparently. Being in two places at once—*apparently*...that would have been child's play.'

He breathed deeply, then said, 'I didn't kill her.'

'So you say.'

'I was with you when she was murdered.'

'Quite...apparently.'

'For God's sake! How, in hell's name...'

'You were capable of killing her.' Her voice became brittle, and cold; as thin and as dangerous as surface ice. She said, 'Don't lie to me, Ralph. You could have killed her...you were certainly capable of it. Just as you're capable of killing me. "Couldn't"—as far as you're concerned—merely means physically unable to...it doesn't mean mentally incapable of.'

The bends in the hill became a little less numerous. Watford spun the wheel, gunned the engine and overtook the lorry. It was unsafe driving; had another vehicle been coming in the opposite direction, there would have been a head-on collision...but there wasn't and the Merc passed the lorry. Watford slammed the lever up, through the gears, and the Merc roared up what was left of the hill.

"Don't take it out on the car,' she said, softly.

'Angela.' The words were chokingly angry. 'You seem to have one hell of an opinion of me.'

'Not a very good opinion,' she agreed.

'I've—I've tried to be a good husband.'

'Have you really?'

'It hasn't been easy. Sometimes, it hasn't been easy.'

'But always profitable...surely?'

'I know...' He stopped as the fury tightened his throat; as it blanched his face and tightened his fingers to a white-knuckled grip of the steering wheel. He whispered, 'I know, bloody well, what all your friends think. All your hoity-toity bloody friends. I've no doubt they sympathise with you, behind my back.'

'Not at all. They're too well mannered.'

'Sneering. Sniggering. Then...'

'At me, perhaps. Not you. I'm the laughing stock, Ralph...not you.'

'And now...And now...' The anger gagged him, again. He took a deep breath, then said, 'And now—to cap everything—you accuse *me* of murdering Ruth. I think you're mad. D'you know that?...I think you're a crazy old woman. Mad! Not to be taken seriously.'

'Seriously enough to marry,' she taunted.

'Dangerous.'

The quick smile flashed across her face, again, and she said, 'The female of the species, Ralph. Old—I'll grant you that—but still the female of the species...and, if you know your Kipling, you know what that means.'

He muttered, 'Sod Kipling!' and relapsed into angry silence.

His driving reflected his mood. It was immoderate and savage. He took corners too fast; his manner of overtaking slower cars was snarling and offensive. It was bad driving—speed, without full control—and with a less perfect car, it would have been dangerous driving.

She sat there. Motionless. Silent. Deliberately goading him with her silence and her imperturbability. In many ways, she had grown to know him better than he knew himself. She knew he was a poor fighter when his opponent could ride his punches; he could exchange insult for insult, but only so long as his insults were accepted. Let them not be accepted *as* insults—let them be taken without retaliation—and his anger changed its direction. He became a spoiled child. He stamped and screamed at his own inability to hurt. And, gradually, his anger burned itself out...upon himself.

It was a trick she'd learned.

Something—one of the many things—she had learned

about this man she had married.

Watford drove, and Watford fumed...and Watford worried. And, gradually, the worry grew into an avalanche and buried much of the anger.

The question still remained; the question Angela had asked, and the question which, so far, he had not answered. Partly because he daren't answer it...but mainly because he *couldn't* answer it.

Why the hell did Pam want him at Little Moysell? What reason was there?...what real, or logical, reason? There had been an understanding—unspoken, but complete—that, after the trial, they'd each go their separate ways. Harry was going inside. Ruth was out of the way...forever! The smash-up—the scandal—had been diverted...but the slap-and-tickle couldn't continue.

What had happened...

Christ, what had happened had been a bloody near thing. A damn sight too near for comfort. Near enough for its memory to bring him out in a muck sweat...even after all this time. As near as *that*.

That day—the day after he'd told Harry; the day after they'd both got blind bloody drunk—when he'd phoned Pam, and said—and said—and says...and says...

He says, 'There has to be a way, Pam. We can't let it happen...not three lives smashed, just because Ruth's been hurt.'

'What about Harry?' The tears are in her voice; despite the metallic distortion of the telephone wires, they are there and he hates for them, because it is time for action, not weeping. It means nothing to him, therefore, when she says, 'Harry's been hurt, too.'

'Harry'll get over it.'

'Everybody "gets over it". Everything.' There is bitterness in her words. 'Ruth will, too ...eventually.'

'You must know what I mean.'

'You mean,' she said, 'you aren't prepared to pay. You've had your fun—we've both had our fun...romping on the rug, together. Now, we've been

presented with the bill. But you don't want to pay.'

'It's not as simple as buying groceries, Pam,' he says, coldly.

'No... I wish to God it was.'

'She has to be stopped.' He pauses, and the pause is of an exact duration; the pause is a silence which is far more meaningful than a thousand words. A little slower, a little softer and very deliberately, he repeats, 'She has to be stopped... somehow.'

She catches her breath. He hears the tiny noise and his mouth twists into a quick, grim smile.

She says, 'Look... where are you?'

'At the office.'

'Are you... I mean, is there...'

'I'm alone.'

'Oh!'

'The switchboard girl's at lunch. Nobody can hear us.'

'Oh!'

'And you?' he asks.

'I'm—I'm alone,' she stammers.

'Good.' He gives a nod of satisfaction. 'Now—listen carefully—here's what I want you to do...'

'No!'

'Pam... listen to me.'

'No. I don't want to know. I don't want to...'

He snaps, 'Shut up!' and the naked anger in his voice quietens her as effectively as a slap across the face.

He says, 'What the hell is it you do want? A divorce case? That's what she's lining up... and I'll defend it.'

'How? How can you...'

'Not win it. But defend it. I'll make her prove every blasted allegation. The lot. Every time. Every detail.'

'What—what good will that do? For God's sake, what good...'

'The muck will stick, sweetheart,' he says, nastily. 'She'll throw a lot at me—and at you... but she'll mess herself up in the process. I'll see to that. She'll hit the headlines. I promise you that. She'll see her picture in all the Sundays... that, too. And all the tit-bits of dirty innuendo. If that's what she wants—and if that's what you want—I'm willing and ready to oblige.'

'And...' He hears the sound of choking—perhaps holding back a sob—then she says, 'And what about Harry?'

He says, 'I'm sorry for Harry, sweetheart. But, I'm not a gentleman. Somebody hurts me—some bitch of a wife decides to put the pressure on—and I hit back...hard. And screw everybody. Including Harry.'

There is a silence. It stretches itself into a full sweep of the second hand of the office wall-clock. He waits...because he knows what is coming next.

She speaks in a quavering voice.

She says, 'You said—y'know—that...that she has to be stopped.'

'I can stop her.'

After a pause, she says, 'How?'

'I need a little help.'

'Wh-what sort of help?'

He teases her, by saying, 'I don't think you'd be interested, sweetheart.'

'Ralph...please!'

'I—er—I don't think you're reliable, sweetheart. In your present state of mind. You might snarl everything up. Y'know...back down, at the last minute.'

'No! I'd do it, Ralph. Anything.'

He waits, with the receiver at his ear. This man is no mean psychologist; he knows the persuasive power of silence; he knows when to talk—and when not to talk...and that, if he waits for these few moments, the mind of this terrified, guilt-ridden woman will bend and she will do exactly as he asks.

She says, 'Ralph?' and there is a moaning quality in her voice.

'Uhu,' he grunts.

'I—I thought you'd gone.'

'No.'

'Ralph—what do you want me to do?...please.'

He hesitates another second, or two, then says, 'Go to the pictures...that's all.'

'What?' And now, there is disbelief. 'Ralph, I'm serious. I want to...'

'Go to the pictures, sweetheart,' he says, gently.

'Y'know...the pictures. Ring Harry. Tell him you're having an evening alone, at the cinema. The Ritz...the six-thirty performance. I'll be there. You won't see me. But I'll be there, sweetheart...and I'll see you. Sit downstairs. The middle of the stalls.'

There is anguish in the words, as she says, 'Ralph...don't joke with me. I'm—I'm serious.'

In a harsh voice, he says, 'This is no joke, sweetheart. If it goes wrong—if any tiny part of it goes wrong—neither of us will laugh for a long, long time...'

He talks. He explains the lie—the perfidy—and, with it a solution. A possible solution. A solution which terrifies her, but whose terror is fractionally less than the only other alternative.

And that evening Ruth is murdered...and Harry snarls everything to hell!

Angela broke the silence of the last few miles.

She said, 'The first decent-looking hotel—or restaurant...pull in.'

'What?' Ralph Watford blinked into the present that part of his mind which had been rooting around in the debris of the past.

'We need a meal,' said Angela. 'I missed lunch. I think you did, too...didn't you?'

'Yes. But...'

'And I have no intention of breaking bread with one of your ex-whores.'

It was a nice restaurant. 'The Wensleydale Heifer', at West Witton; not too far from Leyburn, in the white rose county. The proprietor was a Dane—but, at the same time a naturalised Yorkshireman—who knew how to run a friendly eating-house without making the customers feel they owed him a man-sized favour; who knew how to take good food and made it taste as good as it looked; who knew the difference between grilling and scorching. He was a good host, who kept a good table and a cellar-book of solid, respectable wines.

They sipped what remained of the 1961 Chateauneufdu-Pape, smoked cigarettes and waited for coffee. The dining room was empty, except for staff clearing the place from lunch, prior to preparing it for the first diners, at six-thirty; they'd been lucky... strictly speaking, they'd been too late for lunch but, like all good hostelries, the rules had been bent to accommodate hungry travellers.

Their cigarette smoke swam, in curling patterns, towards the beamed ceiling. The comfort of good food in their stomachs and the warmth from the open fire did much to aid a feeling of well-being. It seemed impossible to continue a hurtful argument in these surroundings; to spit venom at each other while, at the same time, feel such contentment.

Watford leaned a little way across the table, and said, 'All right. I had an affair—of a sort...with Pamela Ogden. But that was before I met you.'

'Before you married me,' she corrected him, mildly.

There was no rebuke in her correction. It was merely a quietly spoken statement of fact; the correction of detail which was no longer of great importance.

It was as if she was uninterested in the subject; as if she found it rather boring—that, or had thought and worried about it so much, for so long, that it had gradually numbed or killed some secret part of her...but, nevertheless, insisted upon factual correctness if, and when, the subject was brought up in conversation.

The furrow of a tiny frown made a perpendicular crease between his brows. He watched her face with casual uncertainty. He was puzzled—a little bewildered— by her tone. By her attitude.

He 'understood' women. All women. Every woman. It was something of which he was proud; of which he sometimes boasted. It was his own peculiar art—one might almost say it was his *profession*...that he 'understood' women.

And now, quite suddenly, he was perplexed. He couldn't 'understand' his own wife...the one woman in the world he claimed to know perfectly.

He gave a half-smile, and murmured, 'After I married you, Angela...after that, no more affairs.'

She drew on her cigarette, and said, 'At least not with Pamela Ogden.'

And, again, it was not a rebuke. It was merely a correction.

The waitress came with the coffee.

She asked, 'Black or white, madam?'

'White,' said Angela.

The waitress poured the coffee and the cream, then asked, 'Black or white, sir?'

'Black.'

The waitress poured the coffee, then left the table. Watford and his wife spooned sugar into their coffees, and Watford said, 'I'm sorry, dear. I don't know what you mean.'

Angela looked politely mystified... as if *she* didn't know what Watford meant.

'About Pamela Ogden.' Watford stirred the sugar into the coffee. 'The—er—the slight affair we had.'

'Ah, yes... before you married me. That's what I said.'

'It's over and done with, sweetheart. A thing of the past... believe me.'

'I do believe you, Ralph.' She placed her spoon alongside the cup, in the saucer, and sipped at the coffee. She drew on her cigarette, then said, 'I believe you... because I've made it my business to find out.'

'You've...' The smoke caught at his throat and made him cough. He turned his head, brought his napkin to his mouth, controlled the coughing, 'You've *what*?'

'Made it my business to find out,' she repeated, calmly.

'You're talking in riddles.' He cleared the last of the roughness from his throat, then added, 'I'm sorry Angela, darling. As I say... you're talking in riddles.'

Her slow smile called him a liar. It also called him a fool... but a fool to be humoured.

She said, 'Don't get excited, Ralph.'

'Excited? Why should I get...'

'And don't cause a scene.'

'Look—why the hell should I...'

'You might.' The smile touched her lips, again, but hadn't the strength to climb as high as her eyes. 'Knowing

you ... you *might*. If you do—if you even look as if you're
going to—I shall walk out of here. I have the car keys. I
doubt—I very much doubt—if you have enough money
to pay the bill. Therefore, if you *do* lose your temper—if
you *do* threaten to make a scene—the embarrassment will
be yours ... all yours.'

'I have no intention,' he said tightly, 'of losing my
temper. I have no intention of making a scene. But, as
your husband, I demand to know what the devil you're
talking about. What the hell all this is leading up to.'

The last few words thinned off into little more than a
breath as their eyes met—level and facing each other
across the table—and he had a moment's terrifying
impression that he could see beyond her eyes and into her
brain ... and what he saw scared the hell out of him!

She had learned compassion ... but compassion which
stopped short at stupidity.

In a lifetime devoted to voluntary social work she had
learned to forgive the seemingly unforgivable; to excuse
the apparently inexcusable. She had listened to lies, when
lies had been pointless and unnecessary. She had seen
filth, where soap and water were both available. She had
witnessed idleness, where work was there to be had. She
knew all these situations, plus envy, greed and sometimes
out-and-out rottenness.

Occasionally—very occasionally—some creepy type
pulled an act which she fell for; told a lie which she
believed; worked a con which she had bought. Occasionally. But, by this time, she'd been at the receiving end of
most things, and each time had been a lesson.

She now knew the difference between being charitable
and being a mug. Over the years she had developed a
built-in filter-system which (merely by listening to the
chosen phrases, the glib moanings and the nuances of the
talk) weeded out the fanny and allowed only the genuine
article free transit to her sympathy.

Thus she had learned compassion—infinite
compassion ... but with it (and as a corollary to the
compassion) she had also learned to hate.

And the hatred, too, was peculiar to herself.

It was not anchored to anger. Rather was it a logical hatred; the residue—the dross—which remained when all compassion had been extracted. It was a soft hatred. A gentle hatred. A slow-working hatred. It has a certain 'genteel' quality... but it was pure, unadulterated and indestructible.

It was the one hatred (the only hatred) which is the true antithesis of love; a hatred without honour, without respect and without emotion.

It was this which Ralph Watford saw in the eyes of his wife—something he had never seen before and something which, by his very nature, he couldn't hope to comprehend... it followed, therefore, that it scared the hell out of him.

She spoke gently. Almost sedately. Except for the words, it might have been any quiet conversation between friends, across a table, in an almost deserted restaurant.

She smoked her cigarette and sipped her coffee as she talked. She watched his face. She noted the draining away of the blood and the increasing pallor. She knew she was getting through to him.

She was satisfied.

She said, 'I believe in honesty. And, by that, I mean old-fashioned honesty. The honesty that can hurt but, at the same time, cauterise. Calvinistic honesty, if you like... not your sort of honesty, which is simply the honesty of self-deception. You're good at it, Ralph. Your sort of honesty. The truth that isn't the whole truth. Your yardstick—that, if it isn't a lie it's the truth—is a very convenient yardstick. It makes the non-lie the truth—but the non-lie is only a half-truth... and real honesty demands far more than that.

'You say—you've just said—that Pamela Ogden was your mistress. Before you met me... that's what you said. By implication, the affair stopped *when* you met me... but it didn't. It continued until we were married... that being the half-truth you missed out. It stopped when we were married—just before we were married—but even that wasn't your doing. She left the district shortly after her husband was convicted for murdering your first wife. After that, the affair *couldn't* continue...because, for a long time, you didn't even know where she was.

'But that isn't the way you tell it...is it? You pick your half-truths very carefully, tell them well, and call it "honesty"...which, by my yardstick, it isn't.

'What you are, Ralph, is a liar. A clever liar...but no less a liar for being clever.

'You're also a womaniser...still. But we'll leave that, for the moment.

'Let's first consider this trip we're making. This visit to Little Moysell...because Pamela Ogden telephoned you. It raises—in my mind—an immediate question. *Why* did she telephone you? Why when, presumably, she has relations—in-laws, friends—did she specifically telephone *you*? Why ask *you* to be there when her husband arrived home?

'Because she's frightened? Of what? Of her own husband? But he wasn't an ogre...was he? In fact—as I remember the case—she gave evidence that he was a very *good* husband. Not the sort of man of whom a woman—especially a woman like Pamela Ogden—might be terrified. She's not afraid of him, Ralph. Whatever the real reason, that isn't it...she didn't telephone you to be with her because she's frightened.

'Indeed, if anything, *he* should be afraid of *you*. It's your wife he killed...remember? And the plea of Diminished Responsibility...to most men—to most husbands—that would have added insult to injury. Ten years—only ten years—for murdering the woman you love...and murdering her in a particularly foul and disgusting manner. Most husbands would want greater punishment...revenge, if you like. Most murderers would be afraid of ever again meeting the husband of the woman they butchered.

'But—apparently—that doesn't apply in this case...and it makes me wonder.

'Therefore, why did she telephone *you*?

'And why did you agree to go?

'The reason—whatever the reason—has to do with Ogden. It has to do with Ogden's release from prison...it *has* to! Which, in turn, means that you're involved, Ralph. Involved with Ogden, I mean. Involved with the man who murdered your first wife . . . now, I wonder how? I wonder how you're involved? Why you're not afraid? . . . why Ogden's not afraid? Why you're not angry? Why—on the strength of a telephone call from *his* wife—you come all this way to meet the man who murdered *your* first wife? What sort of a trio are you? What sort of people are you . . . you three, who have this common bond of a murdered woman?'

She left a gap in her talk, and Watford tried to fill the gap with mock-indignance.

He said, 'You're making bricks without straw, Angela. You're building mountains out of nothing. Your imagination . . .'

'I have no imagination,' she interrupted, quietly. 'Had I imagination—had I ever had any imagination—I wouldn't have become your wife. But I have curiosity, Ralph. And curiosity makes me ask questions . . . questions which lack of imagination forces me to accept as just that. Questions. But no answers. It's why I'm here. I *want* those answers.'

'Not because of Pamela?' He sneered. He tried scorn—one of the weapons with which he was adept—in an attempt to break a way through her barrier of calm. He curled his lip, and said. 'I thought it was Pamela . . . the crumpet I used to romp around with. I thought it was her you wanted to see.'

'Careful, Ralph,' she warned, gently. 'The promise still holds good. I have the car keys. I have the money. Any tantrums, and I'll do what I threatened.'

'You want to see Pamela,' he gloated. 'You want to see the . . .'

'I know all about "Pamela",' she said. Her voice was suddenly loaded with weariness; as firm as ever—as controlled as ever—but tired. She squashed her cigarette into the ash-tray, sighed, then said, 'Pamela . . . and all the others.' She raised her hand a few inches, and went on, 'No . . . don't interrupt, Ralph. I've wanted to say this for a long time. I've wanted to tell you. If only to be fair. Being fair—that may sound strange to you . . . but that's what it amounts to. I wish to be open and above-board, with you—with my husband—therefore you should know. Until now, the opportunity hasn't presented itself. It has now ... so, please listen.'

She paused, to marshal her thoughts; mentally to arrange the words she was about to speak.

And he waited ... because he sensed that something staggering was about to be said.

'I know about your women,' she began. 'Perhaps not all of them ... but enough. Pamela Ogden ... we start with her. By my total, and since we were married, there have been nine others. I'll name them, if you wish ... to remind you. Some of them were married. Some of them were single. All of them were younger—considerably younger—than I am ... which, I suppose, is only to be expected. Nine—ten, with Pamela Ogden ... not counting, I admit, any sudden opportunity you might have seized, and of which I know nothing. I'll settle for ten ... although I've no doubt the number will be added to, as the years go by.'

He rasped, 'You've got no proof. You're ...'

'Ah, but I have.' She smiled. 'You'd be surprised how professional—how—efficient—some of the better provincial private detective agencies are.'

'You bitch! You've had me ...'

'Followed? Watched? Ye-es. I've had you followed, and I've had you watched ... and that's why I can, if necessary, prove what I'm accusing you of. It's also why I think it only fair that you know the price—the ultimate price—of your womanising.'

'Divorce?' Once more he tried scorn and, this time, he was sure it would work. He said, 'Are you seriously threatening to ...'

'Nothing,' she interrupted quietly. 'Certainly not divorce. I'll not be laughed at, more than I am. You have me, Ralph ... until I die. But there are other ways.'

'What ...' He swallowed, then said, 'What "other ways".'

The smile came again. Slow, but soon gone. And not as far as the eyes.

She said, 'Solicitors, Ralph. They live well ... mainly

from elderly women, like me. We all have "our solicitor", and I'm no exception. *My* solicitor has certain instructions. Very specific instructions. For example, when I die—and unless it is from very obviously "natural causes"—he must insist upon a post mortem examination... bearing in mind that your first wife was murdered, that you mourned very little and that, upon my death, you expect to be a very rich man. Bearing all that in mind, he has very specific instructions... to be very suspicious, when he learns of my death.'

'Good God!' breathed Watford.

'He also has other instructions... concerning my will. At the moment, everything I own is to be turned into cash and, after death duties and any other debts, the remainder is to be divided into eleven equal parts. One part for you. One part each, to the ten women who have provided my husband with—er—"favours" his wife couldn't offer. They will be required to attend the reading of the will... as will their husbands, if they are married. The amount—and it is still a considerable amount—will be paid over to them, and the reason for the legacy will be made public.

'My one regret,' she continued, dreamily, 'is that I can't be there when the will is read. That I won't be able to see their faces. Hear their excuses. Watch what some of their husbands might do to you. It is a wicked will—or, so my solicitor keeps telling me—but it is perfectly legal. If it *is* a wicked will, I have no regrets... it is the only way I know of repaying you for *your* wickedness.

'Finally—and then we must go—I think I should tell you that any other mistress will also be included in the will. Your share will drop from an eleventh to a twelfth... and you'll probably have one more husband to pacify. Therefore...' she shrugged. 'Live your life, Ralph. Have your women. But, at least, know that they'll be paid... and by you.'

She stood up from the table, buttoned her coat, and said, 'Right, dear... when you're ready. We mustn't keep Mrs. Ogden waiting.'

THE WOMAN

'MRS. OGDEN'—Pamela Gertrude Ogden—came from the bedroom of 'The Swan's Nest' and flopped into an armchair. She was (to use Thelma's mildly vulgar expression) shagged. She couldn't remember when she'd done so much housework in a single day. She was damn sure the cottage hadn't been as clean as it was now—hadn't looked as cosy—for years... not since she'd come to live in it.

Her nostrils twitched slightly as she caught the aroma which drifted in from the kitchen. Again, it was something new; good food and good cooking... better food and better cooking than *she* could have organised.

Thelma... always bloody Thelma!

The crafty cow must have loaded that damn car of hers up to the gunnels. Junk to clean with, junk to cook with, and food. She must have set off before dawn; she must have spent the last week buying-in and all yesterday loading-up. Organised—y'know... *organised*. Like a military operation. Planned in advance—well-planned...weeks, maybe months, in advance. Even the arrival; parking the car well away from the cottage—smooth-tonguing her way into the place—putting on the all-girls-together act...Christ up a flagpole!

Thelma poked her head around the jamb, and said, 'Finished?'

'Finished,' said Pamela, flatly. 'If this isn't good enough, he can take the next bus back.'

'What?'

'He isn't visiting royalty.'

'Oh!' Thelma tightened her lips, momentarily, then said, 'I'll be with you. Let me check that nothing's burning.'

Pamela said, 'What have you got in there? The fatted calf?'

If Thelma heard, she didn't answer.

There was the sound of pan-lids being lifted and replaced. The faint squeak of the oven-door being opened, followed by the slam of it being closed. The rattle of crockery at the sink. The sound of the tap being run.

Thelma walked into the living room. She was drying her hands on a tea-towel which she'd tied across her front with string, as a makeshift apron.

She stood with her back to the fire, looked down at the other woman, and said, 'Right...for starters, you can cut out the self-pity.'

'Look! What the hell...'

'And you can also stop being bitchy.'

Pamela glared up from the armchair.

'There are,' said Thelma, 'certain basic requirements needed to chase any man hot-foot out of any woman's life. Being a shrew is one of 'em. Self-pity is another. Put the two together, and you won't see his heels for dust.'

'I haven't seen his heels—or any other part of him—for ten years, except in the visiting room of a prison,' said Pamela, bitterly.

'Whereas,' retorted Thelma sarcastically, 'he's been getting an eyeful of *you*, any time he fancied.'

'Don't be a fool.'

'If there's a fool present, it isn't me, girlie.'

'Just what the hell are you up to, Thelma?' asked
Pamela, suspiciously. 'Y'know...just *what*? All this
sob-sister crap. Arriving here, out of the blue. Working
your guts out—making me work my guts out...what the
hell for? What's behind it all?'

'Would you believe, my brother?'

'That's no answer.'

'All right. To give him—and you—a fair-to-moderate
chance of taping up a bad marriage.'

Anger touched the edges of the words, as Pamela said,
'Who says it was a bad marriage?'

Thelma snapped, 'Ask me who says it was a good
one...the list isn't as long.'

'You've got one hell of a nerve...'

'I have one hell of a sister-in-law. But I'm prepared to
be friendly with her...if it'll help.'

Pamela made as if to push herself up from the chair.

'Don't!' warned Thelma. 'I'm here, and I'm staying.
Harry can boot me out, if that's what he wants. You can't.
Believe me, sweetie. I'll slap you down, if necessary. And
don't think that's impossible...I have ten years' edge of
good eating on you. And—come to think of it—it might
not be a bad idea. It's what you've needed for a long, long
time.'

'You hate me, don't you?' Pamela relaxed back into the
chair. She stared her dislike at the other woman, and said,
'You detest me. The woman who took your precious
brother away from you...'

'For an empty promise.'

'...Who gave him something you couldn't give...'

'I'll say! Ten years, behind bars.'

'...Who shared his bed...'

'And couldn't even do *that* too well.'

Pamela stiffened. She watched Thelma with blazing
eyes, then breathed. 'You she-dog! You absolute cow!
You—of all people...'

'Oh, for Christ's sake, shut up.' Thelma waved a hand
in angry impatience. She said, 'You hate me—*if* you hate
me—because I know you too well. I certainly don't hate
you. I'm sorry for you—sorry for Harry...but that's all.'

'It's enough. It's worse.'

'Ye-es. I suppose it is.' Thelma killed her rising anger. She straddled her legs, rested an open palm on each cheek of her rump and warmed her backside in the glow from the fire. She spoke slowly—musingly—as if examining a situation which, until this time, had escaped her notice.

She said, 'Y'know? The crazy part of it? I don't know *why* I'm sorry. No!...that's not quite right. That's not exactly what I mean. Okay, I'm sorry for you—I'm sorry for Harry...but I'm damned if I can find a real reason for the feeling. I'm damned if I can put my finger on one thing—on anything—and say that *that's* why I'm sorry. That *that's* why I sympathise with you...either you, or Harry.'

Pamela muttered, 'Blast you. We don't need your sympathy.'

'No...of course you don't.'

'Keep it.'

'I can't. I can only hide it...and I've done that for too long.'

'We can get along without it.'

'I wonder?' All the anger had left Thelma's voice. All that remained was worry and indecision. She said, 'Pam—for Harry's sake...for my sake. Just for today. Bear with me. Suffer me, if you like. But don't be alone...not today.'

'We—we don't need your sympathy. We don't need your charity. Anybody's!' The last spark of anger was extinguished by the sudden flood of misery and, in a pathetic, little-girl-lost tone, Pamela ended, 'We—we only need each other. That's all. I need him. I hope to God—after all these years—I hope to God he still needs me.'

And then she wept—she wept...she wept...she weeps...

She weeps, as if she will never stop weeping; as if all the misery in the world has turned to tears, and hers are the only eyes through which those tears may escape. She weeps with unbowed head—stiff, and almost at atten-

tion—and the tears run down her cheeks and drip, to stain
the unfastened, unbelted mac with tiny splashes of grief.
She stands, with her arms hanging by her sides, stares at
the policewoman, listens... and weeps.

The policewoman knows of no easy manner in which
to break the news. There is no easy manner. There is only
one way, and that is a hurtful way. To tell it, without
hesitation and without hedging. To deliver it, like a single
kayo blow... and then to wait, patiently, for the recovery.
Any other way merely prolongs the hurt—draws out the
agony... and, in the long run, does no good at all.

The policewoman says, 'Sit down, Mrs. Ogden. I'll stay
with you... if it'll help.'

She nods, and more tears splash the light fawn of the
mac.

She shrugs her arms clear of the mac, holds the mac for
a moment and looks around—dazed—as if wondering
where to place her own coat here, in her own home.

The policewoman takes the coat—gently—and says,
'Shall I hang it up?'

'Over...' She waves a hand, vaguely. 'Over a chair.
I'll—I'll put it in the wardrobe, when I...' She stops
speaking, looks panic-stricken, then whispers, 'When I go
to bed.'

She sits in the chair, and continues to weep. She cannot
stop the tears. She will weep forever. And rightly so. To
have driven a man to this—a good husband—a man as
decent and as loving as Harry... to have driven him to
this!

She deserves to drown—like Alice in Wonder-
land... she deserves to drown in a pool of her own tears.

The policewoman makes tea. Odd—this always
happens—the police service have a great belief in the
recuperative quality of tea... at times of high tension and
at times of great sorrow, they pour boiling water onto tea
leaves. It is the balm to ease all hurts. They make strong,
hot, sweet tea... and think it helps.

And (who knows?) perhaps it does.

The policewoman has found the few bottles of booze
which they keep in the house. She has laced the tea with
brandy. A lot of brandy.

She sips the tea...but continues to weep at the memory of what she has forced her man to do.

She stammers, 'Where is he?'

'At the police station. He'll not—er...' The policewoman looks uncomfortable, tries to smile, fails, then says, 'He's with Detective Inspector Sawyer. Nobody'll hurt him...anything like that. They—er—they just want to question him.'

'He'll not be coming back?'

'No...sorry.'

What a damn fool question! A man murders his next-door neighbour—he stabs her, then shoots her—then calls the police, and makes a full confession...then (Christ Almighty!) his wife is crazy enough to ask whether he'll be 'coming back'.

What a damn fool question!

The policewoman says, 'When they've finished—when Inspector Sawyer's finished questioning him—I'll ask whether you can see him for a few minutes. They might.'

'No!' She suddenly looks as scared as a frightened fawn. 'No...please. I couldn't. I wouldn't know what to...'

'All right. All right.' The policewoman soothes her. 'Not if you don't want to. Not till you feel better.'

'No! Never. I don't want to...'

'All right. If you don't want to see him, nobody can make you.'

And, even at the trial, she cannot bring herself to look at him. She stands in the witness box. She says everything she is required to say. She pleads for him—and every word of her plea is genuine—but she does not turn her head and she does not look at the dock. And, having given her evidence, she walks from the court without once turning her eyes towards him.

Four times. Four prison visits, in ten years. She waits two years...then she sees him for the first time since the murder; they have nothing to talk about, because what they both want to say is (to both of them) a forbidden subject. The second visit (almost a year after the first) is a verification; a verification of the uselessness of that first visit; a repeated mouthing of nothings which goes on for too long. The third visit (with a solicitor) concerns his partnership in the firm; it is a business visit and George, and Thelma, and the solicitor act as a buffer and a shield through which their true feelings cannot pass; she says little—Thelma says far more than she does—and George and the solicitor do most of the talking. The fourth visit (four years ago) is, again, with a solicitor; she needs money and she wishes to sell their house—much of their whole home—and she needs his formal permission; he gives it, without argument—without question—and the visit does not even last as long as the time allowed. And, since then . . . nothing.

Ten years. Four visits. Less than a dozen letters. Not one word of affection. Not one hint of forgiveness. It's sum is a decade of unrelieved suffering. Unrelieved loneliness, without love and without repentance.

'He won't come,' sobbed Pamela. 'Who the hell are we kidding? He won't come. Wherever else . . . he won't come here.'

'He'll come,' soothed Thelma. She was bent, with her arm around the other woman's shoulders. Comforting her. All anger, all impatience gone. In years, she was of Pamela's age but, in wisdom and experience, she was a much older woman. She held the trembling, terrified Pamela much as a mother holds a teenage daughter; spoke softly to her, and was reassuring. She said, 'He knows where you live, and this is where he'll come. Where else? This is his home . . . where else?'

'I—I—I . . .'

'You've had a good cry. It's done you good . . .'

'I—I . . .'

'. . . Now, blow your nose. Spruce yourself up, and get ready for him.'

Pamela was trying to say something.

'He'll come. As sure as night follows day . . . he'll come.'

'R-R-Ralph Watford,' sniffled Pamela.

'Forget him. That's over and done with.'

'B-before you came. Before I knew you were here...'
Pamela wrapped her arms round Thelma's waist, rested a
cheek against Thelma's stomach, and muttered, 'I was
scared. Terrified of what Harry might do... if he came.
I—I didn't know which way to turn. It was where I was
when you arrived—y'know...telephoning. Ralph...
Ralph Watford. I—I—I...'

'You telephoned Watford?'

'Y-yes.' Thelma felt the movement of Pamela's head,
against her stomach muscles, as Pamela nodded.

'What the... *Why?* Why on earth phone *him*?'

'I was...oh, my God, I was so lonely. So lonely! And
so frightened. I—I didn't know what...'

'You goose. You silly, silly goose. Of all the men in the
world. Of all the *people* in the world. To telephone the one
man...'

'I—I asked him to come,' whispered Pamela. 'I asked
him to be here, when Harry arrived.'

'Here?'

'Y-yes.'

'To be *here*...when Harry arrives?'

Pamela nodded. She waited for the outburst; for the
new anger which she was sure must erupt from the other
woman.

Instead, Thelma took a deep breath, stroked Pamela's
hair and spoke quietly...but with utter conviction.

She said, 'Let him come, Pam. Forget him...let him
have a wasted journey. Come to think of it, I've often
wished I could meet him. Since the trial. I've often wanted
to come face to face with that particular animal...preferably up a dark alley.' She paused, then
ended, grimly, 'Don't worry, my pet. Leave Mr Ralph
Watford to me. By the time he gets back to that
whey-faced bitch he married, she'll think he's been
castrated...and she won't be far wrong!'

THE COP

'WHO's at Little Moysell?' asked Sawyer.

He was going off duty for the day. It was closing towards 5.30 p.m. and, twice each week, he allowed himself the luxury of an early-evening finish. It was one of the 'perks' of being a sub-divisional officer. Two days off duty. Three days when (if needed—and sometimes when not only not needed, but not particularly wanted) he wore his uniform until midnight and beyond. And (to counter the self-imposed overtime) two days when he knocked off at a civilised o'clock.

This was one of those days. He'd promised his wife...and she'd go into a prolonged huff if he disappointed her.

He positioned his peaked cap, eyed himself through the mirror in the main office, and asked the question.

Inspector Fenton answered the question.

He said, 'D.O. Ruecroft...from Bagdon Section.'

'Good.' Sawyer straightened his tie.

Fenton hesitated, then said, 'It's meant—er—shelving any real enquiries into the stolen V.W.'

'It'll turn up,' said Sawyer confidently.

'Yes, sir. I hope so.' Fenton didn't seem to share Sawyer's confidence.

Sawyer turned from the mirror, and said, 'I'll be at home all evening, inspector. Anything from Little Moysell—anything at all—I want to know, immediately.'

'Yes, sir,' said Fenton, heavily.

'I hold you personally responsible.'

'That's understood, sir.'

Sawyer nodded his satisfaction, walked from the main office and left Ellerfield Sub-Divisional Police Station. He drove his Citroën Diane from the police station to his home. He was boringly punctilious in his obedience to all and every fiddling detail of The Road Traffic Law; speed limits, Halt signs, Slow signs, Panda crossings, traffic roundabouts—the lot!—he diligently took due notice of them all.

The average motorist would, perhaps, have described Sawyer's driving as 'uninspired'. Even the above-average motorist might have used the same adjective.

The driving typified the man...it typified his whole life.

Ten years previously, he had been an 'uninspired' detective inspector.

Lennox, on the other hand, was a great believer in 'inspiration'. He didn't call it 'inspiration'...he called it 'gut-feeling'. It was something enjoyed and experienced by practitioners of certain professions. Doctors, for example. Barristers. Aeroplane pilots and racing drivers. And, of course, bobbies. Not every member of these professions...but (and always) the 'greats'. It was that mysterious something which made them a country mile better than their contemporaries; it started where logic left off and bridged the chasm between talent and genius. It was (for want of a better description) a sixth sense...but a sixth sense which, when it was on wide throttle, booted the other five senses out of the window. It took those two old and wrinkled chestnuts, 'Truth' and

'Honesty', blew them a loud raspberry, popped their respective rivets and exposed them for what they are...comparatives guyed up as absolutes.

And Lennox had a very strong, and very uncomfortable 'gut-feeling' about the Regina versus Ogden file.

He reached a hand to the telephone on his desk, then spoke to the policewoman on duty at Headquarters switchboard.

He said, 'Now then, pet—can you help me? There's a glorified coal cellar in the basement of this place—not far from the Firing Range—it's called the Archives Section. Know it?...Good. Now—is it on the blower?...Champion. Now—there's an old chap called Peel looks after it. Give him a quick buzz. Then put me through.'

He replaced the receiver, picked up one of the documents from the file and, while he was waiting, re-read it for the fourth time.

The statement made by Pamela Ogden...

...SAW THE POLICE AS I APPROACHED MY HOME ADDRESS. SHORTLY AFTER I ARRIVED HOME A POLICEWOMAN CALLED AT MY HOME, AND TOLD ME WHAT HAD OCCURRED. THIS WAS THE FIRST TIME I LEARNED THAT MY HUSBAND, HARRY OGDEN, WAS HAVING AN AFFAIR WITH RUTH WATFORD. ALL THAT EVENING I HAD BEEN AT THE CINEMA. THE CINEMA WAS THE RITZ CINEMA. THE FILM WAS ENTITLED SHANE. I ARRIVED AT THE CINEMA AT A FEW MINUTES AFTER HALF PAST SIX. I THINK IT MUST HAVE BEEN AT ABOUT THAT TIME. I KNOW THE SHOW STARTED VERY SHORTLY AFTER I SAT IN MY SEAT. I WAS IN THE STALLS. I DID NOT LEAVE MY SEAT THROUGHOUT THE PERFORMANCE. WHEN THE FILM WAS OVER, I LEFT THE CINEMA AND WALKED TO MY...

The telephone bell rang. Lennox picked up the receiver and talked to Constable Peel of the Archives Section.

He said, 'Peel?...This is Superintendent Lennox, here. Now look, old son I need your help. I want the notebooks relating to the Watford killing. The Regina

versus Ogden case . . . All of 'em. I'll give you the list—all
the officers mentioned in the reports and statements—
and the various dates. Get the notebooks together, and I'll
send a cadet down to collect 'em. Okay? . . . Yes, lad.
Now—before you go home to sit in front of a nice warm
telly—have 'em ready for collection within the next thirty
minutes . . . Right—here are the names . . .'

Lennox read names, ranks and (where necessary)
numbers from a list scribbled on a foolscap-sized pad.

Having issued his instructions, Lennox relaxed back in
the desk-chair, held the statement in his left hand and
rubbed the palm of his right hand back, over the bald pate
of his skull until it rested on the nape of his neck.

He muttered, 'Hell's teeth . . . I hope I'm wrong. 'Cos, if
I'm not . . .'

And, at a poky little village called Little Moysell, a certain
Detective Constable Ruecroft (who, strictly speaking,
should have been miles away at Bagdon Section, making
diligent enquiries into the recent theft of a V.W. motor
car) settled back in the front seat of a police-provided
mini-van, fiddled with the tuning knob of a transistor
radio until the endless stream of pop music was coming
through to his satisfaction, then turned down the volume
in order that he might also hear any relevant messages
transmitted via the police wavelength and the speaker
anchored to the roof of the van, just above the
windscreen.

He silently congratulated himself.

It was a soft number; sitting here, listening to the top
whatever-number they plugged these days, when he
should have been asking questions nobody could answer
about a nicked Volkswagen some bloody fool had left
unlocked.

Okay—Sawyer was a prize prick . . . but (just occasionally) his monumental prickery paid unexpected divi-
dends.

And (just to make everything comfy and cosy) it
started to rain.

THE HUSBAND

'THE—ER—"The Swan's Nest",' said Watford.

Angela Watford said, 'A nice name.'

'Think so?' said Watford, sourly.

'Unusual.'

'Yes...I suppose.'

'Where is it?' asked Angela.

'Up a back lane, somewhere.' Watford turned his head and stared out, beyond the windows of the parked Merc. It was a wet world; with wet, and not yet greened, hedgerows; with wet, and not yet leaved, trees; with a wet, and badly surfaced, village street. It was a wet and miserable world, and it matched his mood perfectly. He growled, 'These bloody places. They're all the same. Why the hell anybody wants to bury themselves in a dump like this I'll never know.'

'I, too, am curious,' observed Angela, mildly.

'What?' Watford scowled his incomprehension.

'Why should she?' mused Angela.

'Pamela?'

'That is the only "she" we have in mind, at the moment. Why should she choose to live in a place like this?'

'Out of the way, I suppose. Some people have crazy ideas about...'

'It's one question I might ask her.'

'What?' Watford looked startled.

'Why? Her reason for living here, at Little Moysell. Her *real* reason.'

'Angela.' Watford sounded worried...deep-down worried. He said, 'Take things easy. Please. Ogden—if he's here—when he arrives—Christ only knows what he'll be like. I dunno...he could be a little mad.'

'Insane? Or angry?'

'I dunno...maybe both.'

Angela said, 'Lock anything—anyone—inside a cage for ten years, and they'll come out different. Mad, perhaps...in both senses of the word. He interests me.'

'Frightens you?'

'No—he doesn't frighten me...he interests me.'

'As a social worker, of course,' said Watford, sarcastically.

'No...because I'm your wife.' She allowed a quick, twisted smile the use of her mouth for a moment, then added, 'He interests me because he is the husband of the woman you might have—even *should* have—married.'

'You've already said...he won't be the same man.'

'But an unusual man. I'm sure he'll be *that*.'

Watford grunted. He worked the ignition, then revved the engine of the Merc unnecessarily.

He growled, 'For Christ's sake. Come on—let's get it over with...let's find that bloody cottage.'

THE MAN

How can peace come with pain? How can tranquillity ride in the discomfort of a clapped-out, badly-sprung mini-van? How can a forgotten contentment be rediscovered in the cramped gloom of a not-too-clean vehicle, without windows?

Ogden didn't know.

He only knew it was possible ... and the knowledge was sufficient.

There was (he supposed) certain psychological clichés which the smooth-tongued mind-doctors might have trotted out. An equation with cells. An equation with wombs. Probably even an equation with the grave.

Bullshit!

Happiness had nothing to do with cells—it had nothing to do with wombs—and it had sweet damn-all to do with graves. Happiness? We-ell ... if happiness had to do with anything, it had to do with *people*.

People made you happy...like, sometimes, people made you miserable.

Therefore (logically) his present happiness was despite (not because of) pain and discomfort and a bumpy mini van; his present happiness had a lot to do with people.

With one person in particular.

With Tom Harding.

Holy cow!...and that was something else he'd forgotten. That men like Tom Harding still walked the earth; that, when the chips had all been played, one Tom Harding more than equalled all the pestilence hidden behind prison walls.

Not forgetting a certain medic. A medic whose wisdom had embraced the knowledge that medicine has to do with things far removed from (and, at times, more important than) pills, potions and antibiotics.

From the front of the van, the driver said, 'Little Moysell.'

Also from the front of the van, Harding replied, 'That's the place. I'll tell you where to turn.'

'It's a bit out.'

'You're on time-and-a-half...double-time, before long. You aren't giving favours, son.'

The driver said, 'I had a date.' It was a grumble, but a very mild grumble.

'You've missed it,' said Harding, drily.

'She won't like it.'

'She won't *get* it,' observed Harding. 'You'll go blind all the less quicker.'

The driver chuckled.

He was a young lad; young, and randy, like every other youth of his age. Pleasant, with a happy-go-lucky manner. Ogden guessed him to be footloose and free...and a perpetual source of sleepless nights for the parents of young ladies whose acquaintance he'd cultivated.

Harding turned in his seat, and said, 'Okay, Harry?'

'Fine. Fine, thanks.'

'The legs? Much pain?'

'Nothing to speak of,' lied Ogden. 'I can feel 'em...that's about all.'

'And the arm?'

'Oh, that's comfortable enough, thanks.' Ogden jerked his head, and asked, 'What about your hand?'

Harding grinned. Ogden couldn't see the grin, but he sensed it before the tone carried it on the words.

'This hand,' said Harding, 'is going to earn me more than a few pints of Newcastle Brown. This, and the story of how you burned your legs. And—another thing—the missus'll think she's married a hero...at least, for a couple of days.'

'Compo?' observed the driver.

'These kids.' Harding still spoke to Ogden. 'Booze, birds and bread. That's all they ever think about. Mate, we have produced a generation with three-track minds...supping, shagging and twisting.'

The driver said, 'Don't be stupid. Work it right, you'll get compensation.'

'For an accident we weren't even *in*? For buggering about with a vehicle that wasn't even *ours*? For shoving my hand into somebody else's bloody petrol? I'll get sick pay, son...and be satisfied.'

'You're a mug,' observed the driver, cheerfully.

Harding turned to face the windscreen once more.

He said, 'And you're a driver...so they tell me. Christ only knows who's been kidding you. The way you've changed gear these last few times, you should be a flaming dentist.'

'I'm no Stirling Moss,' admitted the driver.

'Not by a million bloody miles,' agreed Harding.

And, as the daylight faded into the first edge of dusk, the mini van left the main roads and, by twisting his head, Ogden could see the hedges beyond the window on Harding's left. Closed-in hedges, not yet budded by spring. And verges, with their winter's grass still harsh and clumped. And fields, newly ploughed and, here and there, one with its soil harrowed and ready for sowing.

And the bird-wings fluttered in the pit of his stomach...and, for a moment, he wished he could say 'No!'...he wished he could say, 'Stop. Take me somewhere else.'...But he couldn't, because there was nowhere else to go...only Little Moysell...only 'The Swan's Nest'...and the bird-wings fluttered in the pit of his stomach...

And suddenly—as with the onrush of stage-fright—he felt sick, and frightened.

THE WOMAN
THE HUSBAND

It was quite a moment; quite a greeting and quite an entrance.

Watford knocked on the door and, in answer to his knock, the door was opened by Thelma. They eyed each other, the man and the woman, and if reciprocal spitting hatred did now show in each face, their expressions were within cigarette-paper thickness of that emotion.

Thelma spoke first.

She said 'Well?' and the word was like a stone dropped down a deep shaft; as unfriendly—as threateningly dangerous—as the echoed splash of the stone as it breaks the scummed surface of unseen water.

Watford replied with a name.

He said, 'Pamela Ogden.'

'What about her?'

'She sent for me.'

'That was a mistake.'

'It didn't *sound* like a mistake.'

'You've had a wasted journey, Watford,' said Thelma, coldly.

'Like hell I have!'

Angela moved from behind, to alongside, Watford.

She stared hard at the younger woman's face, then said 'We've come a long way, Mrs Simpson. We—I, particularly—have been inconvenienced. We intend seeing Mrs Ogden. We also intend waiting until Mr Ogden arrives home, from prison... unless, of course, he's already here.'

'He isn't.'

'Then, we'll wait.'

'It's a free country, old woman.' Thelma's mouth twisted into a sneer. 'Sit in your car. Wait there... on the road. But not here. Not in the house. Not in the garden. And I'll make damn sure you only *see* him... that neither of you have time to speak to him.'

'Ask Mrs Ogden,' said Angela, gently.

'There's no need to ask...'

'Her preference. Us... or the reporters.'

Thelma caught her breath.

Angela said, 'You know me, Mrs Simpson. I know you. We've met—sometimes we've opposed each other— on various committees of the Townswoman's Guild. I don't bluff. I am—as you've already reminded me—an "old woman". I'm also a pig-headed old woman. If we leave here, without seeing your brother, we shan't wait in the car. We'll find the nearest telephone kiosk, and we'll remind the editor of the local newspaper that Harry Ogden—self-confessed, and very vicious murderer—is due to arrive at Little Moysell, this evening... after only ten years' imprisonment. That, of itself, should deserve at least one paragraph... possibly more. Then—when we get home—I will write letters. One to every national newspaper. Expressing concern that such a man should be free... and so soon. Reminding everybody of the disgusting details of his crime. All the letters won't be printed, of course—but some will... enough. Enough to create—er... *problems*?'

The last word was deliberately emphasised. It had a

soft, but sardonic, question mark attached. It said everything. It demanded complete surrender.

Thelma hesitated. She knew she was licked, but the gall of defeat was almost too much for her.

Then, slowly—grudgingly—she opened the door of the cottage wider and stood to one side. It was a gesture, but without words . . . without a spoken invitation.

As Watford and his wife entered the cottage, Thelma spoke in a low, warning voice.

She said, 'Don't hurt her—don't hurt *him* . . . in any way! Otherwise the newshounds'll have headline material.'

It was odd—it was the damnedest thing . . . Pamela figured it was the damnedest thing. Four of them and, between them, as sweet a collection of dislikes—ranging from mild annoyance to open hatred—as anybody could wish for. And yet, for the moment, they were cemented together. They were fused into a single, four-part unit . . . and by a man who hadn't yet arrived, who might not arrive and whom none of them had seen for years.

It was the damnedest thing!

Take Thelma.

Thelma was—we-ell, hell only knew exactly *what* Thelma was . . . other than Harry's sister. Hell only knew whose side she was on . . . other than her own. That she was furious was obvious; she smoked her cigarette in quick jerky inhalations . . . as if she was stoking some inner furnace and keeping her anger on the boil. But who was she angry with? Christ up a flagpole, who was *she* beefed off with?

Not Ralph Watford . . . there was damn-all about Ralph Watford to bring Thelma up to the boil. She knew him . . . but (come to that) so did half the population of the town they shared. The town they'd once-upon-a-time all shared. Everybody knew Ralph Watford, and the breed of bastard he was. Everybody . . . up to, and including, the scout master's hamster! So, what was so special about Ralph Watford? Except that Harry had done time for killing Watford's wife . . . which (if anybody felt like bursting into flames about anybody else) should make Ralph Watford hopping mad with Thelma Simpson. Not the other way round. So, whoever else Thelma was getting heated up about, it wasn't—or, at least, it shouldn't be—Ralph Watford.

The old lady—Ralph's wife...Angela? For God's sake, who gets mad at a strait-laced old lady? Even a stupid old lady who's married a randy bastard young enough to be her own son? Angela Watford was...Well—what was she?...just *what*? Except for what she was (and, even then, only what she was in relation to the animal who'd bedded her for her bank balance) she was a nice person. A very nice person. Olde Worlde nice...which was a nice sort of niceness. Thelma knew her—had known her a long time...they were both attached to some of the local all-hen get-togethers which catered for the bored women of the district. It made no sense at all to think that Thelma was mad at Ralph's wife. It made no sense, at all.

So-o...who else?

Who else was left?

And maybe that was it. Maybe the arrival of the Watfords had thrown little Thelma more than slightly off-centre. Maybe the truth was there, on the table, at last. Thelma hated the woman who'd pinched her darling brother; the woman who'd toppled her from the top spot in Harry's affections; the woman who—even though she couldn't cook as well as she might, and couldn't keep house as efficiently as she ought—could still plant a high-heeled shoe right up whiz-bang little Thelma's well-groomed fanny.

Come to think of it, that was enough to make *anybody* mad.

And Thelma was good and mad...with somebody!

Nevertheless, they talked...for want of a better description of the lingual short-arm jabs and the vocal infighting.

Watford stood; he was, at least, that much of a make-believe 'gentleman'. He stood, with his hands in his pockets, and with one shoulder leaning lightly against the wall alongside the window. He shared his attention; sometimes being part of the acid-tongued bickering and sometimes watching through the window... peering into the gathering gloom in the hope of seeing the hoped-for arrival of the man they were waiting for.

Thelma sat in the armchair. In some odd way, she made it look like a slightly moth-eaten throne, with herself an ill-tempered queen granting reluctant audience to a trio of annoying subjects. She still wore sweater and trousers, and a smudge of housework grubbiness streaked her face beneath one corner of her mouth. She smoked, one cigarette after another; chain-lighting a new one from the stub of each she finished.

Angela sat on one of the hard, upright kitchen chairs. She sat prim and old-maidishly; knees and feet together; straight-backed; unflurried and with her gloved hands folded in her lap. She showed no facial emotion, and her voice rarely moved beyond a polite conversational level, but some of the things she said, and because she said them without open rancour, ripped old scars into new wounds with the skill of a trained knife-fighter.

Pamela sat on the second kitchen chair. It was her home—her cottage—and it was her man for whom they were waiting... but, of the four, she was the least keyed-up. Emotionally, she'd passed her peak. She was spent—tired... drained of all real resistance. She sat there—already washed, changed and titivated—and, apart from adding a remark or asking a question, waited for her husband... knowing that this exchange of petty dislikes was only the spluttering of the fuse. Knowing that the explosion would come only with the arrival of Harry.

Nevertheless, they talked...

'He'd have left, early this morning,' observed Watford.

'I like your choice of word... "left",' said Thelma, sarcastically.

'What else, for God's sake?'

'As if, for the last ten years, *he's* had a choice.'

'Ten years,' mused Angela. 'For the crime he committed... it's not a long time.'

Thelma snapped, 'You should know!'

'I beg your pardon?'

'It's only a little longer than you've been tied to the goat you married.'

'Oh!'

Watford said, 'What I mean is ... he should be here, by now.'

'He has to find the place.'

'Yes, but ...'

'And public transport to this dump is almost non-existent.'

'I know, but ...'

'*And* he doesn't have a Mercedes-Benz at his disposal.'

'Oh, go to hell,' muttered Watford.

Slowly—softly—Angela said, 'Put that way, it *is* a long time.'

'What?' Thelma stared.

'Ten years.'

'Eh? Oh—well ...' Thelma gave a quick, couldn't-give-a-damn shrug. 'We make our own beds, old woman. If they end up apple-pie, we've only ourselves to blame.'

'Quite.' Angela moved her lips in a quick, whimsical smile. 'By the way, my name's Angela.'

'I know that.'

'I'm older than you are ...'

'I know that, too.'

'... but the expression "old woman" is a little—er ... impolite. Don't you think?'

'Look—if you think I'm going to ...'

'She's a guest, Thelma,' cut in Pamela.

'The hell she's a ...'

'What else is she?'

'She pushed her way in—her and her baby-boy hubby—without an invitation, with being ...'

'And you?' asked Pamela, in a tired voice.

'Me?'

'Who opened the door to *you*? Who invited *you*?'

'Look—are you saying ...'

'I'm saying she's a guest. My guest—and this is my house ... therefore *I* say what she is. She, and her husband—both guests ... treat them as such. Treat them as *fellow*-guests.'

Thelma looked as if she was going to erupt.

She didn't.

Instead, she pushed herself up from the armchair, and muttered, 'There's a smell of burning. I'd better check.'

She hurried into the kitchen.

Take Angela—Ralph's wife . . . Angela Watford.

She, too, was annoyed. Not on the boil—not spouting super-heated steam—like Thelma . . . but annoyed.

Now, why the hell should *she* be annoyed? It made less sense than Thelma's anger. It was illogical, if only because she didn't even *know* Harry. So where was the reason for annoyance—even mild annoyance—based upon the homecoming of a man you've never met, don't know and have no cause to either like or dislike? Okay—it was a very well-mannered annoyance; it went with best china and Palm Court orchestras; it was a very snooty, sniff-nosed annoyance. But it was still there.

But, for why?

Harry had done time for slicing up and shooting Ralph's first wife, then Ralph had trotted Angela to the altar . . . but that was the only connection. And (knowing Ralph) Ruth wouldn't have been painted as the sweet and understanding wife to some dame (even an elderly dame) Ralph had visions of tupping. That wasn't Ralph's way . . . not in a million light-years.

So-o . . . who was *Angela* annoyed with?

Thelma, maybe? They knew each other. They disliked each other. The dislike was some sort of mutual thing; a residue from past clashes . . . or, so it seemed. But (Christ up a flagpole!) this was no time, and no place to rake the ashes from a tin-pot disagreement spawned at some T.W.G. meeting.

Anyway, Angela wouldn't . . . she wasn't the kind.

The old girl had breeding—that, if nothing else—and, however Thelma acted, Angela wouldn't let some unimportant difference of opinion make even more sour what was already . . .

Angela was saying, '. . . very appreciative, Mrs Ogden.'

'What?' Pamela jerked her mind away from speculations. She said, 'I'm sorry, Mrs Watford. I was day-dreaming.'

'Please call me Angela.' She flicked the polite half-smile on and off. She said, 'I was thanking you for describing me as a "guest". I realise that I'm an interloper, but...'

'Not at all. I sent for Ralph. Why shouldn't you come along, too?'

'Thank you.'

Watford growled, 'Great... we'll all be sending each other Valentine cards, next.'

'I still haven't worked out why,' said Pamela, sadly. 'What on earth possessed me to ask Ralph to be with me when Harry arrived home.'

'Memories,' grunted Watford.

'Of your late wife?' asked Angela. She turned to Pamela and said, 'You were friends—weren't you?... Ruth Watford and yourself.'

'Yes.' Pamela sounded awkward. Slightly embarrassed. She said, 'We were—y'know... good friends.'

Watford laughed quietly. To himself—and yet *not* to himself... pretending to laugh to himself, as he gazed through the window, but making damn sure the two women heard the laughter.

'My husband,' said Angela, 'has a weird sense of humour. An odd line in jokes. Death—as far as he is concerned—is either convenient or inconvenient... nothing more than that.'

'I know your husband,' began Pamela. 'Unfortunately, I know him...'

'She knows him a bloody sight better than *you* know him... "old woman".' Watford turned from the window and released all his pent-up fury at Angela. He sneered, 'More than you'll ever know him. More than you'll ever have the red-blooded passion to know any man... more than you ever will have, more than you ever have had. She could give her body... every writhing, sweating inch of it. Eagerly. Willingly. And...'

'Never willingly,' whispered Pamela. Then, to the older woman, 'I swear, never *willingly*.'

'You are kidding yourself, sweetheart,' snarled Watford. 'You are wool-pulling now...as hard and as stupidly as ever. Even now—even *now*—you won't face the truth. You screwed, sweetheart. I have had them—others...scores. And you were always the fastest—easily the fastest—to get the motion under way. When you screwed, you...'

'Shut up!' breathed Pamela, then in a near-scream, she shouted '*Shut up*—you—you...you bloody ANIMAL!'

Thelma came to the door leading from the kitchen. She said, 'What the hell's happening in here?' but nobody answered her.

Pamela bent forward and buried her face in her hands. Her shoulders heaved as she fought to keep back the grief and shame which tried to turn into tears and redden her eyes.

Watford watched. Silently, and with curled lips.

Angela moved a hand from her lap. She leaned across and touched Pamela's arm.

In a calm, soothing voice, she said, 'Mrs Ogden—my dear...he's talking to me. Not you. What he's saying is for my benefit. To hurt *me*. It's...' She paused, then continued, 'it's what we've become. Enemies. I know him for what he is, and I despise him. He knows I despise him...therefore, he tries to hurt me—to humiliate me—by saying wicked things to you, in my presence. Please...' She patted Pamela's arm. 'Ignore him. Ignore what he's said—whatever he says—and he's helpless. He becomes what he really is...an over-indulged and very naughty child, who should have been spanked, hard, but wasn't. Don't cry. Please don't cry for something that happened ten years ago. Today—today is your day, Mrs Ogden...don't let *him* spoil it.'

Pamela moved a hand from her face and clasped the hand which touched her arm.

And a friendship was born. A genuine friendship...as genuine as the friendship Pamela Ogden had once had for Ruth Watford.

THE COP

LITTLE THINGS. The song-writer claimed that 'little things mean a lot'... and that particular lyric-spinner knew his tomatoes. It is the ancient and honourable acorn-to-oak-tree gag and, unlike so many similar fairy tales, it contains some semblance of truth.

Take Detective Constable Ruecroft...

He was no 'acorn', you understand. He had held the title of 'cop' long enough to have become slightly gnarled around the edges, and the sub-title of 'jack' long enough for every last vestige of 'plain clothes' glamour to have disappeared up the spout many moons ago. He was a working detective and (because he had always equated ambition with ulcers, and had never been keen on collecting ulcers) he performed his duties effectively enough to hold down the job, but never efficiently enough to merit being mistaken for any sort of star turn.

He was a cop—he was a jack—he did his job... period.

And, at this particular moment, his job (as decreed by certain beings with grey matter under their helmets) was to sit in a mini-van, in a one-horse village, and watch a lane which led to a cottage.

Thus, his duty... which he performed to the accompaniment of tuned-down pop music coming from a transistor, and while he sipped hot coffee which an ever-loving wife had provided in a Thermos. Boring—but a doddle ... and, anyway, policing *was* boring outside the covers of books.

He hadn't seen the Rover (Thelma's Rover) for the very good and simple reason that the Rover had arrived and nudged its way up the lane towards 'The Swan's Nest' before D.C. Ruecroft's mini-van had taken up a surveillance position.

But he saw the Merc. And, because it was raining, and because, without the engine running, he couldn't use the wipers without the risk of flattening a battery which was already being sucked dry of juice by the parking lights (and which, anyway, was just about on its last legs) he saw the Merc through rain-distorted windscreen glass. He saw it was a Merc. He did *not* see the number plate. He saw it was being driven by a man. He did *not* see that its passenger was a somewhat-past-middle-aged, very sedate-looking woman.

In short, he saw some things, but not others ... which was why he switched off the transistor, unhooked the mike from its housing on the van's dashboard and reported what he thought was the truth.

A little thing...

One of many.

Take the owner of a certain V.W. ...

His name is unimportant. Suffice to say that he was a rate-payer and a tax-payer and that, as such, he expected some sort of value for money. He lived at a semi-rural spot called Bagdon—a community where the householders fool themselves into believing that they are country-dwellers when, in fact, they sleep within sight of grass, work within cubic concrete, and spend half their life travelling between bed and office—and, apart from his mod-con home, the second love of his life was his motor car ... the V.W.

His car had been nicked which (but naturally) made him angry. What made him even more angry was the added fact that (despite the rates and taxes) the cops were doing S.F.A. towards the retrieving of his beloved motor car. They'd visited him, they jotted details into their ever-ready notebooks ... after which they'd vanished into the hills somewhere.

Which wasn't good enough.

Now ...

Sawyer (and, indeed, Fenton) had concluded that this particular car owner wasn't too—er ... 'important'. That, pending somebody having nothing better to do—and pending the missing V.W. being reported abandoned somewhere a few score miles away—he could safely be left to simmer away on his own unimportant hotplate. He didn't have 'pull'. He didn't know people in high places. There was nobody to whom he could ask awkward questions.

That's what *they* thought!

In fact (and one more little thing) the owner of the V.W. was a cat-lover. And not just any old moggy. Russian Blues. As far as *he* was concerned, Russian Blues were the ultimate in sheer animated beauty; they were the cats to end all cats ... they were why cats had been invented, in the first place.

He had three of them.

He had bought them (at one hell of a price ... but he didn't begrudge a penny of it!) from the best breeder of Russian Blues for umpteen miles around. A woman who specialised in prize-winning Russian Blues ... a certain Mrs Lennox.

And (if he remembered rightly) the husband of this Mrs Lennox was some sort of big pot in the constabulary worlds. In this particular force, in fact.

So-o ...

It was about time some whiskers got singed ... via this constabulary big pot ... via the wife of this constabulary big pot...via a breed of cat known as a Russian Blue...

Which just shows (if your name happens to be Sawyer, or Fenton) just how wrong you can *be*!

And how (without plugging the guy's song too often) 'little things mean a lot.'

It was a boozer, and boozers are much the same, wherever they are. Some are flashier than others. Some are quieter, some are noisier. Some call themselves 'road houses'. Some call themselves 'inns'. Some get very nose-in-the-air and called themselves 'hotels', while others crawl up back streets and hide behind the name 'tavern'. Forget it—they are all *boozers*—they all sell beer...and the acreage of chrome and plastic bears no relationship whatever to the quality of the hop-juice or the value given for current coinage.

And beer is beer, and some will argue that there is no such liquid as *bad* beer...there is only good beer, and better beer.

The Falcon sold beer—some of the best beer in the district...which (and because it was handy for County Headquarters) is why it was Sugden's and Lennox's pint-sinking palace.

Sugden took a quarter-pint at a single swallow, lowered the glass and left a moustache of froth on his upper lip.

'I needed that,' he remarked, feelingly.

Lennox trundled his stomach towards a corner table. Sugden followed, and they sat down.

'Owt?' asked Sugden.

'About what?' asked Lennox.

'What the hell do you think?' asked Sugden.

'Where did you pick up the notion that I was a mind-reader?' asked Lennox.

Four questions, and not a single answer. Or, if you like, two questions met by two counter-questions. With any other man in the force—with any other man in the world—Sugden would have exploded verbal lava.

With Lennox it was different. With Lennox it would have been a waste of good energy...and Sugden knew it.

Instead, Sugden tilted his head until he could see

Lennox's legs, below the table, and said, 'Still got the knickerbockers...eh?'

'They'll wear for years,' Lennox assured him.

'When the chief sees 'em...'

'He'll see 'em tomorrow,' said Lennox, quietly. And there was a world of double-meaning in the remark.

Sugden waited.

Lennox tasted his beer, smacked his lips, wiped his mouth with the back of his hand, and said, 'Remember a bloke called Ogden? Harry Ogden?'

'Not off-hand.'

'A murder case. Regina versus Ogden—ten years back...he killed his next-door neighbour. Ruth Watford.

'Aa-ah!' Sugden nodded, slowly. 'Ye-es. Sawyer's case...wasn't it? When he was in C.I.D.'

'Remember it?'

'Now,' agreed Sugden. 'Bits and pieces. Not much...it wasn't much of a flash enquiry.'

'It wasn't *any* sort of a bloody enquiry,' growled Lennox, sourly.

'This morning,' said Sugden. 'When Sawyer wanted to see me. Was it...'

'Not about the case. About Ogden. He came out, this morning. His defence was Diminished Responsibility...it cut his sentence down to ten years.'

'They'll believe owt,' grunted Sugden...meaning courts in general, and juries in particular.

'Some people will,' agreed Lennox...not meaning courts, *or* juries.

And (as has already been mentioned) Sugden knew Lennox, therefore Sugden listened while Lennox talked.

They talked, listened (and, of course, drank beer) in The Snug of *The Falcon* and (as with boozers) once you've seen one Snug you've seen them all; small rooms, tastefully furnished, with subdued wall-lighting, fitted-carpets, Formica-topped tables, upholstered stools and a serving hatch via which liquid refreshment is served at a fractionally higher cost than anywhere else in the establishment.

A middle-aged man, with a bald head, expensive

clothes and a stomach which came near to matching Lennox's shared a corner with a just-past-the-dolly-stage female of about half his age. What he was saying to her could be guessed. What she was saying back to him could be deduced from the periodic shake of her head ... and how long she'd keep saying it could be accurately estimated by the fiscal gleam in her eye and the lengthening periods between each head-shake.

However ...

The would-be-love-birds were the only other persons present in The Snug ... and they had their own problems! They couldn't (and didn't want to) hear what Lennox said. And Lennox and Sugden had seen it too often to be even mildly interested.

Therefore, Lennox talked and Sugden listened.

Then Sugden finished his drink, stood up, and said, 'My call, I think.'

'Same again,' murmured Lennox.

When he'd returned with the refills—and after they'd both tasted to ensure that the brew hadn't deteriorated within the last few minutes—Sugden sniffed, and said, 'He always *was* a prize.'

'But this time—if I'm right ...' Lennox left the sentence open-ended.

'See him,' said Sugden, bluntly.

'Me?'

'It's your bright idea.'

'True,' agreed Lennox grudgingly.

Sugden said, 'Give him a chance ... even *he* deserves a chance.'

'True,' repeated Lennox.

'And, if you're right, hammer him,' said Sugden, nastily. 'Bury the bastard ... it's what he deserves.'

'If I'm right,' sighed Lennox.

'Hammer him.' repeated Sugden.

The cop in question (the man Sugden was, at that very moment, instructing Lennox to 'hammer') was, himself, shouldering his way through a thicket of mental doubts and indecisions.

He drove the Citroën Diane from Ellerfield, towards
Little Moysell, and worried. He worried enough to
produce a nagging ache at the back of his skull; just above
the nape of the neck, and as if his head was recovering
from a recently delivered rabbit punch. A little nauseating
in its refusal to be brushed aside, and something which
prevented clear and unhindered thought.

And yet, he had to think... God knows, at this
moment, and above all else, he had to *think*!

Ogden was back, and he (Sawyer) was way out on a
very long limb.

The message had come through that Ogden had
arrived. The message, as instructed, had been passed on to
him, at his home. He had re-donned his uniform; the
whole shooting-match, including gloves and silver
knobbed swagger-stick. Then he'd given his wife a quick
peck of goodbye, climbed into the car and set off to do
what had to be done.

Which was...?

All right—to see Ogden... but then what? To let him
know that his return had been duly noted... but (again)
then what?

He was doing what he was paid to do—he was doing
his duty—and he had no doubts upon that point... but
what the hell *was* his duty?

Harry Ogden was his duty. That was it... it was as
simple as *that*. Harry Ogden... murderer... lecher... released convict. That was his duty, and the duty of any
hard-working, conscientious cop.

That bastard was under his skin—had been under his
skin for every hour, of every day, for a whole decade. That
blood-splashed kitchen. That hacked and bullet-
shattered corpse. Those eyes—that tone—as the sub-
human responsibile had made his stammered, quiet-
spoken confession. As if words and apologies could undo
what had been done; as if a 'Guilty' plea could wipe away
some of the horror.

That was his duty.

And it didn't matter that other people were blind. That

Fenton couldn't see it. That Lennox couldn't see it. That, in all probability, Sugden wouldn't see it. That didn't matter. Because they were all blind, and they were all wrong. They couldn't see, because they hadn't *seen*. They hadn't seen the corpse, and they hadn't seen the kitchen. They hadn't seen the things that mattered.

And that was it, and all there was to it, and the final answer to everything.

He'd seen the corpse. And *he'd* seen the kitchen.

And, ever since, the man responsible had been crawling around, like some itching disease, under his skin. For the last ten years. But now the itch wasn't there, because the man was out from under his skin. He was free, and in the open.

And, come hell or damnation, there was not going to be a repeat performance of that carnage he'd had to suffer and stomach in that God-awful kitchen.

He was going to stop it. He was going to prevent it.

If it meant detailing a man to watch Ogden every minute, of every day, for the rest of his life, what happened ten years ago was *not* going to happen again.

And, what the hell happened—however much Fenton disapproved, and however much Lennox disapproved, and however much Sugden disapproved—Ogden was going to be told just *that*!

THE MAN
THE WOMAN
THE HUSBAND

IT WAS not at all like any of them had expected.

It crept up on them. There was no immediate fanfare; no Brock's Benefit Night; no sudden and earth-shattering traumatic tremor.

At first, it was a wash-out...as wet, and as miserable, as the weather.

But the climax, when it came, *came*!

Watford was standing alongside the window. His ill-temper had simmered down to scowling sulkiness. He was still peering through the uncurtained glass, but seeing little in the darkness beyond the lighted room.

Then he saw headlights nosing their way slowly up the lane. The headlights stopped within a yard of the rear bumper of the parked Merc. Then the headlights were switched off, and only the parking lights remained.

Watford swallowed then, almost off-handedly, he said, 'He's here.'

Pamela caught her breath, and hurriedly rubbed the back of a wrist across each eye.

Angela murmured, 'Good. I'm glad.' She glanced across at Pamela, smiled reassuringly, and added, 'It's all right, my dear. They aren't red...and you haven't smudged anything.'

'Thanks.' Pamela returned the smile.

Thelma saw, and heard, none of this. She was back in the kitchen.

But nobody moved. Nobody rushed to open the door. Apart from the exchanged smiles of the two women, nobody's expression really altered.

It was as if the build-up had sapped all available emotion; as if what had gone before had tired everybody out and there was nothing left for the *reason* for it all. The women sat in their chairs, and waited. Watford continued to watch through the window and he, too, waited.

Then Watford said, 'No...it isn't him. It's a couple of yobs in a van. Delivering something, by the look of things.'

'Not here,' said Pamela.

Angela said, "Probably the wrong address.'

'Bloody idiots,' grumbled Watford.

Then they relaxed, to continue their waiting.

Somebody knocked on the door.

Watford pushed himself from alongside the window, and growled, 'I'll go.'

As he opened the door he said, 'Look—I don't know what...' He stopped, dropped his jaw for a second, then gasped, 'Christ Almighty! *Harry*... what's happened?'

'Anybody,' said Ogden. 'Anybody under the sun—Pamela, Thelma, George—anybody in the whole stinking world...except *you*. You're the last person on earth I expected to open that bloody door.'

His voice was weak. Low. Sapped of strength by prolonged pain and delayed shock. But the disgust was there, and in the eyes and in the expression and, weak though the voice was, it was the voice of a man who has reached a decision; the voice of a man who, whatever he was less than twenty-four hours ago, is now a complete man.

He was in the armchair, with legs straight and straddled in a narrow V. With each slippered foot resting on a bed of cushions and pillows. With his right arm slung and padded to his chest. Holding a cigarette between the fingers of his left hand, and inhaling and exhaling tobacco smoke in a fight to forget—to ignore— the pain from his legs, and the pain from his arm in order to dominate the quartet who had been waiting for his arrival at 'The Swan's Nest'.

He had been helped into the room by Harding and the driver of the van. He had snarled aside Watford's offer of assistance. He had allowed Pamela and Thelma to settle his feet on cushions and pillows brought down from the bedroom. He had glanced at Angela once ... then ignored her. He had left their questions unanswered, and turned his head aside when Pamela had tentatively touched his face as a prelude to a kiss of greeting.

The only person he had spoken to was Harding, and then only when he was settled in the chair.

He'd said, 'I'll have a fag, Tom ... please.'

Harding had given him a cigarette. Pamela had struck a match, Thelma had flipped her expensive gas-filled lighter and Harding had thumbed the wheel of his home-made lighter.

Ogden hadn't hesitated. It was as if he had not even noticed the other two flames. He'd held the tip of the cigarette in the flame of Harding's lighter, enjoyed a first, deep draw, then murmured, 'Thanks, mate.'

Harding had replied with a solemn-faced nod, then turned to the driver of the van, and said, 'Wait outside, son. I'll be with you.'

The driver had left, without comment.

Ogden had smoked in silence for a few moments, before turning to Watford and saying, 'Anybody. Anybody under the sun—Pamela, Thelma, George— anybody in the whole stinking world ... except *you*. You're the last person on earth I expected to open that bloody door.'

'We're—er—y'know...' Watford flapped his arms a little, and gave a sickly smile. 'We're still friends, Harry...despite everything.'

'Or, because of?' suggested Ogden softly. Contemptuously.

Pamela and Thelma spoke together.

They gestured towards the legs and the arm, and Pamela said, 'Harry, what's happened? Have you had some sort of accident?'

Thelma said, 'Your legs? Your arm? What have you done to them?'

Harding made as if to answer their questions.

Ogden silenced him, with a movement of the hand holding the cigarette, smiled at the two women—first at Pamela, then at Thelma—and said, 'It's something I can't explain. Something you wouldn't understand...neither of you. Let's say—whatever it is—it's cancelled the last ten years...whatever it is.'

'Being a bloody hero,' growled Harding.

'Becoming something more than a number,' corrected Ogden.

'Who is this?' Thelma looked at Harding, with barely concealed dislike. 'Who is he, anyway?'

'This,' said Ogden, deliberately, 'is the first truly decent person I've met for a long, long time. Possibly the first truly decent person I've *ever* met.'

'Oh!' Pamela looked uncomfortably shocked. She cleared her throat, gave Harding a smile which wasn't quite a smile, then said, 'That's—er—that's nice. Mr—er...'

'Harding.' Harding returned the smile which wasn't quite a smile.

'Mr Harding. But...' Pamela paused, moistened her lips, then continued, 'Well—y'see, Mr. Harding... We've been—we've been waiting...All of us—we've all been...Y'know...Waiting for Harry. And...'

'He stays,' interrupted Ogden.

Harding said, 'Look, mate. I don't want to...'

'If you don't mind, Tom.'

'Well—no—I don't...Y'know—I don't...'

'All right,' said Harding quietly. He looked at Pamela,

then at Thelma, then at Watford and, finally back to Ogden. He nodded, and murmured, 'If that's what you want.'

'He stays,' repeated Ogden, to the others.

Thelma snapped, 'Harry, don't be such a damn fool.'

Watford said, 'Look—he's a complete stranger...'

'Not to me.'

'...so why the hell should he...'

'*He stays.*' Ogden spoke each of the two words very deliberately. He turned his head, grinned up at Harding, and added, 'Don't worry, if they don't like you, Tom. With these bastards that, of itself, is a recommendation.'

Harding moved his head in a single nod, as if he already understood.

There was a moment of stunned silence.

Then everybody—even Angela—made as if to speak, and all at the same time. There would have been a bombardment of words—a four-part explosion of objection—had anybody actually spoken.

They didn't... and the timing was split-second perfect.

As their mouths opened, so did the door of 'The Swan's Nest' and all four, and Harding, turned their heads as Sawyer marched, unannounced, into the cottage.

THE MAN
THE WOMAN
THE HUSBAND
THE COP

THEY had expected Ogden, alone. Instead, they had
Ogden, plus an ally and Odgen, plus an enemy. The odds
(as they had expected them) were going to be four-to-one
but, instead, they were four-to-three...because Sawyer,
although he was opposed to Ogden, was also opposed to
them, if for no better reason than that he saw them as
Ogden's friends. And Harding, the stranger—the man
none of them knew—had a larger-than-life don't-give-a-
damn personality which eclipsed even that of Thelma.

The odds, therefore, were just about even.

Sawyer didn't know this, and Sawyer was doing what
he would have described as 'his duty'.

He was finding it difficult. His forte was not 'leaning';
he was not (and never had been) one of those bull-in-a-
china-shop coppers who don't give a toss—whose
shoulders are broad enough to shrug off anything, and
everything up to, and including, a Home Office enquiry—

whose eyes are hard enough to cut glass and whose voices can make a threat out of an innocent remark about the weather . . . he wasn't one of *them*!

He was a 'book man'. And, for the first time in his life, he was venturing beyond the covers of 'the book'. He was treading unknown territory. At first, timidly . . . almost apologetically. Feeling his way. Watching faces— particularly the face of Ogden, himself—and assessing reactions from expressions. Choosing his words carefully; skirting around any possible double-meaning.

But (and above all else) saying what he truly believed had to be said . . . and, to that extent at least, having the guts to defy convention.

Lennox, on the other hand, was hopping mad . . . for *Lennox*. Not being of the rip-roaring fraternity—being built more for comfort than anger—he rarely lost his cool and, even then, not far and not for long.

Nevertheless . . .

The woman in his life had given him some stick, the minute he'd walked into the house; bucketsful about some fool from Bagdon who shared Mrs Lennox's passion for a certain breed of pussy-cat. The said fool having had his motor car pinched. The said fool wanting to know why the hell his motor car hadn't yet been recovered . . . indeed (as far as the said fool could make out) wasn't even being looked for. And where was all this high-powered coppering everybody talked about, these days? And what the hell were the hobbies of Bagdon paid for, anyway? And wasn't it time some half-baked, dopey-looking, sloppy-minded, over-subsidised detective had a rocket up his rectum?

All this (and more) Lennox's wife passed on to Lennox.

All this (and more) Lennox tried to pass on to the Bagdon D.C. . . . but couldn't. Because (on Sawyer's personal instructions) the Bagdon D.C. was keeping his bum warm in a van at Little Moysell.

Nor could Sawyer, himself, be contacted . . . he, too, being on his way to Little Moysell.

Little Moysell. it would seem, was a busy little village.

It was attracting coppers faster than a honey-pot attracts ants.

And now Lennox was hurrying to add himself to the Little Moysell copper's convention. He leaned over the steering wheel, as far as his stomach would allow, cursed every traffic light which was inconsiderate enough to show red as he approached and, periodically, muttered, 'He must be out of his tiny mind. He must be bloody *mad*!

Sawyer stood, not relaxed—not quite relaxed—alongside the armchair in which Ogden sprawled. He held his swagger-stick at hip-level, horizontal and in front of his thighs. He held it in gloved hands, and his grip on the stick prevented any slight tremble of the hands which might have given a clue to his own feeling of uncertainty, and the gloves covered up any whiteness of the knuckles caused by the grip on the stick. He was like a shipwrecked man, clinging onto a spar, and hoping to God he hadn't lost the ability to swim.

He said, 'I would like to make one thing clear. In fairness to you. In fairness to all concerned.'

'Inspector.' Angela spoke, for the first time for almost thirty minutes. She said, 'Would you mind clarifying that remark?'

'*Chief* inspector,' Sawyer corrected her.

Angela bobbed her head in silent apology, and said, 'Chief inspector.'

'Which remark, madam?'

'About being fair . . . to "all concerned". Exactly what do you mean by the words "all concerned"?'

'All of you.' Sawyer moved his head and glanced at their faces in a swift, smooth arc of embracement. 'Friends of Ogden, here . . . I assume you're all his friends. Therefore, I mean all of you.'

'Really?' Angela looked mildly amused . . . but interested.

'I think,' said Thelma, grittily, 'that you have the nerve of hell itself. Coming in here. Flashing your petty little authority around. Standing there, and . . .'

'Leave him.' Ogden cut in on the haranguing build-up. 'He's come a long way. Let him say his piece.'

'Always,' murmured Angela, 'with the proviso that he doesn't forget the law relating to slander.'

'The truth,' said Sawyer, pompously, 'is rarely slanderous, madam. I speak to—and of—Ogden, here. Where it concerns you. Any of you. I trust you will take it in the spirit...'

'Get on with it,' growled Harding.

Sawyer turned to the one person in the room he didn't know, and said, 'I don't know who you are, but...'

'I,' said Harding, warningly, 'am the bloke who isn't going to bugger about with slander...anything daft like that. I'm the bloke who—one-handed, or not—will knock your teeth down the back of your throat if you step too far out of line. Now—let's have less excuses for what you're going to say, before you say it...and *say* it. Just be warned, that's all. I never have had that much time for coppers. So, if you deserve a good thumping, that's what you'll *get*. Right?'

'A colleague of Ogden's, of course,' sneered Sawyer. 'One of his criminal acquaintances, I've no doubt.'

'Look, mate—I've given you fair warning...'

'Leave it, Tom.' Ogden's face was grey with pain. His voice was tired...carrying weariness of this long and eventful first day of freedom. He looked at Sawyer, and said, 'Now—for God's sake—you've come here for a purpose. To say something. Say it...then get out.'

Sawyer looked down and into Ogden's face. There was a moment's silence, as their eyes met—like the first crossing of swords, before a duel—then Sawyer gave a little cough and continued to do 'his duty'.

He said, 'You're a convicted murderer, Ogden. That much is a fact. Not untrue. Not slanderous. A simple fact. You were sentenced—you were sent to prison for a term of fifteen years—ten years ago...good conduct, as usual, has earned you remission. Ten years in prison, for a particularly foul murder. Not a long time...'

'No?' said Ogden, bitterly.

'Not in my opinion.'

'Not in—er—*your* opinion.'

'I happen to believe in hanging...in certain cases,' said Sawyer, grimly.

Ogden said, 'So do I. Mine was one of them. There were moments—days, and sometimes weeks—in that "not a long time" of ten years when I wished, with all my heart, that hanging hadn't been abolished. Something you wouldn't understand ... but the truth, nevertheless.'

'Am I supposed to believe that? To believe ...'

'You're not supposed to believe *anything*,' exploded Thelma. 'You, and you're kind. You believe what you want to believe ... and nothing else. Not one damn word. If you don't want to believe it, it's a lie ... period.'

Sawyer turned to her, and said, 'You're his sister. Am I right?'

'You're right,' snapped Thelma.

'Thelma Simpson?'

'You're still right.'

'You didn't give evidence, at the trial ... am I still right?'

'I wasn't asked.'

'Quite. You weren't asked.' Sawyer's expression showed contempt. 'And one of the reasons you weren't asked was that you couldn't be trusted. You couldn't be trusted to tell the truth ... even on oath. That, as I recall—as it was later explained to me, by Ogden's own solicitor—was the main reason he daren't call you as a witness. Even as a character witness. And you have the audacity to lecture *me,* on the subject of truth.'

'You, and every other ...'

'Ah, but she's changed.' Ogden cut in on Thelma's furious rejoinder. The eyes in his pain-whitened face were mocking as they glanced around the room of the cottage. He said, 'This room, Sawyer. The smell ... the smell of good cooking. It's all Thelma. Not my wife. She couldn't do it—she could never do it ... only Thelma.'

Thelma said, 'Look—I don't see what business it is of ...'

'It's an act of atonement.' Ogden continued speaking, as if Thelma's interruption hadn't been uttered. 'A sort of expiation for the sin of greed. The greed of herself, in the name of her husband. Her husband—George Simpson, my brother-in-law ... a weak man, Sawyer. Dominated by his wife. And his wife was an ambitious wife. She liked good living... still does. Oh, she'd have told lies in the witness box. Of course she would. To get me off the hook. Back into the business. A gimmick—y'know...an accused murderer serving behind the counter. I know— I know...she had other reasons. More honourable reasons. But they were only temporary. A psychiatrist would know what to call them...I don't. Some sort of mental defence mechanism, I suppose. A false reason, for a motive—a reason her own mind made her be- lieve...because she was subconsciously ashamed of the real reason. Something like that. Involved. Like every- body else's thought process—yours, mine...every- body's.'

Ogden's mouth curled into a slow, wry smile, as he ended, 'And how do I know this, Sawyer? We-ell—despite what you say—ten years is a long time. Time to think. Time to work things out. And, in ten whole years, she only visited me once. Just the once. And with George, her husband. And a solicitor. And all the documents drawn up, to buy me out of the partnership with her husband. An accused murderer is one thing. But a *convicted* murderer is another... bad for business. I signed—I sold... at their price. No arguments. Symbolic, I suppose. A symbolic death...a symbolic "topping". A self-imposed death penalty. But—y'know what?... I think it boomeranged. What she'd done. What she'd made her husband do. Greed and love, Sawyer. I doubt if they can both live in the same mind... not without driving some poor devil crazy. And I think the love—the love we had for each other, as kids—countered the greed and ripped her apart. Years of it... years of a punishment even I didn't suffer. And all this...' Once more, he glanced around the spotless room. 'It's an atonement. A penance. A plea for forgiveness. She knows what truth is, Sawyer. She's learned... the hard way.'

There was a silence. It stretched itself out, like a quivering steel wire, to near-breaking point. And every eye watched Thelma's face, and every person in the room knew that Ogden had torn the scar from a badly healed wound to reveal the pus of hidden shame.

Angela stooped and picked up her handbag, from the

floor alongside her chair. She opened the handbag, took out a silver flask, unscrewed the top and held the flask out, towards Ogden.

She said, 'For medicinal purposes, Mr Ogden. Brandy. Forgive the liberty, but I think you need it. You look as if you're in pain.'

'Thanks.' gasped Ogden.

He tipped the flask to his lips, swallowed, then held the flask to return it to Angela.

Angela said, 'Keep it. You may need another drink.'

Sawyer seemed to realise that, in some way, the conversation—his 'duty'—had been snatched from his control. He straightened his back slightly, gripped the swagger-stick more firmly and gave a nod towards Ogden's strapped and bandaged arm.

'What happened?' he asked.

'Something else you wouldn't understand, mate.' Harding answered the question.

'I've already warned *you*,' snapped Sawyer. 'I don't know who you are, but...'

'Harding,' growled Harding, dangerously. 'Thomas Harding. Driver by profession, Newcastle United supporter by birth, beer drinker by inclination.' As he talked, Harding fumbled, left-handed, in the hip pocket of his trousers. He produced a battered wallet, held it towards Sawyer and continued, 'That's who I am, mister police *chief* inspector. You'll find it on my driving licence, if you care to check. Damn-near thirty years on the road ... and not a conviction. No trouble with the police of any sort ... and you can check *that*, when you get back to your police station. And what I *don't* like, is being called a hook. I'm clean, mister police *chief* inspector. Not because I haven't been caught. Because I'm honest ... and it's as easy as that. So-o—I don't like being called a hook. Not by you ... not by any bugger. So, watch your mouth, mate. Watch what you say. Watch what you suggest. I dunno about the others. Maybe they're bent—maybe they're straight ... I wouldn't know. Harry, here. I met him, today. First time. What you think about him isn't important—not to me ... I make up my own mind. He's a bloody good bloke ... as far as *I'm* concerned. He pays his way. He doesn't rabbit on too much. He's good company. He has guts. From what I've seen of you—y'know...first reactions. First reactions. *You* might be more of a man, if you were a bit more like Harry.'

Sawyer refused the proffered wallet.

He muttered, 'I have my duty to do...and, I'll do it.'

'Do it,' said Harding, gruffly. 'Just don't include me in it...that's all.'

'Judas Christ, they're all the same,' grunted Lennox, irritably. He shoved his feet on brake and clutch as one more traffic light moved up to scarlet as he approached. 'Red—red—red...all the bloody same.'

He sat in the car, glared at the traffic lights and, gradually—like the first rays of a rising sun topping a mountain peak—the glare turned to an expression of wide-eyed enlightenment.

The inconvenience of a series of traffic lights had triggered off a grumble. The grumble had formed itself into random words. The words had formed themselves and been mouthed. The mind had caught the words, examined them and placed them alongside a problem that same mind had been grappling with.

And the solution to the problem had been there...all the time.

Ask a cop how he solves an involved crime and, sometimes, he'll be honest. He'll say he doesn't know; that it's a knack—that it comes with experience—that it's a gut-feeling coupled with hard graft.

True. But sometimes he knows, because...

And that's all. *Because.*

As with Lennox.

Because (and for no good reason at all) a series of traffic lights had been a bloody nuisance.

The lights turned to green and Lennox eased the car forward.

He was in a hurry. He wanted to reach Little Moysell before Sawyer jumped in with both feet and landed in sewage over his head.

Sawyer could feel the shifting; the gradual movement of

alliances—like the near-imperceptible easing aside of tiny grains to allow the sinking into soft sand—and, for the first time since he'd entered the cottage, he felt the stirrings of vague uncertainty.

He still did not think that what he was doing was wrong—he was still convinced that his visit was an unsavoury, but very necessary, duty ... but (perhaps?) that he had, so far, *done* things wrongly. Or, if not wrongly, a little imperfectly. That (perhaps?) he had not been careful enough—not been wise enough—in his choice of words and, because of this unwisdom, had lost some of the vitally necessary objectivity.

He was also puzzled at the illogical presence of at least two people at 'The Swan's Nest'.

He turned to Watford, and said, 'May I ask you a question, sir?'

'What?' Watford looked startled at being suddenly spoken to.

'A question,' repeated Sawyer. 'Something which is puzzling me.'

'Certainly ... certainly,' said Watford.

'Why are *you* here?' asked Sawyer.

'I'm sorry. I don't follow.' Watford frowned.

'The husband of Ogden's victim,' explained Sawyer.

'Oh! I see ...'

'But now, *my* husband,' said Angela, quietly.

'Ah—er ... yes.' Sawyer looked momentarily embarrassed. Then he said, 'I—er—I heard. I was told about your marriage to Mr Watford. Shortly after the trial, wasn't it?'

'Shortly after the trial,' agreed Angela.

'As I recall,' said Sawyer, 'you were together—you and Mr Watford—at the cinema when Ogden murdered Mrs ... When he murdered the first Mrs Watford.'

Angela nodded her agreement.

Watford said, 'The Ritz, chief inspector. The film was a western.'

'*Shane*,' said Ogden, softly.

'What's that?' Sawyer turned and frowned his disapproval at the man he'd come to interview.

'The film,' said Ogden, 'was called *Shane*. Watford and his present wife were in the circle—Pamela, my own wife was in the stalls... while I was busy murdering the first Mrs Watford. The film, chief inspector, was called *Shane*. You must remember the name. As far as everybody here is concerned it's a very important name... a very important film. If it ever does the rounds again, I must remember to see it. You, too, chief inspector. You, too, must see it... it marks a milestone in your life, too.'

Sawyer narrowed his eyes and, in a warning voice, said, 'Don't get impudent, Ogden. I didn't come all the way here to...'

'You've no damn business here!' exploded Thelma.

'Madam, I will not...'

Pamela said, 'Please go, chief inspector. You've done harm. More harm than you've done good.'

'I'm sorry. Mrs Ogden. I have a duty...'

'To hell with your so-called duty!'

'Mrs Simpson, I won't...'

'Please,' pleaded Pamela.

Watford rasped, 'For God's sake, Pamela. Don't crawl. The pompous bastard has no legal right to be here in the first place.'

'Mr Watford. I know my rights. I know what I'm allowed to...'

'I know what I'm *going* to do, before long,' growled Harding.

A voice said, 'Sawyer.'

Thelma glared her loathing at Sawyer and almost screamed, 'Get out! Get out of here, before...'

'Quieten down, Mrs Simpson. You won't help matters by...'

'What "matters"?' asked Angela. 'As I see it there is no valid reason for this...'

'Keep out of this, Mrs Watford.'

'*Sawyer!*'

'Why the devil should she keep out of it? She—all of us—question your right to barge in here and...'

'Mrs Simpson. This is a last warning. I will not...'

'Please. Please, go. Leave us in peace.'

'You've been asked to leave, Sawyer. You've been asked. Now you could be thrown out. That's what I...'

'Be advised, Mr Watford. Don't be foolish enough to...'

'SAWYER!'

It was as near a thermo-nuclear explosion as it is possible to get, given only lungs, throat and a mouth. It sent a tidal wave of sound ripping through the room and drowned into silence every last whisper of the rising babble of lesser voices.

And there he was, having entered the cottage through the door which Sawyer had, inadvertently, left off the latch. After the verbal bomb-blast, every other mouth became, momentarily, slack-jawed and every head turned to see what the hell could make so much noise. And there he was... looking for all the world like Old Man Beelzebub himself, padded out and tarted up in plus-fours, zingy pullover and a bow tie.

Lennox had arrived.

It is odd. It is something no copper—no writer, no *anybody*—can ever satisfactorily explain. It defies mere words. It leaves descriptive prose at the start-line. It is always the genuine article... for the very good reason that it can't be imitated.

But (whatever 'it' is) some men, and even a few women, have it.

In the thespian world, men like Richard Burton, Orson Welles and Peter O'Toole have it by the bucketful. In the political arena, Churchill had it... and so had Nye Bevan. It has to do with stature but, at the same time, has nothing whatever to do with physical proportion. It has to do with magnificence, but mere ugliness is no bar to its presence. It can never be learned; men are born with it, and they retain it until their last breath... that, or they never know it.

Top-line coppers have it. Not all of them, but those who do are top-line coppers *because* of it. It is a quality which is immediately apparent; it sets them apart; when they join a group, all other members of that group become nonentities; when they give an order even the most bloody-minded of flatfeet never, for one moment, dream of disobeying that order. Within that most select of all clubs, The Police Service, these men are legendary. They perform miracles of crime detection . . . and they do it almost off-handedly. When they interview (and if they throw the switch and go onto full power) the interviewee is sweating cobs before the first question is asked. They can pick the one truth from a bundle of lies as certainly, and as accurately, as a well-trained pointer can pick a game bird from its hiding place in the rough.

Lennox was such a man—such a copper—and, within five minutes of his arrival, he had every other occupant of 'The Swan's Nest' in the palm of his chubby, fat-fingered hand.

He stood on the hearthrug, with his broad backside enjoying the full heat from the blazing fire, with his brogued feet planted wide apart and, as he stripped the cellophane from a cheroot, he grinned down at Ogden.

It was a wry grin—without much humour—and it was returned with a look of sadness mingled with pain.

'Ten years, old son,' murmured Lennox. 'A small lifetime. Now—tell me . . . was it worth it?'

Ogden tried to send the grin back to the fat detective superintendent. He didn't quite make it but, instead, he moved his head in a single, tiny shake.

'No . . . it never is.' Lennox sighed, and added, 'Bugger what *you* did for a pastime.'

He shoved the cheroot into his mouth, patted his pockets for matches, then muttered, 'Ta,' as Harding held out the flame of his home-made lighter for the tip of the cheroot.

They waited. Some knew—some guessed—what was coming . . . and the others knew that *something* was on its way. Something important. Something climactic. Something which was going to make the next few minutes some of the most important minutes of their lives.

And yet, Lennox started on a happy note—and why not? . . . Lennox was, basically, a very happy type.

'Y'know,' he said cheerfully, 'it doesn't often happen. Like this, I mean. Outside books, that is. In books—all right—everybody ends up on some scuttering little island, somewhere. Else in a country mansion. Else on a grain...summat like that. Agatha Christie. Any of you people Agatha Christie fans?'

He looked round, enquiringly.

Angela said, 'As a matter of fact, I am. I've read most of her books.'

'Me, too, ma'am.' Lennox smiled happily at Watford's wife. 'I reckon she's just about the best in the business. Y'know...All the suspects gathered neatly together. All ready for the pay-off line. Everybody on edge, wondering who's done it. Our Agatha...she's a cracker when it comes to concocting brain-teasers. But—y'know...real life. It doesn't often happen like that. It's usually a bit more messy. A bit more—er—"iffish"...to use cricketing jargon. Come to think of it, I've never known it before. Not in real life. All the suspects together, in the same room.'

He paused to enjoy a long pull on the cheroot.

Watford said, 'suspects? What suspects?'

'You lot,' said Lennox, and he accompanied the answer with a quiet—almost private—chuckle.

'Suspect to *what*?' asked Watford.

'Murder, old son...what else?'

'Sir.' Sawyer spoke from the back of the room. His voice was tight and high-pitched. He cleared his throat, but the voice came out as tight and high-pitched as before, when he said, 'With respect, sir. I don't see...'

'You will, Sawyer,' said Lennox, drily. 'Hang about, son. You *will*.'

'Murder?' said Watford, softly. 'Whose murder?'

'We-ell, now...' Lennox began his head polishing-neck-rubbing-jaw-scratching routine with his free hand. 'Let's start the ball rolling with a murder enquiry. A ten-year-old enquiry. Sawyer's...when he was a detective inspector. I've—er—examined the file. Exhumed it, you might say...from its grave under Headquarters. It's all there. I've read it. Every word. Statements, pocket books, reports...the lot. And photographs. Everything. And it made ve-ery interesting reading.

'Take the statements. You—Watford—you made a

statement. You—Mrs Ogden—you made a statement. You—Ogden—you, too, made a statement.' He looked at Angela, and said, 'You—Angela Finkle, as was . . . right?'

'Right,' nodded Angela.

'You, too, made a statement. And . . . y'know what? It's a good job—a *bloody* good job—none of you were cross-examined on the strength of those statements. It's a good job Ogden wasn't represented by an even moderately competent defending lawyer. He'd have skinned the lot of you, alive.'

Angela said, 'My statement was true, superintendent. If you're suggesting that *my* statement was in any way . . .'

'I'm suggesting, ma'am, that you did what everybody else did. That you made a statement to Detective Inspector Sawyer. That Detective Inspector Sawyer typed it out . . . maybe dictated it. That you read it. Then you signed it. Am I right?'

Angela nodded, and watched the fat detective's face through slightly narrowed eyes.

'Is there anything wrong in that, sir?' asked Sawyer. 'The procedure is correct. The manner . . .'

'The language,' interrupted Lennox. 'The sheer undiluted, ticky-tacky police jargon. Nobody talks like that, son. Nobody! Not even coppers . . . exceptwhen they're grass green, and giving evidence for the first time. Let me remind you. Ogden's statement—he's just nipped next door to see his fancy woman, and she's told him she's up the spout . . . 'We held a short conversation, during the course of which she informed me that she suspected that she was pregnant.' Angela Finkle's statement—she's in the pictures, with her boy friend, and she sees Mrs Ogden for the first time . . . 'Ralph Watford was sitting on my right. I remember he pointed out to me that Pamela Ogden was in the downstairs seats.' Mrs Ogden's statement—she's just got home, from the pictures, and she's been greeted by the news that her husband's knifed and shot the woman next door, after also being told that old Ogden, here, has been having it off with the dead woman on the side for God knows how long . . . 'This was the first I knew of the matter'—meaning, the murder—'This was the first time I learned that my husband, Harry Ogden, was having an affair with Ruth Watford.'

'I'm not criticising the procedure, Sawyer. I'm criticising the language. Everybody said what they wanted to say—agreed ... but everybody said it the way *you* wanted 'em to say it. Which means the statements were true ... but not wholly true. It was Harry Ogden, *à la* Detective Inspector Sawyer. Pamela Ogden *à la* Detective Inspector Sawyer. Angela Finkle *à la* Detective Inspector Sawyer. The whole bloody file was *à la* Detective Inspector Sawyer.'

'It was the truth,' croaked Sawyer.

'No! It was "The Gospel according to Sawyer" ... which made it one hell of a long way short of the truth.'

'Sir, I must object. I cannot stay here and be subjected to ...'

'You're going nowhere, Sawyer,' growled Lennox, warningly. 'What you did, ten years ago—what you allowed to happen—concerns every person in this room. It also concerns the force, and the reputation of the force. You're staying, son. You're going to sweat it out ... and, if you've never had an order in your life before, you can take *that* as one.'

Sawyer stood rigid for a moment, then breathed, 'Yes, sir,' in a voice which was almost a whispered moan.

And, suddenly, the 'funnies' were over. The cheerfulness was a thing of the past—something that had never been—and the podgy man in the ridiculous clothes was a wizard, capable of performing feats of magic ... but whether good magic, or bad magic, had yet to be determined.

Lennox stayed his straying hand by shoving it deep into a pocket of his plus-fours. With his free hand, and as he talked, he weaved smoke patterns in the air with the cheroot, occasionally pausing in the talk and in the smoke-weaving to raise the cheroot to his lips, inhale, then add a secondary pattern as he allowed the inhaled smoke to filter freely from his nostrils.

He said, 'First destroy. First knock down ... then re-build. Clear the ground—level it flat ... then, use the same bricks to build a new house. We'll do it that way. So-o—for a start off—we'll see what we've got. We'll check the joints, and see how well they fit. We'll see what Sawyer—what *all* of you—claim happened, ten years ago. Briefly...

'Ogden's wife telephones him, sometime during the day, saying she's going to the cinema. Watford, and his present wife, also go to the cinema that same evening. The same cinema. Watford sits with his present wife throughout the performance. They see Ogden's wife...and are certain she didn't leave the cinema.

'Meanwhile, back at the Ogden's place, Ogden comes home from work. He nips next door—to Watford's house—for a quick slap and tickle with the first Mrs Watford. The first Mrs Watford has news for him. That she's in the club. That he—Ogden—is the daddy-to-be. Tempers get out of control. Ogden grabs a knife and goes for his lady friend. He stabs her—what is it?—seven times...blood all over the place. But she won't snuff it. So he dashes back into his own house, gets his gun, returns to the Watford's abode, and finishes her off with a couple of bullets. Exit the first Mrs Watford.

'Then...surprise!—surprise! Ogden cools down, realises what he's done, and gets the big idea. Telephone the nick, tell 'em he "found" the body...and hope they'll believe him.

'He does—and they don't...followed by a quick confession and ten years behind granite. That, as I see it, is what we're all expected to believe. Right?'

Lennox swept enquiring eyes around the room, but nobody offered an answer to the last single-word question.

Lennox drew on his cheroot, then continued, in a soft, dreamy voice, 'Seven goes with a knife. Two goes with a bullet. And him a master butcher—and a marksman with Christ knows how many cups and medals to prove it and we're expected to believe *that*? A butcher knows where to put a knife, folks...a lot of people still think Jack the Ripper was a butcher, and he did a damn sight more than just kill! A butcher wouldn't need seven stabs. Just the one...two, at most. Then, bingo!...maggot-meat. He'd know where to stab. He'd know where to shoot. And, if he was a marksman—a class shot, with trophies to prove it—he'd know where to aim ... and he wouldn't need two pulls on the trigger.

'You're all following, I hope.' Once more Lennox eyed his audience, questioningly. Once more the question remained unanswered. He inhaled cheroot smoke, looked across the room at Sawyer, and said, 'And that kitchen. I've only seen photographs ... but I can guess. Tell 'em about the kitchen, chief inspector. Tell 'em. You saw it. I've only seen photographs. Come on ... tell 'em all about that kitchen.'

There was a moment of silence.

Then Sawyer muttered, 'It was—it was ... *horrific.* Blood. Everywhere. On the floor—on the walls ... everywhere!'

'But not too much where it should have been,' taunted Lennox.

'S-sir?'

'On his clothes. A trail—marks of some sort—between the two houses. Maybe not that ... it was raining. I think. Right?'

'It—it was raining, sir,' mumbled Sawyer.

'But not raining heavily enough to wash pints of blood from his clothes ... surely? There should have been more ... surely? And nail-parings—you didn't take any ... why not? There should have been blood there, too ... surely? Blood on the soles of his shoes ... surely? Blood in the welts ... surely? Blood on his hands—on his arms—on his face—somewhere on his skin surface ... surely? All that blood—blood everywhere, and on everything—but so little on the man who used the knife ... is *that* what you're saying?'

Sawyer remained white-faced and silent.

'Is that what you're saying?' repeated Lennox in a hard voice.

Sawyer closed his eyes, took a deep breath, let it out then, in a voice heavy with defeat, said, 'No, sir.'

'What *are* you saying, chief inspector?' There was no mercy in the question; no mercy in the tone.

'I—I ...' Sawyer tried, but it wouldn't come.

'I don't hear you, Chief Inspector Sawyer,' rasped Lennox. 'Speak up, please.'

From somewhere—from some unplumbed depths of his soul—Sawyer dredged up the last remnants of dignity. He held himself with something approaching pride and, when he spoke, his voice had been scoured clean of all pomposity.

He said, 'It would seem, sir, that I made a mistake. It would seem that, on your interpretation—an interpretation which I accept—that, ten years ago, I conducted an enquiry...without an open mind. I did the inexcusable. I decided who *I* thought was responsible, then I slanted the evidence to prove that I was right. I searched for something short of the whole truth. As a result, an innocent man was sent to prison. I will not insult that man further by either apologising, or asking his forgiveness. If you're right—and I think you are—what I did was unforgivable.' He paused, then ended, 'My resignation will be on your desk, tomorrow morning, Superintendent Lennox. It won't help matters...but it may keep some of the shame away from the force itself.'

In some strange way the speech—delivered by a man like Sawyer—made the rest of them feel they'd witnessed a death. It made them feel awkward. Sad. Interlopers at the bereavement of a stranger.

Ogden was the first to speak.

'Forget it, Sawyer,' he said, gently. 'I will.'

'Ah, but *we* can't,' said Lennox, heavily.

Angela said, 'Superintendent, the man made a mistake...that's all. A serious mistake—agreed...but no more than a mistake. We're all entitled to make mistakes occasionally.'

'Not coppers, ma'm,' said Lennox, sadly. 'Not mistakes of that size...it ain't allowed.'

'Who knows about it, except us, in this room?' pleaded Angela. 'Mr Ogden has already...'

Sawyer broke into the plea, and said, 'Thank you, madam. But Superintendent Lennox is right. Such mistakes are not tolerated in the Police Service. They can't be...ever!'

There was another period of hush. Silence, as what had

been said—and the implications of what had been said worked its way into their minds.

Then, Harding spoke.

He spoke as a simple man—as a rough-hewn man—and with the honesty of such a man. He spoke haltingly. Feeling for words—fumbling for a way in which to express himself—but quietly, gruffly and with no intention to hurt.

'Look—tell me to mind my own business... I'll shut up. You people—except for Harry, here—I don't know you... come to that, I reckon you could say I don't even know Harry. But I do. Better than most of you, I reckon. Those legs—that arm—he saved a man's life. And then, he didn't even stop to ask the man's name... and that makes *him* a man by my reckoning. So-o, I know him—y'know... I *know* him. They rarely come as good. They don't come better.

'And now—as I hear it—he's just done ten years inside... and for summat he didn't do, in the first place. Ten years! That's a hell of a long time. I was in the war—North Africa, Italy—and I was away from home for nearly four years... and *that* was a long time. It's a yardstick, see? Summat to measure it by. *Ten* years... that 'ud have sent me round the twist. And that was in the army—not in clink... so it gives you some idea. It gives *me* some idea.

'And the copper who sent him down. Harry, here, doesn't want the copper to suffer. Y'know... wants everybody to forgive and forget. Me?...' He glanced at Sawyer, gave a quick, lopsided grin, and said, 'Sorry, mate. I'd want to stand an' watch 'em slice your balls off. Not like Harry... I don't have his nature.

'But, what I was saying is this. Y'know—according to this fat copper... according to what he said, at the start. Whoever did what Harry's supposed to have done— whoever killed this woman—they're here, in this room. Some bastard who committed murder, then sat back and let some other poor sod suck the hammer. One of you lot... one of *you*.'

'Easy, old son,' murmured Lennox.

'Oh, no!' Harding stared at the fat detective's face, and met him, eye for eye. 'You've got your principles, mate. I've got mine. I got into this lot accidentally ... because I offered Harry, here, a lift. All right—I'm in it ... for whatever reason. I'm in it. So-o, I'm gonna saw *my* two inches off ... unless Harry tells me to belt up. And maybe not even then.

'You, mate ...' He nodded at Watford. 'I wouldn't trust you as far as I could throw you. You're a wide boy. I reckon you'd make a bloody good pimp ... begging your pardon, missus.' He glanced, apologetically, at Angela.

'He would,' agreed Angela, softly. 'He'd make an excellent pimp.'

Harding returned his attention to Watford.

He said, 'I reckon you could commit murder, mate. I reckon you could do it ... without much effort. And, I reckon you could stand by and see another man sent down for it ... I reckon you could do that, too. You're the sort. I've met you before—not you, personally ... but your kind. Lower than a snake's belly, mate. That's you.'

Watford opened his mouth to reply but, before he could speak, Harding continued.

'It's a good job for you, mate—as I see it, it's a good job for you—this lady was with you, when your missus was done in.' He bobbed his head at Angela. 'She doesn't tell lies—not them sorta lies ... not her sort.'

Angela murmured, 'Thank you, Mr Harding.'

'I am,' said Watford, angrily, 'Harry's friend ... his best friend. I'm the man who ...'

'The man who screwed "Harry's" wife—behind "Harry's" back ... that sort of a friend,' interrupted Ogden, bitterly.

Watford said, 'Look—why should I be here, if I'm not ...'

'Because I sent for you.' This time Pamela interrupted. 'Because I weakened—panicked—sent for you ... and you *had* to come.'

'You're no bottle, mate.' Harding curled his lips as he spoke the words to Watford. 'It shows ... like a mucky stain all down your front. You and Harry? Friends? That'll be the bloody day! You could have killed her, mate. Easy. But this lady says you were with *her* ... so that lets you out. She says Harry's wife was there, too ... so that lets *her* out. I'm not all that keen on coppers, but I can't see Sawyer, there, doing it ... So that lets *him* out. So—as I see it—There's not much left.'

'Me?' suggested Lennox, amiably.

'Don't be bloody stupid.'

And everybody looked at Thelma.

Thelma went white, then red, then white again. She seemed incapable of speech. For the space of a dozen heartbeats she seemed suddenly to be inanimate; to be devoid of life, and as bloodless, and as dead, and as cold as a frozen vegetable.

Then she spoke and, when she spoke, she spoke with her eyes as much as with her voice; disbelieving eyes which went with a disbelieving voice.

'You—you can't,' she whispered. 'God Almighty—you *can't* ... you really can't believe *that*!'

'You knew him, I think,' said Angela, wearily.

'My brother? What the hell sort of ...'

'No—not your brother ... my husband. You knew him.'

'Oh!'

'You *did* know him,' repeated Angela.

'*Him!*' Thelma glared loathingly at Watford as she made the word a spitting insult. 'Everybody knew that animal. Everybody. What he was, what his morals were like and what an utter bastard he was. Of course I knew him.'

'I think we should get to the truth of this thing,' said Angela in a flat emotionless voice. 'I think we owe that, to all present. Tell me, Mrs Simpson, how well did you know my husband?'

'What?'

'How well did you know him?'

Watford said, 'For God's sake, Angela.'

'I would like to know.' Angela looked at Thelma as she spoke. 'Not for the sake of idle curiosity, or because I wish to embarrass you. I think we should know—all of us, here in this room—if only because we seem to have embarked upon a great soul-baring session.'

'I did not...' Thelma forced the words out, from behind clenched teeth. 'I did not know him from *underneath*. He didn't "have" me ... if that's what you're asking.'

Angela smiled—a thin, meditative smile—then said, 'The act of copulation. These days, there are so many ways of saying it, and of describing it. Your brother uses the word "screw", whereas you use the word "have"— both innocent and inoffensive words—and there are, of course, many other expressions ... all descriptive, I suppose but, to me ...'

'An old and embittered woman, married to ...'

'No,' counter-interrupted Angela. 'An old-*fashioned* woman—that, if you like ... but also a woman with a modicum of respect for the English language.'

'All right!' blazed Thelma. 'If you really want Lady Chatterly talk, you can have it. We didn't ...'

'Hold it, missus!' Lennox cut in, and waved the furious Thelma into silence. He beamed his good humour, widened his grin, then said, 'You're liable to shock somebody. Me, for example ... I live a very sedate life. me, the wife and the cats. It wouldn't do for me to pick up naughty words. Anyway ... we believe you. *She* believes you.' He nodded his pumpkin-round head at Angela. 'She's having you on, pet. Maybe getting her own back for something ... you'll know what, better than me. So-o— ease up, eh? ... stop putting your blood pressure at risk.' He paused, then added, 'He didn't. And *you* didn't.'

'It seems to me ...' began Harding.

'Harding, old son,' said Lennox, patiently, 'you may be a red-hot lorry driver but, as a detective, you pong. You couldn't detect your way to the heavyweight champion of the world ... not even if he was knocking hell out of you.'

Harding looked cross.

Lennox said, 'Watford's present wife is a lady. So was Watford's first wife. It's a knack he has. But Ogden's sister didn't kill the first Mrs Watford ... any more than Ogden did.'

'Oh!' Harding looked vaguely disappointed.

'So-o... Lennox twisted his pot-bellied trunk enough to toss the remains of the cheroot into the fire, turned, eyed the assembly with benevolent good humour, and said, 'If you'll all belt up for a few minutes... eh? And let the old man have a quick squint through the keyhole.'

Later—much later—when what was happening, and what was being said, had become something the posh novelists might describe as 'the events of yesteryear', none of them could decide. About Lennox... whether he was a willing executioner, guyed up as a clown, or a clown whom fate had jockeyed into performing an unwilling execution job.

Not once did the smile leave his face. Not once did the tone of his voice take upon itself the expected sombre quality of a man who is piecing together the splinters of a ten-year-dead crime and, at the same time, revealing an involved, but obvious, mixture of injustice, incompetence, fear, shame and downright idiocy.

He was Touchstone, with his fingers caressing the noose—or he was Jack Ketch in the costume of a buffoon... and none of them ever knew which.

He started simply. Jokingly. Like the star turn on the Northern Clubs' circuit; grabbing his audience with the first gag, prior to giving them what they are waiting for and building up to a climax which brings a storm of applause. He was that much of an artist, and he was as sure as himself of *that*.

He said, 'The Yanks have a phrase—they have a lot of phrases... they have the knack. "Let's drop it on the carpet and wipe our feet on it for a little." That's a neat phrase... don't you think? A nice, rounded way of saying something. I like it. It means—we'ell... it means what I've spent most of today doing. Wiping my feet on a crime file. Regina versus Ogden. It's been there, on the doormat, and I've been rubbing all sorts of muck into it with these beetle-crushers of mine. And—y'know what?... you'd be surprised. How much I know about you people. You folks who were around, when Ruth Watford was murdered. Just by wiping my feet on you... you'd be surprised how much I've learned.

'You, for example.' He spoke directly at Ralph Watford. 'A bit of a lad with his pants off...eh? But bored—y'know...bored to hell. Maybe not aware of it, but that's what it boils down to. Bored...and a bastard. That is a very explosive combination, son. It makes for nastiness. It makes for vandalism. It makes for crime...and, sometimes, it makes for murder.

'And how do I know these things? We-ell, now...let me draw a few diagrams.

'Your present age, forty-one. I know that—I've read your statement—you were thirty-one at the time of the murder. Thirty-one years old, at the time we're interested in. Thirty-one years old, married to a good-looking wife, a couple of years his junior, but out with a woman old enough to be his mother... that's the picture. Out with the older woman, for what? A spot of bish-bash-bosh? No-o...not this one. Not as *I* read her, and not as I read *you,* son. But—y'see—thirty-one is a very nice age. Not too old for the dolly-birds. Not too young for the mature women.

'But not this time...right? So-o, the question is, what are you doing prancing around with Angela Finkle? And the answer *has* to be wrapped up in pound notes. Bread. Loot. Which, with a woman as old, and as wise, as Angela means marriage. Marriage. The promise of marriage. Or, at the very least, the prospect of marriage. She isn't a dope, son. Her cash is strictly anchored to a wedding breakfast. You know it. I know it. You knew it ten years ago...and, at that time, you had another woman as a wife.'

Lennox stopped talking for a moment, and smiled quizzically at the scowling Watford.

Watford stayed silent.

Pamela suddenly said, 'You're doing a great job of character assassination, superintendent.'

'Is that a fact?' Lennox switched his enquiring beam from Watford to Pamela.

'Wouldn't you call it that?' countered Pamela.

'Tell me.' Lennox's ready grin took on overtones of wickedness. 'Are you feeling left out of things, pet?'

'I don't know what...'

'Because, we can deal with you next, if you like. You and Watford go together...don't you?'

Pamela didn't answer the last, throw-away question. She took a deep breath, closed her mouth, tightened her lips and waited. She knew—they all knew—that *she* was next.

'Watford's here.' Lennox observed the obvious with the apparent innocence of a puppy. He raised an eyebrow at Pamela and asked, 'Who sent for him? You?'

Pamela didn't answer.

'Not Ogden's sister,' said Lennox. 'Not after the verbal pasting *she's* just given him. Not Ogden, himself. According to what was said, ten years back, Ogden was having an "affair" with Watford's wife—Ogden *murdered* Watford's wife...therefore, not Ogden. Not your husband. Not Sawyer...I can't see him sending for him. Not Harding...as far as I know, Harding hasn't met Watford before this evening. I can't see him coming uninvited. Not to meet the man who—supposedly—murdered his first wife. The man who—supposedly—was having an affair with the murdered woman. And, for the same reasons, I can't see his present wife thinking it was a good idea. So-o, somebody sent him an invite—who?...who else, but you? And—if you—*why* you?'

Lennox left a space into which somebody could have slipped an answer.

Nobody did.

'Pamela Gertrude Ogden,' mused Lennox. 'The witness who stood up in court and said beautiful things about a husband who had just admitted playing fast-and-loose with Ruth Watford...and who had just pleaded guilty to murdering the said Ruth Watford. Y'know what, sweetheart?...I don't think you're that forgiving. I don't think *any* woman is that forgiving...not when what is euphemistically called "the physical side" of a marriage hasn't certain kinks in it. Not so soon after the event. After a while...maybe. After she's had a few extra-marital romps—a bob-for-nob exercise...maybe. But not so soon. It's not on, lady. It's not part of the female make-up.'

'You're sex-mad,' sneered Pamela.

'Could be.' Lennox nodded, cheerfully. 'My wife breeds cats . . . we watch it all the time.'

'From you, that is one hell of an observation.'

The remark came from Watford. It was hurled at Pamela, and it was all it was meant to be . . . a deliberate and hurtful retaliation for what had been said before the arrival of either Sawyer or Lennox. Something the police didn't know. It was a shot in the back, from the shadows and—because Watford was rage-maddened, and because Watford was stupid—it was also the break-through for which Lennox had been searching. The last peice of the jigsaw. The final hammer-blow with which the podgy detective superintendent could nail tight the lid of the coffin.

Touchstone, or Jack Ketch? They never knew. They could never decide. They only knew that this fat, smiling, stupidly-dressed, head-bobbing copper was just about the most deadly—just about the most cheerfully astute—creature on God's good earth. And that now he *had* them—and *knew* that he had them—and that his words were like a killing-bottle in which was imprisoned somebody who had committed a ten-year-old murder.

'How's the legs, son? How's the arm?' Lennox switched his attack to Ogden. He nodded towards the flask which Ogden still held in his unbandaged hand. He said, 'Take a swig, son. You're going to need it.'

Ogden sighed, then raised the flask to his lips.

'Look,' said Harding, harshly, 'if you're gonna . . .'

'Shurrup, lad.' Lennox used a bored and long-suffering voice. 'Just listen . . . eh? Stick to lorry-driving, and learn.'

Harding closed his mouth, and contented himself with a prolonged glare.

Ogden wiped his mouth with the front of the wrist whose hand held the flask, and said, 'Is it necessary?'

'What do *you* think?' asked Lennox.

'I've done ten years. They can't be given back.'

'They should never have been taken away.'

'Let's say I've learned my lesson.'

'No bitterness?' Lennox sounded mildly surprised.

'I don't want vengeance,' said Ogden.

'I said bitterness.'

'Wouldn't *you* be bitter?' asked the killer, heavily.

'I wouldn't have done it, in the first place.' Lennox answered the killer's question, without taking his eyes from Ogden's face. He continued, 'Ogden, old son, it doesn't work that way. The law doesn't believe in punishment by proxy. The right person, or nobody... that's the way it goes.'

'I suppose,' said Ogden. He sighed, then repeated, 'I suppose.'

Lennox said, 'All that crap about you having an "affair" with Ruth Watford. That's what it was... crap. Right?'

Ogden nodded.

'A reason. Y'know—a motive... something to keep Sawyer happy.'

Again, Ogden nodded.

'I'll make a guess,' mused Lennox. 'This bit *has* to be guesswork. It's not in the statements. But Watford's here... when he shouldn't be. And he's just said something... which he shouldn't have said. So-o, it's guesswork. My guess is that you turned the coin over. That you weren't having an affair with Ruth Watford, any more than she was pregnant... any more than she claimed that you were the father. That, in fact, it was the other way round. That your wife was having an affair with Watford... and that Ruth Watford tumbled. Turn the coin, and there's a ready-made motive. Not much of a motive—not strong enough to bear close examination... but, if you played it well, it wasn't likely to be examined. A motive—of a sorts... that was enough. A confession, followed by a guilty plea, would do the rest.' Lennox paused, then said, 'How am I doing, son?'

'You're doing fine,' said the killer, softly.

Watford said, 'It doesn't prove anything,' and his voice rode near-panic breathlessness.

'It gives a reason for *you* being here,' said Lennox. 'It sweeps the cobwebs from *one* corner. You were invited... by Ogden's wife.'

'So? What the hell does that...'

'After all this time?' Mockery and contempt shaded the edges of Lennox's smile. 'You are a bit of a museum-piece, Watford old cock. You really *do* know the ladies. You can twist 'em around your little finger. All of 'em. All types ... all age groups. Not many men can. A lot claim it ... but that's a different thing. You *can*! Ten years ... and you're still the one she yells for. After what you did. After what you organised. It was still *you*.'

'I'm—I'm his friend.' Watford motioned towards Ogden. 'Damn it all—that's what I am ... his friend.'

Ogden twisted his head to stare up at Watford.

'Not a second time,' he said, grimly. 'Once, is once too many. I hate you, Watford. I despise you. If my legs weren't ...' He sighed deeply, then ended. 'I'd kick your lying teeth in.'

'All right!' There was desperation in the killer's voice. 'All right ...'.

'I don't believe it.' Angela interrupted the killer's outburst. She looked at Lennox, and said, 'Superintendent, you dress outrageously and you behave like a music-hall comedian, but we're all afraid of you ... myself included.'

'Surely not, ma'am.'

'Don't mock me, superintendent.'

'Ma'am, I'm not enjoying this.' All humour left Lennox's face. He spoke soberly, and with a touch of self-hate. He said, 'What I'm doing is more than righting a wrong. I wish that's all it was ... I'd be happy. But I'm also crucifying a fellow-policeman. It's necessary, but that doesn't make it any less painful.'

'That one?' Angela glanced contemptuously at the white-faced Sawyer. 'That pompous, self-opinionated popinjay? I still cannot understand why he came here, in the first place. To gloat, perhaps. To rub salt into wounds which—or so it seems—were never earned. If he'd done his duty, ten years ago ...'

'He *did* his duty!' blazed Lennox. 'For half his life—more than half his life—he's done his duty ... what he considered to be his duty. Honestly. Without corruption. Without being too concerned about whose corns he trampled on. He wouldn't hold the rank he

holds, otherwise. But he's human—he makes mistakes—
and, ten years ago, he was conned into making a mistake
which will now cost him his job—cost him his
pension—and make him headline news in every scandal-
sheet in the country.' Lennox paused, then snarled, 'And
lady, *you* helped in the con. *You* made it possible . . . because you made a statement which was a lie.'

Angela exchanged anger for anger.

She snapped. 'I think you're out of your mind. I
think . . .'

'How many times have you seen Pamela Ogden?'
rasped Lennox.

'I don't see what . . .'

'How many times?'

'Three times, if you must know.'

'First time?' Lennox's questions had a whip-crack fury.

'At the cinema. On the evening of . . .'

'Second time?'

'In court. I was in the public gallery, when she . . .'

'Third time?'

'Tonight. This evening, when we . . .'

'Twice,' snapped Lennox.

'I beg your pardon?'

Lennox lowered the tempo of his tone, as he said,
'You've only seen her twice, ma'am. The first time—God
only knows who it was you saw—some woman, similar
build, same colour of hair, with a white mac. You saw her
from behind, and above. At a cinema—before the lights
lowered—and on an evening when they were showing a
first-class film. I'll take you to any cinema—showing that
sort of film—and, from behind and above, I'll show you a
woman who, from that angle, looks remarkably like
Pamela Ogden. Wearing a white mac. Just as long as you
don't see her face . . . it'll be her.'

Lennox turned to face Pamela, and said, 'But you
weren't there . . . right, sweetheart?'

'No. I wasn't there,' agreed Pamela, heavily.

'You'd been conned into telling your husband you were
going . . . right, sweetheart?'

Pamela nodded.

'While, in fact, you stayed at home and butchered Ruth Watford . . . right, *sweetheart*?'

Once more, Pamela nodded.

They pitied her . . . all, but one of them. They listened to her as the tears coursed down her cheeks, and she tried to explain; as she stumbled her way through the reliving of the nightmare, and the ten-year agony which followed that nightmare.

'It is—it was . . . him. Watford. It was him! He rang me, and said . . . He threatened what he'd do if Ruth . . . She had—she had to be seen. And I pleaded with her. I—I—I swear to God, I pleaded with her. And then—and then things got out of hand. And there was this knife. This—this knife . . . And—and—oh my God! *She wouldn't die.* I kept—I kept . . . But she just wouldn't die. And—and—and I couldn't leave her. I mean—I couldn't . . . I couldn't just leave her. So I—so I . . .'

'You ran home.' Lennox's voice was gentle and filled with compassion, as he took up the story and granted her the tiny mercy of silent misery. 'You knew where your husband's gun was . . . of course you did. You got it, and finished her off with bullets. Then, your husband arrived. Unexpectedly. Saw what had happened . . . and talked you into letting him take the blame.'

'She was my wife,' said Ogden, simply.

'And while you were being interviewed?' asked Lennox. 'When Detective Inspector Sawyer first questioned you?'

Ogden almost smiled, as he said, 'She was in the bath. Cleaning herself up. I—er—I had to get them out of the house . . . to make things look as if she'd come from the cinema.'

'Nobody saw her arrive home.' Sawyer answered the unasked question in a flat and dead voice. 'The lights came on. The officer waiting thought he'd missed her—thought she must have used the rear door . . . it didn't seem important. Then the policewoman called. We searched the house later.'

'Too late,' observed Lennox, wrily.

'Much too late, sir,' admitted Sawyer. He moved his shoulders in a tired shrug. 'And now?'

'Take her in, chief inspector . . . the case is still yours.'

She offered no resistance. She allowed Sawyer to take her gently by the arm, and she walked like a soulless thing; without complaint and without expression other than the tears which still spilled from her wide open eyes.

As she passed Thelma, Thelma moved. Nobody expected it and, if they had, it was too sudden a movement to have been stopped. The blow was open-handed, but it carried all the frustrated power which, for the last ten years, had been building up as hatred. It left an imprint of scarlet along one side of the pale face but, for what good it did—for what pain it seemed to cause—it need never have been delivered.

Pamela didn't even blink.

'That's enough!' warned Lennox. 'She hasn't enjoyed it, either.'

Sawyer and Pamela left the cottage.

'I suppose,' murmured Angela, 'it's why she buried herself here.'

'Shame,' said Lennox, sadly.

Angela said, 'I, too, know something about shame.' As she spoke she stood up. 'She'll need a friend. Do you mind?'

'No. Tell Chief Inspector Sawyer I said so.'

'Thanks.' Ogden held out the flask, as Angela made to move towards the door.

Angela smiled, and said, 'Keep it, Mr Ogden. Please. Not as a gift, but as an apology for my own part in this stupidity.'

Ogden nodded.

Watford moved as if to follow his wife.

'The police car, Watford,' said Lennox.

'What?' Watford looked startled.

'A little matter of Conspiracy to Murder . . . plus anything else I can think up within the next few hours.'

Watford breathed, 'Oh, my Christ!' and his defeat was absolute.

Angela moved her head in a slow nod at Lennox, then

said, 'Thank you, superintendent. You're right of course... we shouldn't be afraid of you. With luck, I'll be dead before he finishes his prison sentence.'

'With luck, *he* will be,' countered Lennox, grimly.

The Watfords left the cottage. At the same time... but not together.

'And now...' began Thelma.

'And now, little sister,' interrupted Ogden, 'you, too, can go. I want a clean break... everything! I'm not the man you knew. I'm not the man you used to dominate. I don't intend to become that man again. Get out of my life—please... and stay out.'

Thelma was going to argue, but Lennox beat her to the words.

He said, 'Statements, Mrs Simpson. They're the bane of a copper's life... and we'll need one from you.' He turned to Ogden, and said, 'Be in touch, son. In your own time... but be in touch.'

'In my own time,' agreed Ogden, quietly.

Lennox guided Thelma from the cottage, and Ogden and Harding were left alone.

'Well?' demanded Harding.

'Sorry, Tom.' Ogden looked rueful. 'Dragging you into family squabbles. Y'know...'

'Don't talk like a berk.' Harding waved his uninjured hand at Ogden's legs. 'With that lot. How the hell can you cope?'

'I'll manage. I'll be able to...'

'I know a nurse,' said Harding with a grin. 'A bit out of practice, but she still knows her kit. She'll get you right... no time at all.'

'If you mean what I think you mean...'

'Away, man.' Harding's grin grew into a chuckle. 'She's nursed me through all the ailments I've had since I married her.'

'She doesn't know me. You've no right to...'

'She'll send me back for you. You don't know our lass. She will... she'll send me all the way back, to fetch you. And *she's* the boss.'

Ogden returned the grin, and said, 'You poor, hen-pecked bugger.'

'Don't I know it. But—we have a spare bed-room... and I've always fancied a lodger I could trust. I'll feel happier on the overnight runs.'

'Tom, I still think...'

'Have you ever tasted Newcastle Brown?' asked Harding.

'No. That's one drink I haven't yet...'

'Lucky man. You've the high moment of your life ahead of you.' Tom Harding held out his unbandaged hand to help Ogden from the chair. 'Come on, mate. That young sod waiting in the van... he's already on double-time. If we keep him much longer, the firm'll go broke paying him his wages.'

*   *   *

'The Swan's Nest' stood empty in its wilderness of a garden. In the kitchen a meal cooked, then burned before the spluttering fat ignited from the Calor gas flames. The flames spread, and hissed a little as the rain hit them and were turned into tiny puffs of steam.

It was an isolated village... a long journey for the nearest fire tender.

By the time the brigade arrived the cottage was an inferno and, by the time the fireman left, it was gutted to four walls surrounding black and sodden debris.

It was the end of a cottage.

The end of an agony.